# ANGEL BLUFF

## A DAVENPORT HEIRESS MYSTERY

JILL SANDERS

Angel Bluff

This is a work of fiction. Names, characters, organizations, places, events, and incidents are either products of the author's imagination or are used fictitiously.

Text copyright © 2022 Jill Sanders

Printed in the United States of America



ANGEL BLUFF

DIGITAL ISBN: 978-1-945100-42-0

PRINT ISBN: 978-1-945100-55-0

Copyeditor: Erica Ellis – inkdeepediting.com

# SUMMARY

Morgan wakes in the hospital broken and confused, with no memory of the last four years. Dazed from the meds, she's stunned to learn that she's married to the sexy green-eyed man haunting her dreams. Just one look from this hot bad-boy causes her entire body to react. But who is this guy? What was their relationship like? Men like this don't usually fall for her. Did he have had something to do with the accident? Unsure who to trust, she returns to her ambivalent family only to be caught up in a web of lies, drama, and deadly deception.

Liam can't believe his good fortune. Orphaned at birth, and homeless for most of his teen years, he managed to claw his way out of the slums to become a multi-millionaire before the age of twenty. He then stumbles upon the love of his life in a chance encounter on a rare night out. After convincing her to leave her overbearing family for him, the stage was set to live happily ever after. But now someone is hell-bent on taking everything he holds dear. With the details of

Morgan's accident becoming more clear, he'll have to fight to keep her safe and convince her that he's worthy of her trust and love once again.

# CHAPTER ONE

*Darkness approaches from outside. I feel no light inside me strong enough to resist it."*
**Christopher Pike**

T he first thing Morgan saw when she woke was a pair of sexy green eyes looking down at her. Somehow, the color seemed to pierce into her mind and remained a beacon through the many days of fog and pain that followed.

She was lifted and moved several times before silence finally surrounded her and she drifted into a deep, dark slumber. The next time she woke, it was to the sounds of a woman shouting and low voices arguing. The noise caused her head to ache so much that she moaned, gaining the attention of everyone in the room.

"Morgan." A blonde woman rushed forward and bent over her with concern flooding her eyes.

Morgan? It sounded familiar. The woman's face looked familiar too. As did the dark-haired man who moved next to the blonde woman.

Then it hit her. These were her parents. Her mother's hair, which was normally perfectly manicured, was tied back in a ponytail. She could honestly say she'd never seen that on her mother before.

She was still wearing the latest fashion, as usual, but her shirt appeared wrinkled, which was totally out of place. Her mother's face showed no signs of worry and was toned and flawless, thanks to Botox and a team of plastic surgeons.

Her father also appeared a little disheveled. His dark hair appeared as if he'd run his finger through it and his button-up shirt was wrinkled and untucked from his dress pants. This was also unusual

"Mom? Dad?" she croaked out. Her throat was sore and raw, and the rest of her body was numb.

Her mother gasped and covered her mouth. "We're here, baby." She leaned in and kissed her.

"What...?" she started, but her throat hurt too much to continue.

"You were in an accident," her father said, wrapping an arm around her mother and pulling her close to his side. "You've been in and out of a coma for the past week."

An accident? She'd been unconscious for over a week? She tried to remember anything about an accident but came up blank. Actually, at this point, all she could remember was her parents' faces. She wasn't even sure she could remember their names at this point.

She swallowed a few times and when her throat felt better, she asked, "How am I?" She'd tried to move a few times and hadn't been able to, which worried her.

"They have you strapped down with all these tubes," her mother said. "The doctor assured..." Her mother dropped off as another face appeared on the other side of the bed. Her mother glared upward, and Morgan followed her gaze with only her eyes.

There, standing a few feet away, were those green eyes that she'd dreamed of. The man belonging to those eyes was looking back at her, but no matter how hard she tried, he didn't look familiar at all. Outside of the pulsing memory of those green eyes.

He was tall. He towered over her father, who stood at five-ten, so the man must have been over six foot. He had warm honey-colored hair that was cut short on the sides and a little longer on the top. He too appeared to have run his fingers through his hair, as it was a little messy. Then again, it could be the style he was going for. It did make him look sexy and a little mysterious.

He had a full beard that was trimmed short against his face. And such a perfect face it was. His chin was... well, delicious. His nose was slightly crooked, and even that was sexy.

"Morgan?" the man said, looking down at her. His green eyes scanned her face and when they locked with her eyes, she could almost feel the pain behind them in her soul.

Her heart jumped in her chest, causing her breathing to double, and the machines she was hooked up to sent off warning alarms. Suddenly, the room was filled with the sound of loud beeping, which only increased her heart rate. That set off another machine in a vicious cycle that she had no power to control, and panic ripped through her entire body.

"I told you," her mother gasped. "You need to leave. She's not ready to see you," she barked out.

The green-eyed man glanced up at her mother, breaking his connection with Morgan, which caused a wave of different emotions to flood through her.

Her heart was beating so erratically at this point, she was beginning to feel dizzy.

"You need to leave," her father said as Morgan shut her eyes and tried to steady her heartbeat before her heart burst out of her chest.

Morgan waited for the man to decline or fight back. She didn't know why, but something in her gut told her that he should fight for the right to be with her. Instead, she watched through tear-filled eyes as he left the room without so much as a backwards glance.

"There, he's gone now," her mother said with a sigh just as a nurse came rushing through the door the man had just disappeared through.

Morgan closed her eyes and tried to steady her breathing. A soft beep signaled that another dose of medicine had been injected into her veins through the tubes in her arm.

"You'll get some rest," her mother said as the nurse started to take her vitals. The woman's cold fingers on Morgan's wrist were the first thing she'd felt in a while. "You'll see, you're going to make a full recovery. We'll take you home, you'll get some rest, and then you'll get some... help. Then everything will be back to normal."

Morgan lay there, listening to the rhythmic sound of the machines and wondering just what normal was. Who exactly was that sexy green-eyed man? Why did he look so lost? So lonely? Was he someone important to her?

It took two more days before she could sit up in bed and swallow something solid. Even then, her mother had to cut the chicken into very tiny bits and feed her since her jaw was so sore.

Most of the time, she was in a drug-induced slumber, in and out of consciousness. She only saw and remembered half of what was going on around her. She didn't know if anyone visited her except for her parents, who appeared daily and told her how things would be once she was able to go home.

She couldn't even conjure up an image of her bedroom or the home she lived in. Hell, she was even questioning what she looked like. So far, all she could come up with was that she had dark hair like her father.

She desperately wanted to look in the mirror but was too afraid to. Instead, she focused on getting back some of the memories that she'd lost.

On the sixth day after waking up, she had short visits from her friends, Kimber, Leanne, and Reagan, whom she remembered easily once she saw each of their faces. Memories came flooding back the moment they stepped into the room. If she'd been standing, they would have knocked her over, that's how powerful it was.

Kimber Lafyette had been the first one to walk through the door. Morgan and Kimber had been best friends since second grade. They'd attended the very prestigious Westlake Private School in Beverly Hills, which is where they had met Leanne Blyton in fifth grade. Reagan Hope had joined their group a year later.

The four friends had been inseparable since then.

"There she is." Kimber rushed over to bounce on the end of Morgan's bed. Pain shot up her left leg, which was in a massive cast.

Actually, both of her legs were in casts, along with her right arm. Her right arm was the only limb not wrapped in plaster and in immense pain.

"Oops." Kimber chuckled.

Kimber was the one friend out of the four that was always getting them into trouble. She was a true agitator. She'd cut her long brown hair into an extremely stylish bob in high school and had stuck with the style, which not only suited her but had also started a trend.

"Hey, you break her, you buy her," Leanne said, moving over and setting a large vase of red tulips on the table next to Morgan's bed. "How are you doing, sweetie?"

Leanne was the comedian in the group, the one person who always brought the humor and the laughs. Her long blonde hair was pushed back away from her face, letting her natural beauty to blind everyone who saw her.

Morgan joked back, "She can't afford me."

"I can," Reagan said, setting down another vase of red flowers, then looking down at Morgan. "In the shape you're in, I'd bet your parents would take half off." She tilted her head, sending her medium-length dark-auburn hair to fall over her shoulders. "You look like shit."

"Leave her alone," Leanne said, taking Morgan's left hand. "She's alive. That's all that matters."

"I haven't had the courage to look at myself yet," she admitted to her best friends.

The three of them were silent in return.

"I think we should help you out first, before you turn the mirror on yourself." Leanne pulled out her purse. "Ladies, it's makeover time," she said cheerfully.

For the next hour, her three friends tortured her by washing her hair in one of those buckets you either puke in or set your feet in to soak. It took some doing, since there was apparently a lot of caked dried blood that had been missed by the nurses' sponge baths.

"You have a serious bump back here," Leanne said, gently running her fingers over the base of Morgan's head.

"Yeah, I noticed." She groaned and tried not to sigh too loudly at the feeling of getting clean. In truth, having her hair washed felt so good. She'd asked her mother about getting to the bathroom several times in the past few days, but she had discouraged it and made it very clear that she wasn't capable just yet. "I wanted to shower, but..." She shrugged and then motioned to her legs. "I can't walk at the moment."

"How do you pee?" Leanne asked as she gently combed through Morgan's long dark tresses.

"I..." She frowned. "I'm not sure. I mean, I don't really feel a lot yet from my waist down." She motioned to her legs. "Maybe I have a catheter?" She shrugged.

Her three friends glanced at one another. "Ewww. Gross," Leanne said, causing them to giggle.

"But you can feel? I mean, you'll be able to walk, right?" Kimber asked soberly.

"Yes." She nodded, then for show, wiggled the toes on both of her feet. Her friends relaxed and sighed a little.

"That's good," Kimber said cheerfully. "I'd hate for you to be a cripple for the rest of your life."

"There," Leanne said. "I'm done combing your hair. Since we don't have a blow dryer, you can let it air dry. Now we just need makeup."

"Step aside, girls, this is my specialty." Reagan sat on the edge of the bed.

Morgan sat still while her friend did her best. Reagan wasn't lying—if you ever needed makeup done, she was the best woman for the job. Reagan's grandmother was Dame Lillianna Hope, a silver-screen actress who won the hearts of the American people with her wartime movies. She had also been a pinup model, and later in her career had been in several popular television shows.

Lillianna had made enough money to set up her family for multiple generations, then she'd gone and married one of the richest men alive at that time. The family was not only Hollywood elite, but they were also practically royalty.

Reagan's mother, Beth Hope, riding on her mother's coattails by keeping the name, had followed in her mother's footsteps and for the past twenty years had been a long-running character in one of the top five soap operas.

Reagan herself had done plenty of commercials and guest spots on her mother's show when she was younger.

Half an hour later, Reagan smiled down at her. "There, that's the best I can do to hide the bruising." She laid a hand on Morgan's cheek. "You almost look like yourself."

"Almost?" Morgan asked. "I think I'll take that mirror now." She held out her hand, and Kimber placed a compact in it.

"Just remember," Leanne said, "you're alive."

Morgan nodded. "Thank you." She held the compact to her chest. "Thank you for coming. For being here, by my side, after all these years."

Her three friends smiled back at her, and Leanne bent over and wiped a tear from her cheek.

"That's what friends do," Reagan said softly as a tear slipped don her cheek.

Taking a deep breath, Morgan opened the compact and for what seemed like the first time in her life, looked at her reflection.

From what she could remember about herself, she normally had small, narrow features. Her nose was short and perfectly symmetrical. Her eyes were spaced an ideal distance away from one other and were a rich warm honey color. Normally, she had the slightest of dips directly in the middle of her chin.

Now, however, her face was extremely swollen. She had

no dimple in her chin, her cheeks were large, and even the bridge of her nose was far too wide.

Reagan had done her best to cover the bruises, but Morgan could still see that they covered the majority of her face and forehead. Her eyes were swollen as well, making them look closer together.

She didn't look like herself. Tears filled her eyes, blurring the vision of herself in the compact.

"Hey," Leanne said, rushing to wrap an arm around Morgan's shoulders. "It's okay. You're okay."

Morgan felt her other friends embrace her as well as more tears flowed from her eyes, no doubt ruining the makeup that had just been carefully applied to her face.

"What happened?" she cried. "I just can't remember anything."

"It could be worse," Kimber said.

"You're alive," Reagan added.

"We're here for you," Leanne said, holding onto her.

"What's happened?" a deep voice said, causing the friends to ease away. "Is she okay?"

Morgan used her good hand and wiped the tears from her eyes, smearing some of the mascara. There, standing at the end of her bed, was the sexy green-eyed man.

She'd asked her mother about him, but her mother had only grown upset, and her father had said that they would tell her about him later. Later kept getting pushed back and each time she asked, her mother grew increasingly frustrated until Morgan stopped asking.

"Yes, she's just..." Leanne started.

"Finally gotten a look at herself for the first time," Kimber finished explaining for Leanne.

"It's Reagan's makeup job," Leanne said, bumping her

friend's hip. "I think she's losing her touch as a makeup artist."

Reagan smiled and took Leanne's hand, then Kimber's. "We were just...leaving." She tugged on their hands. They gathered their belongings and shoved them haphazardly into their bags.

Less than a minute later, her room door shut behind them, leaving her alone with the man, who was still standing at the end of her bed, looking down at her.

"Are you okay?" he asked her, his voice sexier than she'd remembered.

She felt her heart kick hard in her chest, and she willed the machines not to go crazy this time. When they didn't, thankfully, she nodded her head.

"Everything is so... swollen." She felt her face flush.

The man frowned. "Does it hurt?" he asked, not making a move towards her.

"No, the pain meds are pretty much dulling everything."

"That's... good." He frowned even more, then moved his eyes from hers to roam over her body. "I wanted to come back when you were awake, but your parents..." He sighed and looked down at his hands. Since he didn't finish, she assumed that she should have known what he was talking about.

At this point, she was slightly embarrassed that she didn't know who he was. Obviously, she should have pressed her parents further.

"Are you sure you're, okay?" he asked, finally moving towards her.

"I'm..." She thought back to her swollen face. To the strange appearance that had looked back at her in the mirror. Then she thought of her friends' words. "I'm alive."

He pulled the chair closer to the bed and started to take her hand in his. When he noticed the tubes sticking in her hands and wrist, he stopped and made fists and rested them on his knees instead.

"I've asked the doctors when they'll release you." He looked down at his balled hands.

"You have?" she asked with a slight frown. She wanted to ask why, but he continued.

"Unfortunately, your parents know your doctor and the hospital staff personally, and the nurses won't tell me anything other than it's up to the doctor to release you so you can go home." He reached out and ran a finger over the back of her ring finger.

"They took your ring?" he asked, frowning up at her.

"My...?" She glanced down at her swollen fingers. There, where his fingers brushed her skin, was an obvious white line where a ring had been.

She felt her breath hitch as the realization dawned on her that this man was her husband, and she didn't even remember his name.

# CHAPTER TWO



It absolutely killed Liam to see Morgan this way. Every part of her was either swollen, discolored, or broken.

He could see the pain behind her eyes, even though she was denying it.

He knew everything about her. Understood what every look, every little sound she made meant.

When his eyes returned to hers, she was looking at him strangely.

"What's wrong?" he asked her, moving slightly closer.

She opened her mouth to answer, only to have her mother burst through the door.

"I told the nurses that I didn't want you in here alone with her," Victoria Davenport said as she stormed into the room, looking irritated. Actually, since the moment he'd met her, she'd always looked that way, at least around him.

He didn't know if it was his presence that she found annoying or the fact that her daughter had gone against her wishes when she'd married him a little over a year ago.

"I'm allowed to be in here with my wife," Liam said firmly. "You may be her mother, but I'm Morgan's husband." He stood up, ready to fight.

For the past week, he'd allowed her parents and the nurses to persuade him that it was in Morgan's best interest that she not have too many visitors. He'd been allowed to check in on her, but only when she'd been in a deep drug-induced sleep.

He'd fallen for her family's lies. It was luck, actually, that he'd come today at a different time than he normally did. His intentions were to just poke his head in to see that she was okay before he headed out to a meeting. Then he'd seen she was being visited by the quad squad, as they always called themselves.

Obviously, Morgan's best friends had been trying to lift her spirits. He could tell that they'd done something to her hair and makeup. She was a great deal less pasty and bruised looking than she'd been since the accident.

To him, the makeup and hair didn't matter. She was still the most beautiful person in the world. It was a huge relief, just knowing she was alive and safe.

Why then did he feel so scared to reach out and touch her?

"Until we know more..." her mother started. She glanced over at Morgan, then lowered her voice, as if Morgan wouldn't be able to hear her even though she was sitting up, looking directly at her mother. "We don't want you alone with her."

He knew exactly what she meant. Since the moment the details about Morgan's accident had come into light, her family had questioned his involvement. He was pretty sure it was the reason they were doing everything they could to keep him away from her.

"Why?" Morgan asked. "What do you mean by until you know more?"

He glared over at Victoria then turned to Morgan and sat back down. Taking her hand in his, he took a deep breath and said, "Because your accident—"

"Was so terrible," Victoria broke in, giving him a look.

"What do you mean?" she asked, looking down at their hands.

Victoria sighed, and Liam watched a softness wash over her as she turned her attention to Morgan. "Your accident is something we didn't want you to worry about. Your father and I are making sure that it's investigated to the fullest."

"If you didn't want her to worry about it, you wouldn't have just brought it up," he added sarcastically.

Morgan glanced between her mother and him, then said, "I... don't remember anything."

"We know, dear. It's probably for the best, seeing as it was very horrific," Victoria said soothingly.

"No, I mean..." She turned to him, her eyes filled with sadness. "I don't remember you."

He felt his heart sink, and he frowned down at her. "What?" He shook his head.

"I can't remember you," Morgan added.

It took a moment to process this. He would have thought it one of Morgan's jokes, but the look in her eyes told him otherwise. A lump formed in his throat, his gut twisted, and his heart broke at the thought of all they had being gone in a single moment.

He didn't know what he would do if he couldn't remember everything Morgan was to him. Everything she'd done to drag him from the darkness that had been his life and bring him into the light.

And he'd been so far down in the darkness, he hadn't believed anyone could help him.

He'd grown up an orphan, never knowing who his parents where or why they'd given him up in the first place. His records showed that he'd been dropped off at a firehouse in the middle of a winter storm in Bend, Oregon.

He'd been passed from one orphanage to another and at the age of six had ended up just outside of Los Angeles, where he'd met Ryder Tripp and Sean Wilson.

Ryder was a skinny black kid who always had a black eye thanks to him being so good at sports that the other boys always took out their frustrations on him.

Sean was a mouthy know-it-all type that usually let his mouth get him into trouble. He had a knack for knowing just when to run away, but not before getting in that perfect, witty jab.

Liam had been the silent, shy one, who, when nervous, stuttered a little and always looked down at his shoes when talking with someone new.

The three boys had instantly become best friends. To this day, he remained in contact with Ryder on an almost daily basis.

During their early teenage years, Ryder had gotten even better at sports, mainly basketball. Sean and Liam, even though they liked playing with Ryder, had more interest in computers, specifically programming. Liam loved learning programming languages and had learned to use as many as possible.

During their early teen years, he and Sean had self-taught themselves how to write computer code on any computers they could get their hands on. They would often skip classes and sneak to the computer lap just to write silly games, trying to impress one another.

Sean had always tried to outdo Liam, but Liam was so much better at programming and always had the better game ideas and programming skills. Sean's games were usually filled with bugs or didn't work at all when he tried to show Liam.

Shortly after the three friends turned sixteen, they decided they could no longer handle the rules at the orphanage and had stopped going back there at night. They'd stopped attending school as well, and only went whenever they wanted to use the computer labs or the locker rooms to shower or steal clothes.

Living on the streets of LA hadn't been as hard as he'd thought, at least not while the weather was warm. That first winter, Liam had dreamed of the nights he'd spent on the orphanage's hard, smelly cots.

Then one night, he'd gotten an idea to write some security software. It had been a particularly cold night when he and Ryder had broken into a new car to get warm and sleep. He'd spent the entire night messing with the onboard computer, using the busted laptop that he'd found in a dumpster. The thing only worked when he held the screen at an odd angle, but he'd didn't care. It was useful enough to hack into the car's system and learn everything he could about it.

Sean had lost interest in programming and spent most of his time surfing or chasing girls. He'd hooked up with a few girls and would spend nights with them or at some of his other friends' places, not once inviting them to tag along. There were months that neither Ryder nor Liam heard from Sean.

Liam sacrificed everything when he'd been sixteen and

seventeen to write and finish the software in hopes that someone would have some use for it. Sean had initially helped Liam out with a few ideas and some of the programming. Even then, partnering with Sean had been a given. No matter what happened, Sean was his brother.

Liam had spent a lot of time on chat boards, talking about the benefits of the program, which he called ESP, Electric Security Platform.

When Sean had come to him one evening shortly after Liam had turned eighteen and demanding Liam buy him out, Liam had given him everything he could, which was less than five thousand dollars, which he'd saved from his job as a parking garage attendant. He'd worked so hard for that money and had planned to purchase a used laptop so that he could finish working on the software from anywhere.

He would have never believed that four months later, one of the largest electronic automobile manufacturing companies would purchase his security software to install on their new electric cars. In one week, he'd suddenly become a millionaire and he'd only been nineteen at the time.

He'd gone from living on the streets to owning a Fortune 500 company in less than a six-month period.

The first thing he'd done was get an apartment for Ryder and himself. Someplace downtown. Someplace nice.

Ryder had been working at an old boxing gym, helping clean up after hours. He'd fronted Ryder the funds to purchase the gym when the owner had wanted to retire.

Sean hadn't come around for almost a year and when he did, he'd been drunk and had started a fight with Ryder. So he'd kicked him out, and they hadn't seen much of him since.

For the next few years, he'd traveled, spent a lot of his new money on things. He'd been wasteful and stupid. Then, he'd grown bored and started tinkering with code again. Well enough, that he'd gotten so good at it, the people running his old business had come knocking. He'd answered the call, since there wasn't anything else to do.

He'd found Morgan a few years later, when he was twenty-six. He'd never imagined that his life could keep getting better. He didn't deserve someone like her. Every day he woke up with her next to him, he'd pinch himself just to make sure it was real.

Now she was telling him that everything they had, everything he'd meant to her, was gone.

"You don't remember me?" he asked, trying to understand what was happening. When he'd walked in, Morgan had been laughing and joking with her friends, whom she'd obviously known. Plus, she seemed to know her parents.

"No," Morgan said softly.

His hand dropped from hers. "What..." He looked up to Victoria, who was frowning at her daughter. "Did you know about this?" he asked Victoria.

Now it all made sense. This was why they were keeping him away from Morgan. They had finally found a way to get him out of Morgan's life, for good.

Was he going to stand for it? What could he do if Morgan didn't remember him? There was no way he was going to let go of her. Morgan was the best thing that had ever happened to him.

Whatever happened now, he was going to fight for her. Fight for their love. If the roles were reversed, he knew without a doubt that she would do the same.

"No, of course not," Victoria said with a slight gasp. "I

think it's time you left," she said quickly. She opened the door, motioning for him to leave.

"No," he said firmly. Then he turned his attention back to Morgan, who was looking at him with pain and confusion in her eyes. "I'll leave only if Morgan wishes it."

"Morgan, dear," Victoria said, moving back over to her daughter's side. "You're tired. I think it's time you got some rest."

Morgan looked between them. "Mom, I think I'd like a moment alone with..." When she frowned up at him, his heart broke a little more. She really didn't remember him. She didn't even know his name.

"Liam," he said softly. "Liam Taylor. You're Morgan Taylor." He took her hand in his again.

"Liam," she said, her frown slightly increasing. "I'd like a moment alone with Liam." She turned to her mother. "Please."

Her mother glared at him, then straightened her shoulders, a move he knew she did when she wanted to appear more powerful and in control.

"I'll be just outside the door," Victoria said, more as a warning to him.

"Thank you," Morgan said. She turned to him.

When the hospital door shut behind Victoria, Morgan asked. "Are we really married?"

He smiled and softened. "Yes, we married on March twentieth of last year."

She continued to frown and then asked, "What is today's date?"

This time he was the one frowning. "It's June eleventh." If she couldn't remember him and didn't even know the date, what else had she forgotten. Had the doctors checked her out completely? Memory loss was no little thing. He vowed once he left her room to hunt down the damned doctor who had been in charge of checking her out and have a word with the man.

The Davenports were an elite family. Hell, Morgan was an actual heiress. Surely, they had gotten the best doctor to look after her. He'd tried to push his way into her care from the moment he'd found out about the accident, but her family was... well... overpowering.

"You really can't remember me at all?" he asked her, wishing to take her hand again, but just the thought of her not knowing his name made him refrain. He didn't want to scare her.

"No." She shook her head slightly. "But then, I didn't really remember my parents at first either. Even with Kimber, Leanne, and Reagan, it took a moment for their names to register."

"The quad squad," he supplied as relief washed over him. If she had issues remembering everyone else, most likely it would just be a matter of time before she remembered him.

Morgan shifted, then chuckled. "Yes, I'd forgotten we called ourselves that. See?" She reached out and touched his hand, then jumped back slightly as if the touch shocked her. "I'll remember you. It's just... I'm so confused right now."

"Right." He smiled, trying not to let it affect him, then reached over and took her hand in his. "I'm sure you'll remember everything once you're home."

This time when Morgan frowned, he knew what was coming before she said anything.

"I... my parents..." she started, only to have the door open again. This time Victoria had brought Doctor Ellis. The man had been Morgan's doctor since birth. He not only went out of his way to make house calls for the family, but Liam was pretty sure they were the sole reason the man hadn't retired yet.

"What's going on here?" the older gray-haired gentlemen asked. His tone sounded as if Liam had been torturing Morgan. His eyes accused him of such as well.

"We were just discussing when I can take my wife home," he said, standing up.

Dr. Ellis moved over to Morgan's side. "Morgan, your parents and I think it's best if you went home with them. They're more prepared for your physical needs. They've hired a physical therapist and live closer to the hospital and my offices." The doctor glanced up at him. "I'm sure your husband doesn't wish to hinder your recovery and sees that this is the best course of action."

"The best course of action is for her to be home with me," Liam said, glaring over at Victoria.

"It's not up to you," Victoria said. She rushed over to Morgan's side and laid a hand on her casted leg. "It's up to Morgan."

Everyone in the room looked down at Morgan in silence.

"I... think... I need some rest," Morgan said slowly. "I'll decide tomorrow."

For a moment, Victoria appeared as if she was going to push Morgan, so he jumped in, not wanting to give her time or to pressure Morgan into making a rash decision.

"Rest." He took Morgan's hand in his and then lifted it to his lips. Even her right hand, the only thing on her body not in a cast, was completely covered in bruises. He let his lips rest on her knuckles and closed his eyes against the pain he felt knowing that she was in such deep pain. Knowing that she'd forgotten how much she meant to him. "I'll see you tomorrow." He made a point to let his eyes lock with hers. He'd just have to show her all over again. Have to prove to her that he was worth giving him a chance again.

Fighting back the emotions, he straightened and left the room without another word.

The first thing he did after leaving the room was to hunt down her wedding ring. One of the nurses gladly presented a bag of her belongings that had been cut or taken off her after her accident.

He slipped her wedding ring onto his pinky finger, determined to get to the bottom of finding out more about the care she was receiving. He wanted to find out what sort of tests they'd run on her.

Not really knowing where to start, since the Davenports pretty much owned the hospital, he pulled out his cell phone and called the only other person he trusted.

# CHAPTER THREE

*When you light a candle, you also cast a shadow.*
**Ursula K. Le Guin**

There was too much for Morgan to process while her parents were still in the room talking to the doctor. She may have forgotten Liam and the life she'd had with him, but the memories of her parents were strong.

She knew at times they were overbearing, obnoxious, and protective. But there was no doubt in her mind that they had her best interests in mind.

She could either return to something she knew, something that was safe, or trust in the life she'd chosen over a year ago, even though she couldn't remember having made such a choice.

"Mom." She groaned sightly and rested her head back, closing her eyes. "I'm tired and my head hurts."

"Here, honey, let me get you some more—"

"No." She jerked her eyes open just before her mother could hit the small button that dispensed her pain meds. "I don't want to fall into a deep drugged sleep. I want some quiet time so I can think." She looked over to her father and added, "Please?" She made sure to look a little pathetic.

"Victoria, I think we should go. Let's let Morgan get some rest." He walked over and took Morgan's mother's arm and started gracefully pulling her towards the door.

The doctor had left shortly after Liam had gone. No doubt he'd just been there to make her parents' point in the first place.

Morgan mouthed a thank-you to her father as they left the room.

When she was alone in the room, she closed her eyes and ran over her options. She tried searching her memories for any sign of her past with Liam. She pulled up his face in her memory and tried to remember his touch, his scent, anything.

A few minutes later, totally frustrated, she glared down at her casts and wished more than anything that she could get up, walk over to the window, and see outside. What was the weather like? It was June. Was it sunny or raining? She couldn't tell from her position.

The hospital room was large, no doubt a private suite her parents had arranged. They made huge donations to the hospital each year, so she was sure the hospital had been eager to help.

She frowned. Why? Why did they always make donations to this hospital? She searched her memory and an image of a small baby wrapped in blue flashed so quickly in her mind that she had to reach up and touch her temples when pain pulsed there.

"I have a brother," she gasped. "Aaron." She smiled when she remembered his name and relaxed back as an image of him filled her mind. Then she remembered how Aaron had fought for the first few years of his life in this very hospital. Leukemia. She remembered. She'd been four years old when he'd been born and six when he'd disappeared into the hospital for over a year. He'd come back so small, so fragile, that she hadn't been allowed to play with him for an entire year after.

So why hadn't Aaron come to visit her yet? Maybe he had come, as Liam had mentioned he had visited her when she'd been asleep.

Why was she having an easy time remembering her friends and her family but still couldn't remember a thing about Liam?

She didn't know how they'd met or fallen in love. She couldn't even remember her wedding day. That hurt since she'd always dreamed of her special day. She'd imagined being treated as a princess, having a huge extravagant wedding at the country club or maybe even a destination wedding.

One thing she could clearly remember was daydreaming about the day she'd walk down the aisle. Now, she'd just learned that not only had the memory of falling in love for the first time been ripped from her, but so had the memory of the most important day of her life.

As tears rolled down her cheeks, she desperately wished to be surrounded by familiarity.

As she drifted off to sleep, that thought consumed her mind until she woke. Her body was riddled with pain, and her head ached from the tears the night before and the indecision.

When her parents showed up shortly before dawn, she was so desperate to make it all stop that she caved in and told them that she would allow them to take her home after the doctor agreed that it was okay for her to leave the care of the hospital.

Someone must have told Liam before he entered her room. The look on his face was a cross between hurt and anger. The anger was focused completely on her mother. Morgan noticed that Liam managed to say only a few words to her his entire visit.

During the two hours he sat by her side, her mother never moved from her spot in the corner. She couldn't remember ever being chaperoned before and wondered why her mother was acting so strange now.

She'd wanted to ask her once they were alone, but she'd fallen asleep shortly after lunch and when she woke next, she was alone in the room.

Her conversation with Liam flowed easily enough. He filled her in on what he'd learned from the doctor and nurses about her health, something her parents didn't even talk about with her. She asked him questions about how they'd met, but each time, her mother would cough, and Liam would softly tell her that he'd remind her when they were alone.

Something told her that if it were up to her mother, they would never be left alone.

Nurses came and went. The doctor visited her once a day, usually first thing in the morning.

A physical therapist, Carolynn, a rather muscular black woman with a cheerful smile, came in just before dinnertime and talked to her about what she could expect once she was allowed to go home. She didn't know how the woman expected anything from her since both of her legs were in casts.

When she told Carolynn this, she just laughed.

"Oh, honey, only one of these will stay on once you leave here." Carolynn tapped the heavy plaster on her right leg. "This is just wrapping to keep the sutures clean," she told her, then she turned over the file she was looking at. "See here?" She pointed to a diagram of a body. On it were red pencil marks on the body. "These lines are where you had stitches." Then she pointed to black lines on what Morgan assumed were the bones. "These are breaks. Your right leg has three breaks, here, here, and here." Carolynn pointed to spots on her fibula twice, one low by her ankle and one high near her knee and then her tibia once right in the middle. "These breaks are common in car accidents where legs get pinned behind the steering column." She sighed. "It'll take a lot of hard work, but you'll be up and walking in no time."

"What about my arm?" she asked, looking down at her left arm.

"You aren't left-handed, are you?" Carolynn asked.

Morgan nodded. "Afraid so."

Carolynn chuckled. She flipped a page and then showed her the chart that showed her upper body. "Solid break in your radius. No pins, but you'll need the cast on for about six weeks. Your leg cast will have to be on longer. You'll be given crutches and you might need to use a cane for a while too."

Morgan frowned at that thought. Canes were for old people. Weren't they?

"I..." she started, but then she stopped and shook her head.

"Go on, honey," Carolynn said, motioning. "If you can't say it to your therapist—even your physical therapist—you shouldn't say it anyone." She giggled.

Morgan smiled briefly, then said, "I'm struggling with memory loss."

Carolynn's eyes softened. "That'll happen with cases like yours. Your entire body is fighting hard to get back what was taken in a flash. Be patient, it'll all come back to you. The more you stress over it, the longer it'll take." Carolynn sighed and then stood up. "Now, enough chit-chat. How about we get down to work? Let's get you up on your feet."

"I..." Morgan felt the blood leave her face. "Am I ready?"

"Honey, I guess we'll find out," Carolynn said with a laugh.

It took some doing. Carolynn had to cut the bandages off Morgan's left leg first. When the fresh air hit her skin, Morgan shivered and instantly wished for the security back.

"You'll get used to it," she assured her. "The nurse will be in after to change these bandages." She ran her fingers over the small, soiled bandages over Morgan's thigh and knee areas. "This all looks good enough to get you up on your feet. Or well, foot." She chuckled again. "Here." She handed her a crutch and then showed her how to prop it under her right arm. "It'll take some doing, but we'll have you going to the bathroom on your own in no time."

Carolynn took Morgan's right elbow and helped her stand on her left leg. The first thing Morgan noticed was how strong her leg felt under her. Sure, the skin pulled and itched under the bandages, but she didn't feel like it was going to buckle underneath her. The second thing she noticed was how much shorter she was than Carolynn.

"What honey?" Carolynn asked her when she noticed Morgan's face.

"I guess I didn't remember how short I was," she admitted, and Carolynn burst out laughing.

"Honey, I'm six-four. Everyone's short standing next to me."

Morgan smiled. "Good. For a moment there, I thought I'd lost a few inches."

Carolynn was smiling when the door swung open, and Morgan's mother came in. The moment she noticed Morgan standing, she rushed over and grasped her waist.

"What on earth is going on here?" she demanded. "Who are you? You can't just come in here and force my daughter—"

"Lady, you'd better back off now," Carolynn warned. "You're going to make us all fall, and I know you and I are strong enough right now to handle that, but this poor child isn't."

Morgan saw her mother's eyes narrow. "What authority do you have to come in here?"

Carolynn's eyebrows shot up, then she held up a finger silencing her mother. "Morgan, why don't you have a sit while I go on out into the hall and have a nice chat with your mother?"

Morgan was so dumbfounded that this woman was able to silence her mother that she fell backwards onto the bed and nodded her head.

"Good. Don't you go anywhere. I'll be right back," she added with a wink. Then she turned and walked out of the room.

Her mother stood there, looking between Morgan and Carolynn, when Carolynn said from the doorway. "Well? You coming?" Her mother flinched slightly and then stepped out of the room.

When the door shut, Morgan sighed and closed her eyes. It had felt so good to stand up. To be off her backside. For the past week she'd done everything she could to relieve the weight on her hips and butt area. But with the heavy casts, all she could do was slightly shift her weight from butt cheek to butt cheek.

Even now, just sitting straight up was a huge improvement.

About two minutes later, the door opened again, and Carolynn walked in with a smile on her face.

"Well, now, let's see how well you do at walking," she said cheerfully.

Morgan was so eager, she started to get up by herself. Carolynn rushed across the room, laughing, and helped her.

"Yeah, you're ready." She helped her put the crutch under her arm again.

She made three trips from the bed to the bathroom before all of her energy drained out of her.

"That's good for tonight," Carolynn said, helping Morgan sit on the edge of the bed. "Better than even I thought you'd do."

Morgan was smiling when the door opened again. This time her mother had Dr. Ellis in tow.

"There she is now," Carolynn said cheerfully. "Your daughter just made three trips to the bathroom. She's going to be running marathons in no time." Carolynn winked at her. "I'll be back tomorrow around the same time." She nodded to the doctor and her mother. "I'll just go see if they have your dinner ready."

Carolynn quickly left the room.

"Are you okay?" her mother asked, rushing over to help Morgan shift a pillow behind her back.

"Yes, it felt good to get up." She sighed and rested her head back. "I'm tired now, but it felt good."

"You shouldn't have pushed yourself," her mother said. "Herold, don't you agree?"

Dr. Ellis was too busy reading Morgan's chart to answer.

"Mother, I'm fine. Besides, I got to use the bathroom."

She sighed. "It felt wonderful. Carolynn says that with some help, I'll be able to shower tomorrow."

"No!" Her mother almost barked it out. "Herold, you simply have to stop that woman."

"Carolynn is one of our top physical therapists," Dr. Ellis said firmly. "I'm the one who put her on the schedule to start working with Morgan today. If all goes well tomorrow, you'll be able to take Morgan home the day after."

Her mother was silent for a moment, and Morgan could see the wheels turning in her mother's head.

"Very well, but I'm going to insist I be here next time," she said firmly.

Dr. Ellis shrugged slightly as he set her chart back down. "How are you feeling?" he asked Morgan.

"Good. Tired. Hungry," she answered.

The doctor nodded slightly as he frowned down at his watch. "Good, good," he said before leaving.

Her mother sat next to her while someone brought in her tray of food.

While she ate, her mother told her all about how they had set up her bedroom for her.

"We've gotten a state-of-the-art adjustable bed. You'll have an around-the-clock nurse at first, then the best physical therapist," her mother continued. Morgan half listened, but the more she ate, the more tired she became.

Halfway through her meal, she pushed the tray aside and shut her eyes while her mother continued to talk about the arrangements that she'd made for her grand return.

In her sleep, she dreamed of her childhood. Questions that she'd had during the day were answered once her eyes closed. But the only answers were from the time before Liam. Nothing of her life with him or her feelings towards him ever crept into her slumber.

The following day, Carolynn was back, only this time Morgan's mother was right there, commenting on everything Carolynn tried to get Morgan to do. Her mother complained about how she thought the woman was forcing Morgan to work too hard.

Morgan wanted to tell her mother to sit down and not interfere, since she was enjoying the exercise. She hated being dependent on someone else and wanted some of her freedom back.

Almost half an hour after Carolynn walked in the room, she left again.

"I don't like how that woman is forcing you to do things you're not comfortable with," her mother complained when they were alone.

"Carolynn wasn't forcing, and all I was doing was standing and walking," she pointed out.

Her mother was currently fluffing her pillows after she'd spent a few moments readjusting Morgan's right leg. She knew that her mother was hovering but figured that she would allow it, considering the circumstances.

"I'll just go and see about getting you some lunch," her mother said once she was done adjusting and readjusting everything.

"Thanks," she answered, silently wishing for a panini and an iced caramel mocha for some reason.

A few moments after her mother left, there was a knock on the door and Liam walked in.

"How are you feeling today?" he asked, stepping inside.

Her eyes zoned in on the cup and bag he was carrying, and her heart did a little flip in her chest. Thankfully, they had removed all of the sensors attached to her chest once they'd determined she was in stable condition.

"I'll be doing much better if that's an iced caramel

mocha," she answered, silently wishing it was, but unsure if it would be since she didn't know how much of her life she'd shared with the man.

When Liam chuckled and held out the cup towards her, she felt her entire body weaken at his sexy grin. God, the man apparently knew her. Right down to her favorite drink. Then again, she supposed it wasn't hard. Hell, most of her friends knew how she liked her coffee drinks.

"It is. I know it's your favorite, as well as"—he held up the bag— "your all-time favorite sandwich, a chicken panini with spinach and extra pesto." He pulled up the chair and sat next to her, then dug in the bag and pulled out a sandwich for her and one for himself.

She looked down at the wrapped sandwich from her favorite sandwich shop and her favorite drink and felt her eyes start to burn. She avoided looking at him as she hid her emotions. Liam really did know her.

"Hey," he said, taking her hand, "it's just a sandwich."

She felt stupid. She'd done her best to hide her emotions, but apparently, he even knew how to break through that barrier.

"Where's Victoria?" he asked, with a slight frown.

"Vict..." She frowned and then sighed. "That's my mother's name." She felt a huge relief wash over her. "Victoria Davenport." She slumped back a little on the pillows.

Liam's frown grew. "You're just now remembering that?"

She nodded, then took a sip of her drink and sighed as the cool sweetness filled her mouth and gave her happy little feelings. "Yes." She looked at him. "My parents' names are Victoria and Thomas Davenport. I have a younger brother, Aaron Davenport." She smiled as more memories washed through her. Memories of her teenage years. Of family holidays taken overseas. Of the house her parents own in Paris, the one in Hawaii. So many more memories. "I'm Morgan Renee Davenport. Sixth generation heiress to the Davenport legacy, which goes back to England, where one of my ancestors was kin to a king."

"No," Liam said in a low voice as he took her hand again. "You're Morgan Renee Taylor, my wife. The woman that I fell in love with and the person I plan on spending the rest of my life convincing to love me in return."

# CHAPTER FOUR

*Everyone is a moon and has a dark side which he never shows to anybody.*
**Mark Twain**

Over the next few days, Liam spent as much time with Morgan as he was allowed. She'd been moved to a private room, and he'd visited as often as he could without interfering with her parents, since he didn't want to argue with Victoria. The woman didn't like anything he did and took any opportunity to voice her dislikes.

Even on their wedding day, Victoria had pulled him aside moments before the ceremony and had berated him about the low number of guests he had in attendance.

When he'd stepped out and stood up front with the preacher, he'd tried not to focus on the dozen friends sitting on his side of the aisle versus the hundreds that crowded together on Morgan's side.

Morgan had pulled him aside later that evening at their reception and assured him that his handful of friends were far more valuable than the hundreds of strangers that had come at her parents' request.

"Don't let my mother get to you," Morgan had said, wrapping her arms around him.

"About what?" he'd asked. She'd looked so amazing that day. Like the fairytale princess he'd first imagined she was that night when he'd met her. The satin V-neck wedding dress that she'd picked out had been so her. It had an open back, and he'd enjoyed running his fingers over her soft exposed skin the entire time they danced at the reception.

"My mother is obsessed with guest lists. She believes the success of an event can be calculated based on the sheer number of butts in chairs." Morgan had rolled her eyes to show him she thought it was ridiculous.

"I'm not worried," he said, but in truth, Victoria's words had stung. He didn't have a family to share the day with. All he had was a handful of friends that he trusted. People who knew what he came from, where he'd been in his life. Where he was now.

Since he'd struck it rich, as some of them had joked with him about, he'd learned who he could trust and who he couldn't. Some people had come into his life shortly after he'd hit it big. It had taken him a while to figure out that they were only there because of his position or his money.

He'd tried dating and it had been as big of a disaster as some of those friendships. When he met Morgan, he'd already written off the possibility of finding someone.

Morgan had tilted her head slightly when he said he wasn't worried, and he knew that she'd read right through his defenses.

"Okay, I might have been a little worried," he'd admitted, then he smiled. "But all that matters is this." He'd lifted her hand and looked down at the perfect one-carat diamond solitaire ring that he'd picked out for her. Then he'd lifted her fingers to his lips and kissed them. "Us. You're my wife and I'm your husband." He'd pulled her to him and had kissed her.

They'd laughed when loud clapping and cheers interrupted them. It had been the second-best day of his life, the first being the day that he'd met Morgan.

Sine the moment he'd met her, Morgan had a way of making him feel special. Like he was worthy of being loved.

Almost a week after Morgan had woken up, he walked into the hospital and was halfway to her room when a nurse stopped him.

"She's not here. Your wife was released first thing this morning," she said in passing.

He stopped dead in his tracks as her words sank in. Then he rushed forward to her door and looked into the empty room.

Pulling out his phone, he dialed Victoria. When she answered, he barked out, "You took her home?"

"Well, hello to you too, Liam," Victoria said in a calm voice.

"She wasn't supposed to be released until tomorrow," he replied.

"Well, Dr. Ellis agreed that it was okay for us to take her home a day earlier." Victoria added, "I could have sworn I told you yesterday."

"You know damn well you didn't." He punched the elevator button. "I'm coming over."

"I'm sorry, that wouldn't be a good idea. Morgan's very tired from all the excitement this morning. She's resting now and can't take visitors," Victoria said cheerfully.

"I'm not a visitor. You will not keep my wife from me," he growled out and hung up.

He ignored her phone calls as he drove from the hospital to the Davenport estate.

The huge iron gates at the bottom of their drive were shut and when he buzzed the security box, their butler, John, answered.

"Hey, John, it's Liam. I'm here to see Morgan," he said quickly. He liked John, even though the man was a hard-ass most of the time. He knew that he was just doing what Victoria had requested.

"Sorry, sir, I've been given instructions—"

"John, let me in," he said firmly. "I'm not playing any of Victoria's games. I'm here to see my wife."

John was silent for a moment, then the gates opened slowly.

How many times had he driven up this drive when he'd been seeing Morgan or in the past year? Fewer than a dozen, he figured as he parked in front of the stone steps that led up to the iron front doors.

Unlike the modern home that he and Morgan had chosen for themselves last year, which was almost an hour away in the hills, the Davenport estate was a little more dated, historical looking. It was made of white stone and surrounded by palm trees.

The inside was just as grandiose as the outside, with a lot of iron, stone, and marble.

When he stepped up to the iron doors, John was there, holding the massive door open for him.

"I'm to lead you into the study," he said firmly.

Ignoring the man, he stepped inside and headed for the massive marble staircase. He knew that Victoria would have put Morgan in her old rooms upstairs.

He was halfway up the stairs when John said, "Sir, she's not up there. She's in the guest wing."

Glancing down at the man, he followed him through the main entryway and living space down a long hallway with stone archways. There were no pictures or paintings here, as if the space had been simply forgotten or not used often.

This was an area of the home that he'd never been in before.

"Madam thought it would be easier for the Mrs. to be in rooms downstairs and that are closer to the gym. She's arranged for the physical therapy sessions to begin first thing tomorrow." The man said all this quickly, as if he didn't want to be caught giving information to the enemy.

"Thanks, John," he said as he stood outside a heavy wood door.

John nodded and then quickly disappeared.

When Liam opened the door, Morgan was sitting up in bed, reading.

She glanced up and smiled at him. "You made it. Mother told me you had work."

He frowned as he crossed the room and, without thinking, bent down and kissed her. Part of him hadn't wanted to admit it, but for a moment, he'd been worried that he'd lost her.

Victoria Davenport was a very powerful woman. If she didn't want him to see Morgan again, he knew in his gut that she'd do anything to keep them apart.

Feeling Morgan's lips under his softened that worry slightly.

Hearing someone clear their throat behind him, he stiffened and pulled back.

"I left instructions—" Victoria started

"Let's make one thing clear," Liam said, straightening. "For now, Morgan wants to recover here, but at no point will you bar me from seeing her again, unless it's her specific wish." He waited until Victoria glanced down at Morgan, then narrowed her eyes ever so slightly.

"I'm just doing what's best—"

"Morgan can decide what's best for her," he said, a little more firmly than he'd intended. He turned to Morgan, and he felt his heart soften just looking down at her. "If you don't want to see me, you can message me yourself." He pulled the surprise he'd brought for her out of his pocket.

She took the cell phone box from his hands and looked down at it.

"Your phone was lost in the wreck, but I had them pull everything from your last backup. I got you the newest model." He smiled as she opened the box.

"Thank you," she said.

To his horror, her eyes began to water.

"Hey." He sat on the side of her bed and touched her shoulder. "What's all this about?"

She chuckled and shook her head, then set the phone down on her lap to wipe her eyes with her good hand.

"It's just..." She motioned to the phone. "I remember this photo."

He looked down at the image of the beautiful French Polynesian sunset with their dark silhouettes kissing in front of the light and smiled. "That was on our honeymoon," he said softly. "That's us." He picked up the phone, used her code to unlock it, and opened the images. "Here are more." He showed her. As they scrolled through the images, her mother left the room.

"I... don't remember any of this." Morgan set the phone down after frowning at some of the images they'd taken on their honeymoon.

"It'll come back to you." He touched her hand, running his finger over the spot where her wedding band used to sit.

He noticed that her fingers were less swollen. Actually, her face was almost back to normal as well. There was still a lot of bruises, but they had lightened in color.

She'd obviously been able to shower, and her hair was now back to its normal sheen and style. Her face was still bare of all products, which highlighted the bruising. Still, she was the most beautiful thing he'd ever seen.

"How are you feeling?" he asked her, shifting to sit a little closer to her on the king-sized bed.

"Good." She tucked the phone against her side. "I didn't even remember this room." She glanced around.

He chuckled. "I didn't even know it existed."

"Good, I'm not the only one then. I was sure I would remember everything about this house. For the most part I do. I mean, I remember the day we moved in here. I remember having swimming parties, a few birthday parties, and I even had my very first kiss standing outside the iron doors." She smiled. "I was—"

"Sixteen. Bobby Lincoln," he supplied. "I know."

She frowned and then tilted her head. "Okay, so... we've established you know everything about me."

"Almost everything."

"Since I can't remember... how about you spend some time telling me about you."

He thought about it, then nodded. "Okay, what do you want to know?"

She was silent for a moment. "Your family? Are they from around here?"

He frowned and felt the punch in the gut that always come when he had to explain his past.

"I'm an orphan," he said simply.

Morgan frowned. "I'm sorry." She shook her head.

"It's okay." He took her hand in his again. "I was abandoned as a baby in Oregon. I grew up in several different orphanages until I was placed in one in Los Angeles."

"What about adoption?" she asked.

He shrugged. "I was too disagreeable."

"I doubt that," she said with a frown, and he remembered her saying the exact same thing the first time he'd told her about his past.

He looked down at their hands and felt as if he could never explain to her how much she'd meant to him over the past two years. How was he going to show her? What could he do?

More importantly, was her family going to allow him to get close to her again. They'd done everything in their power to keep them apart the first time and if today was any hint of what was to come, he doubted Victoria was going to play nice this time either.

"What happened when you graduated high school?" she asked.

"I didn't. When I was sixteen, I quit school, ended up getting my GED instead. I thought it was the smartest move, only..." He frowned. "We couldn't handle all the rules at the orphanage and decided to try heading out on our own. So..." He shrugged. "We moved out."

"We?" she asked with a slight frown.

"Ryder, Sean, and me. We had grown up in the orphanage together and were best friends. We got our GEDs at the same time. We had a plan, well, Sean and I did at any rate, to start our own software business. Ryder was already working at the gym full time, and I had a job in a parking garage. Still, it wasn't enough to keep us in the apartment we'd tried to rent. We lived there all of three days. They kicked us out after they found out we were all underage."

"Where did you live?" she asked, concern lacing her voice.

He shrugged. "In shelters, on the street. During the winters, we'd stay at the gym Ryder was working at or break into cars to stay warm."

"How terrible," she said, and he felt her fingers tighten in his.

He remembered telling her all this long ago. They'd talked about every aspect of his past over the last two years. She'd told him all about her past as well. How she'd been raised in privilege, had taken family vacations to so many places he'd only dreamed of going.

He'd promised himself when he was younger that if he made it in life, he'd see all those places. He'd traveled for the first couple years after the initial buyout.

Then he'd gotten lonely and bored and returned home. When he'd been offered the job of CEO of his old company, ESP, he'd jumped at it. He'd never really wanted to sell in the first place, but all those zeros on the check had dazzled him.

He'd never been happier than when he was running the business he'd started that night long ago. Until he'd bumped into Morgan.

Before he could explain how he'd finally made some-thing of himself and gotten off the streets, there was a knock on the door, and Aaron strolled in.

He didn't hate Aaron, but he didn't exactly like him either. He tolerated the guy.

He was twenty-two and as spoiled as any person could be. Liam didn't know how Morgan and Aaron could be related. There hadn't been an ounce of spoiled attitude in

Morgan from the moment he'd met her, whereas Aaron acted as if the entire world owed him everything.

"There you are, sis," Aaron said casually. "I'd heard you'd returned home." He glanced over to Liam. "Already bored of him and marriage?"

"Aaron?" Morgan dropped her hand from Liam's and reached out for her brother as tears filled her eyes. "Aaron." She half squealed his name.

Liam could see that she was genuinely excited to see her brother, while Aaron appeared bored and slightly annoyed.

"Yes, still here, sister." He walked over to her side of the bed and let her take his hand in her own.

"Oh, wow, I..." Morgan shook her head slightly, then wiped the tears from her face. "You've changed from my memories." She tilted her head slightly.

"I just got a haircut," Aaron said with a slight shrug. "You look absolutely horrible," he said calmly. "I can't believe you'd let anyone see you in such a state."

Morgan reached up and touched her hair.

"Don't mind him. You look radiant," Liam interjected as he took her hand in his. But he could tell that her brother's words had already affected her, like they had always done.

"Aaron, don't you have somewhere to be?" he asked.

"Nope," he answered quickly, sitting on the side of the bed. "Mom tells me that you're staying here indefinitely," he added with a slight inflection in his tone.

"She's here until she is well enough and decides to come home," Liam replied.

"Right." Aaron chuckled. "If Mom ever lets you go again." He stood up. "Well, I'm bored." He walked out without another word.

Morgan was frowning at the door. The lighthearted mood from earlier was long gone.

"Hey, don't let Aaron get to you," he said, taking her hand again.

"Has he always been like that? In my memories..." She shook her head. "He was different."

"I've known him for almost two years and in that entire time, he's been..." He motioned with his free hand. "Pretty much the same."

"I..." She shifted and pulled her hand from his. "I'm tired now."

He felt a stab in his chest, but she did appear tired, so he nodded. "I'll stop by tomorrow."

He stood up and glanced around the stark white room. He mentally made a note to have a bunch of her favorite flowers delivered to cheer up the place.

Their home was so different from her parents' house. Her mother decorated everything in white, cream, or taupe. At their home, Morgan had always added bright hits of cheerful colors—blues, greens, and red, her favorite color.

He leaned over her and brushed his lips against hers. He felt her stiffen and then relax against him.

"You'll remember me," he said softly. "You'll remember everything. I promise."

She nodded and then shifted slightly before closing her eyes.

When he stepped out of the room, Victoria was standing there, waiting for him.

"We need to talk," she said, and without waiting for him, she walked down the hallway.

# CHAPTER FIVE

*Look at how a single candle can both defy and define the darkness.*
**Anne Frank**

Morgan was sitting on the edge of her bed the morning after returning home. Nothing felt familiar to her. She'd hoped that when she returned to her parents' home, she would remember more.

But instead of staying in her old rooms upstairs, she'd been wheeled into this guest space that she didn't even remember the house having. They were decorated in stark colors. Even though the intent was to make a guest feel welcomed, they actually did the opposite. The starkness of everything made her feel less comfortable than she had in the hospital.

The windows were too far away to really see outside, and the blinds were closed, only allowing in a sliver of light at the bottom.

She desperately wished to sit outside in the sunlight and had no way of getting there by herself, as the wheelchair she'd been wheeled in on had been quickly taken away. She didn't trust herself yet using the crutches.

Ann, her mother's maid and housekeeper, had wheeled in a tray of breakfast almost an hour ago. She'd promised that she'd return to help her shower and clean up, but she hadn't come back yet, and Morgan was getting desperate to head to the bathroom.

Ann was a middle-aged woman who had more of an eagle eye than her mother. The woman saw all that went on around the house. Nothing ever got by her. Even when Morgan had been a teen, she remembered Ann finding out about the slightest infractions happening around the home.

She waited another five minutes before grabbing her crutch and standing on her own. She slowly made her way to the bathroom, mindful to not slip on the gleaming white Italian marble floors. After using the toilet, she felt good enough to wash her face and comb her hair on her own.

She stopped short of showering, since it would take wrapping her leg and arm in plastic, a task that had taken both Ann and her to accomplish yesterday before Liam had visited.

She was making her way out of the bathroom when the crutch snagged on an area rug. She let out a quick scream and closed her eyes, waiting for the pain she knew would come from the fall. Only it didn't come. Instead, a deep chuckle had her jerking her eyes opened.

"I guess my timing is perfect," a male voice said directly behind her.

There were strong arms wrapped around her, holding her steady, and she relaxed.

Her initial belief that it had been Liam who had caught her dimmed when the man spoke again.

"You shouldn't try walking on your own this early in your recovery."

She craned her neck and looked into dark brown eyes. The man was handsome. Not rugged like Liam, but a slick, sleek handsome. He was obviously a man who paid a lot of attention to his looks. His hair was slicked back and styled, and his beard was neatly trimmed. Still, he was damned good-looking, and her heart jumped. Or maybe that was due to the fact that she'd almost fallen?

Either way, she was a little breathless and instead of responding to him, she nodded as he helped her to the side of the bed.

"There, that's better," he said with a smile. It was then that she noticed he was wearing black scrubs with a white embroidered Beverly Hills Physical Therapy logo.

"I'm Grayson Moore, your physical therapist." He knelt beside her.

"Morgan Dav— Taylor," she corrected quickly.

She had been playing her married name over in her head since the moment Liam had corrected her. Morgan Taylor. Mrs. Liam Taylor. It sounded... right. Deep in her soul, it sounded good. Which was something. Right?

"I know." Grayson chuckled. "As I said, I'll be your physical therapist."

"Right," she sighed and remembered her mother mentioning that she would start therapy today. "I'd hoped to shower before..." she admitted.

"Today we're going to start off light. I think we'll be okay." He examined her cast, then touched her exposed toes one by one. "Everything looks good. You're getting good blood flow. How about your hand?" He reached up and took her fingers in her left hand, wiggling them one by one.

She watched the top of his head as he concentrated on the task.

"I don't like the color of your fingers. I might suggest we remove this cast and let your arm air a little, then get you in a breathable one." He finally looked back up. "I'm hoping that little show earlier wasn't a sign of how good you are at walking with those," he said with a smile as he nodded towards the crutch, which had fallen when she'd tripped earlier.

She smiled. "It got snagged on the rug." She motioned to the thick area rug at the base of the bed.

"Right, we'll just get it out of the way then so that doesn't happen again." He had just started rolling it up when her mother walked in.

"What are you doing?" her mother asked Grayson.

"I'm removing an obstacle that your daughter has already tripped on," he said firmly as he set the rug aside. He turned back to Morgan. "Now, let's see your skills." He handed her the crutch.

Morgan's mother watched her walking across the room for all of a minute before she got a phone call and left again.

"Good," Grayson said encouragingly. "Not bad." He helped her sit back down. "We can't start the real fun until after your cast is off, but there's plenty we can do in the meantime. How's your other hand?" He knelt in front of her and took her right hand in his, then turned it over several times. She winced with pain. "Yeah, we can start here," he said to himself as he continued to twist her arm back and forth.

By about the fifth time, she felt her tight muscles relaxing a little.

Still, it was a painful process and even other parts of her body were starting to ache.

She was just about to suggest that he give her a break when Liam stepped into the room, a huge armful of colorful flowers in his arms. He took one look at Grayson kneeling at by Morgan's feet and frowned.

"Can I help you?" Liam asked, setting the vase of red tulips down on the dresser.

She was so happy to see the color in the room that her eyes never left the flowers while Grayson explained why he was there and what he was doing.

"I think we've done enough for today. I'll be back tomorrow. I'll talk with your mother about getting that cast removed today and get you fitted for something that will allow your arm to breathe a little more," Grayson said before heading out.

"Thank you," she said, turning her eyes away from the flowers and mentally comparing the two men.

Her earlier assessment had been right. Where Liam was more rugged and raw looking, Grayson was slick, refined, and, no doubt, her parents' idea of a perfect son-in-law.

She had fallen for Grayson's type in the past. She could remember at least that much. Ron had been her second boyfriend. He'd come from a very wealthy family. If she remembered correctly, his father had been in the stock business. Anyway, Ron had been well dressed, and she'd fallen for his charms. But on their second date, if it hadn't been for the self-defense classes her father had insisted on, she would have ended up a rape victim. When he'd started ripping off her clothes after she said no, she'd punched Ron so hard, he'd had to have rhinoplasty surgery to fix his crooked nose.

It had taken her almost a year to trust enough to go out on another date. Even then, she'd made it a double date with Leanne.

Having her trust ripped away at such a tender age somehow transformed her from the spoiled rich heiress that she'd been her entire life into something else. Someone a little more cautious and appreciative.

Which is why, she assumed, she'd fallen for Liam. He was the complete opposite of the poshness she no longer found appealing.

Even though he was wearing a gray suit today, there was a rawness to him, and she could tell that, no matter how well he dressed, it would always be there.

After Grayson left, Liam turned to her.

"You look like you're in pain." He walked over and gently lifted her casted leg onto the bed. He helped her shift over and even propped a few pillows behind her head until she was comfortable.

"Thank you," she said with a sigh. "I suppose I am in pain," she admitted after a moment.

"Where does it hurt?" he asked, sitting beside her.

"My arm." She held up her unbroken arm. "Grayson made me realize how much I'd been holding my body still. Not using my muscles in the past few weeks has locked them all up. He was helping me release the tension in this arm."

Liam took her arm in his hands and her mind instantly compared the two men once more. Grayson's hands had been cold and soft. Liam's were warm and had a few calluses on the palms, as if he was used to working with them instead of sitting at a computer writing software.

Another difference was that Grayson had pushed her muscles to the limits, while Liam gently rubbed them, easing her pain. She released a low moan and leaned back on the pillows as his hands moved slowly over her arm, avoiding the bandage that covered the cuts on her elbow area.

"We need to replace these bandages," Liam said, standing up. He walked into the attached bathroom and came back with a box of medical supplies her mother had purchased.

Sitting beside her again, he gently removed the soiled bandages. The moment before he released the last layer, she looked away.

"Have you seen this?" he asked gently.

"No." She closed her eyes.

"It's not as bad as I'd thought it would be," he replied. "You can look. I know you're squeamish with blood, but there really isn't any now. I cleaned the dried blood away."

Taking a chance, she opened her eyes and looked. He was right, it wasn't as bad as she'd thought it would be. There was a thin line that almost made a Y on her forearm just below her elbow.

"See," Liam said, running a finger gently over it. "I don't think you even need a big bandage anymore. We can put a couple Band-Aids over it instead."

She nodded her head and held up her arm for him to finish working on.

"Let me take a look at the one on your head next," he suggested once he was done.

She hated the large bandage that had been wrapped around her head since the moment she'd woken up.

Reaching up, she touched it and winced. "I..." She felt tears sting her eyes.

"Hey," he said, gently taking her hand. "I'm here. You probably worked yourself up about the one on your arm. This one probably isn't bad either."

Closing her eyes, she took a deep breath and nodded,

then focused her eyes on the pretty red flowers sitting directly across from her while he worked.

"Thank you for the flowers," she said once he'd removed the soiled bandages.

He glanced over at them and then smiled back at her. "There are three more vases in my car. I couldn't carry them all in at once."

"There are?" She felt her heart flutter at the thought of having more color in the room. Just knowing that Liam knew her enough to understand that she craved color, something cheerful in the room, had her smiling.

"I'll bring them in after we're done." He returned to the task. "I know how much you love color, and this room is as drab as the rest of your mother's decorative skills."

She chuckled and then winced when her head hurt.

"You're in pain. Didn't they give you something for it?" he asked.

"It's in the bathroom. I was supposed to take it with breakfast but..." She didn't want to tell him that she'd forgotten. That Ann had yet to come back and help her shower. Instead, she shrugged and tried to hold still as he removed the last barrier.

"Okay, this one's a little nastier. You'll need to keep some bandages over it, but I'm sure I can do better than this big thing." He tossed the wad of gauze into the trash bin. "Want to see?"

"No, I'll pass. Until it's nothing more than a tiny scar, I don't want to look," she admitted.

She was slightly surprised when he cupped her face and waited until she met his green eyes.

"No matter what, you are the most beautiful thing I've ever seen. No scars could ever dim your shine." He smiled at her as his eyes slowly ran over her face.

She may not remember Liam, but one thing was perfectly clear—he meant every word he'd just said to her.

She remembered the first kiss he'd given her at the hospital and the one last night. She'd been so shocked at how familiar his lips had felt against hers. How wonderful he'd smelled and tasted when she'd licked her lips once he'd left. She'd instantly wanted more. Craved it. Even now, her eyes moved down to his lips as he finished cleaning the wound.

When he was done, he brushed his lips over the bandage before straightening up.

"I'll go get the rest of the flowers," he suggested.

She nodded since she didn't know what else to say. Suddenly, she felt very nervous around him.

When he was gone, she took a couple of deep breaths until she felt a little steadier. It took him three more trips and, when he was done, the entire room smelled of flowers and was so bright, she couldn't help but feel cheerful.

"That's much better," he said, sitting beside her again. "You always fill our home with fresh flowers. In the spring and summer, they're usually from our own yard."

"Where do we live?" she asked, suddenly realizing she knew nothing about the home she'd built for them.

"Our place is up on a hill overlooking the Pacific on one side and the city on the other. The area and the home were called Angel Bluff by the architect who designed and built it. There are pictures of our place on your phone."

She had looked through a few photos on the phone before her mother had come in and she'd hidden the phone under her pillow. When she'd woken the next morning, the phone battery was dead, and she hadn't been able to plug the charger in since it required bending over and getting to the plug behind the nightstand.

"I couldn't plug it in. I guess the battery ran out." She took the phone out and handed it to him. "The box with the charging cable is in the drawer."

"You didn't get to look at any of your hundreds of pictures?" he asked with a smile.

"Did I really take that many pictures?" she asked, and as an answer, he laughed as he pulled the nightstand out and plugged in the phone.

"I'll let you decide. It might be in the thousands," he joked as he sat beside her and handed her the phone.

She waited until the phone booted up then frowned down at the screen. Yesterday when he'd handed it to her, it had been unlocked. Now it was asking for a code to get into it.

"What's wrong?" he asked, watching her.

"What's the code?" She showed him the screen.

"Your birthday," he answered easily. "It was set to our anniversary, but since you probably didn't remember that date, I had them change it when they cloned your phone from the backup."

She smiled as she unlocked the phone. "When did we get married?"

"The official date is March twentieth," he answered with a smile. Then he nodded to the phone. "Did you find those pictures?"

"No, I only had a chance to look at a handful of photos. We appeared to be at a few charity events. There were some of several pieces of art." She scanned the photos and found the images.

"Yes, you've been working with a few charities. Helping them set up events," he answered.

"My job?"

He frowned. "No, more of... a hobby. You're donating

your time to help out on some pretty worthy causes. It was your mother's idea to get you out of the house."

She frowned up at him. "Why did I need to get out of the house?"

He looked down at his hands and avoided her eyes. Whatever he was going to say next, she had a gut feeling that it was either going to be a lie or an excuse.

# CHAPTER SIX

*We can easily forgive a child who is afraid of the dark;*
*the real tragedy of life is when men are afraid of the light.*
**Plato**

The guilt he'd felt the moment he'd found out about the accident surfaced again, and he avoided Morgan's eyes.

"I've been... working a lot lately," he answered finally. "You were growing restless and when your mother suggested helping out"—he shrugged and looked at her phone— "you jumped at the chance."

Thankfully, Morgan didn't press him further. Instead, she silently scrolled through the photos. When she chuckled, he glanced over at an image of her and her friends.

"You and the quad squad crew hang once a month. It's sort of mandatory," he replied with a smile.

"Where are we?" She showed him an image of the four friends sitting by the pool, sipping drinks.

"That's our place," he said easily.

"What?" She frowned and looked at the image again. "We have a pool?"

"Yes. Why? Do you remember something?" he asked eagerly.

"No, it's just..." She set her phone down and frowned at him. "What do you do for a living?"

"I'm the CEO of Electric Security Platform, the company I started when I was sixteen, shortly after I turned eighteen, I sold the company." he explained. "When my company was first bought out, I sold it for over a hundred million." The amount still caused him to smile.

Morgan's eyes widened. "You went from breaking into cars to stay warm at night to being a multi-millionaire?" she asked and when he nodded, she laughed. "Now I know why my mother hates you," she said between giggles. "You're new money."

"Yeah," he sighed. "That sums it up. Shortly after we started dating, you explained how your parents would never think of me as anything other than a broke orphan who happened to be in the right place at the right time. They treat me as if my money will run out soon. The first time we invited your parents up to the house, your mother made a point to let me know how much she hated the modern architecture. Not to mention what she thought of your interior decorating skills."

"Oh, tell me there are pictures of the inside of our home in here. I've always dreamed of decorating my own place." She picked up her phone and scanned through the images.

"There are plenty of pictures. Each time you add a red throw pillow or a hot blue rug, you snap a photo." He smiled as he nodded to her phone.

She chuckled and showed him a picture of red throw pillows on the soft gray sofa in their main living room.

"We decided to keep the main furniture a solid color so we didn't go crazy trying to match everything. You like core colors with hits of cheer," he said, using her exact words.

She smiled. "That sounds like me."

"That's because it is you." He glanced at his phone when it chimed, reminding him of his meeting.

"Problem?" she asked.

"No, just... I have to head into the office." He tucked his phone away and stood up. "My number is in there." He motioned to her phone. "I'd love to hear from you. I'll stop by again tomorrow."

She nodded slowly, setting her phone down.

He thought back to when he'd walked in to see the dark-haired man kneeling before her, holding her arm, and frowned. "Don't let that therapist push you too hard."

"I won't." She wiggled her good arm and stretched it. "It feels much better now. Thanks for rubbing it and for changing my bandages."

He nodded. He wanted to tell her that she should be home, that if she was home with him, he wouldn't let her go without anything. He would have even made sure to be there to help her full time. But as he got ready to go into the office to meet with the board, he realized that maybe it was best, at least for now, that she remained here.

"If you need anything. Let me know." He leaned in and, before he kissed her, he paused to look into her eyes. "You don't know how thankful I am that you're okay," he said. When she nodded, he smiled and brushed his lips across hers.

Each time he kissed her, he was reminded of how lucky he was. "I love you," he added and then he turned and left the room.

He had a few moments before he had to leave and went in search of Victoria.

She was in her office on a phone call, but when she saw him in the doorway, she made an excuse and hung up.

"What are you doing back so soon?" she asked him with a frown. "I thought Grayson was in with Morgan?"

"He was, then he left. I changed her soiled bandages and massaged her sore muscles after that therapist caused her pain. I thought you said you were taking care of her. If you're not capable..." He dropped off.

Victoria slowly stood up, her eyes narrowing as she walked around her desk. The woman oozed old wealth, from her stylish hairstyle, which probably cost more than most people's rent each month, down to her designer outfit and shoes, which for sure cost more than most people's cars.

"Morgan is perfectly safe here," she replied while crossing her arms over her chest.

"She told me that she's been waiting for a shower. Where is Ann?" he asked. Victoria had claimed that the housekeeper would be watching out for Morgan around the clock.

"She had to run an errand this morning," Victoria said. "Grayson was going to handle—"

"What?" he broke in, feeling his temper spike. "Giving my wife a shower? Changing her bandages? You'll trust a perfect stranger to handle those simple tasks for Morgan, but not her husband?"

"No." Victoria waved his statement aside and smiled one of those fake smiles he was used to getting from her. "Grayson is a friend of the family."

"Morgan had never met him," he supplied, knowing that she would have mentioned the man if she had.

"No." Victoria sighed. "Thomas and I have known of his work at the hospital for a few years. We trust him."

"Forgive me if I don't," he said firmly. "We agreed yesterday that Ann would be watching out for her. I don't want some strange man in charge of bathing or caring for my wife."

Victoria's chin rose, as did her left eyebrow. "Ann will be back shortly."

Just then there was a quick knock on the door and Ann appeared. The middle-aged housekeeper was one of the few in the house that Liam actually liked and respected.

"I'm sorry, ma'am, my errand took longer than I thought it would," she said as she came into the room and set a folder down on the table. "I'll just head in and help Morgan with her morning shower."

"Thank you, Ann," Victoria said with a slight sneer aimed at Liam.

When Ann had left the room, his phone chimed again.

"You'd better get to work." Victoria smiled.

"I meant what I said," he said firmly. "If Ann can't watch out for my wife, I'll hire someone myself and take her home." He didn't give Victoria a chance to respond before he left the room.

The route back into the city to the offices of Electric Security Platform was clogged with traffic, and he walked into the boardroom almost ten minutes late.

"Sorry for the delay," he said and sat down at the head of the table. "Where are we at?"

An hour later, as he sat in the office that he normally only used once or twice a week, he felt like throwing something.

Having his life's work torn apart was nothing new. After all, the software used in most of the hybrid cars that were on the streets today was nothing like the code he'd written all those years ago.

But the possibility of having it hacked... that was something he would not stand for.

How could he claim to be a security platform if it wasn't secure?

Where was this new information coming from? Robin, one of his staff members, had gotten a tip that their latest update had a weakness. The rumors were that several cars had been hacked into. So far, nothing was officially reported, and no cars had been stolen because of the weakness. But still, it was enough information to damage his and the company's reputation.

This new dilemma meant that he would be working overtime once again to personally go through the latest code line by line if he had to.

Since there was no time like the present, he started shortly after the meeting. Lunch and dinner were delivered to his desk as he worked. The next time he blinked, the sun was coming up, almost blinding him through the massive windows of his office.

Standing up and stretching, he glanced at his clock and cursed. He knew without a doubt that he had to get a few hours of sleep before he went and saw Morgan. Transferring his work to his laptop, he walked out just as Cheryl, his personal assistant, was walking in with a bag of bagels and some coffee.

"I'll take these to go. I'm heading home for a few hours rest, then off to see my wife," he told her. "If I had any meetings..."

"I'll reschedule or cancel. Drive safe," she said as he walked out.

Hiring Cheryl was one of the best things he'd done for

the business, besides creating the software in the first place. The woman almost had a second sense about things.

As he drove up the hill, he thought about the times he'd taken Morgan for granted. Nights he'd returned home late, too late. She'd been fast asleep, and he hadn't even had a chance to tell her goodnight or kiss her before bed.

Dinners that he'd had to cancel because of late night meetings or updates that had needed to be pushed after hours.

The guilt from the night of her accident tried to surface but he pushed it back, swallowed it like a huge pill. He couldn't think about that now. He didn't have the ability with the lack of sleep and the worry about Morgan's health.

He pulled through the security gates and headed up the long drive to the house, which sat on top of the hillside. There was a five-car garage that sat lower than the main section of the house. In that building, there was a hallway leading from the second floor of the garage to the basement of the house.

The second floor of the garage held his at-home office, where he spent the majority of his days working when he didn't have to go into the office. There were four bedrooms there too, which were deemed guest rooms or staff rooms. There was even a kitchen.

They'd had a few parties where they'd filled those rooms and the other four guest bedrooms in the main house.

The home boasted two large garages. One detached that could hold five cars and one attached, which also had room for five cars. Occasionally they parked up at the main house, but for the most part, they liked to leave the cars down in the lower building.

As he parked the car in his normal spot, he frowned over at the empty place where Morgan's car normally sat.

The pain in his chest deepened. He needed to shut down for a few hours before he drove back into the city and saw her.

He climbed the unique triangular stairwell and stopped on the middle floor. He went into the kitchen and grabbed a slice of cold pizza and a bottled water and took them upstairs with him.

He dumped his laptop on his nightstand, toed off his shoes, and removed his shirt and belt as he ate the cold pizza and washed it down with water. Then he fell onto the bed face-first.

He woke when his cell phone chimed. Fumbling for his phone, he answered the call before looking at the caller ID.

"You think this is over?" the deep voice hissed at him. "I found you, mother fucker."

The line went dead before he had time to respond. Instead, he tossed his phone down and cursed. Sitting up, he dragged himself into the bathroom and stood in the shower.

He knew what was coming next. The messages, the additional phone threats. He'd have to change his number once again.

This wasn't the first call he'd had like this. From the moment he'd sold ESP, there had been threatening calls. At first, he'd taken them personally.

At one point, he'd even believed the threats were coming from Sean. After all, it had been only a matter of months after he'd paid his best friend off that he'd struck it rich.

Sean had, when he'd found out, come to him demanding his share. But Liam had spent those months rewriting everything they'd created after he'd found several serious errors. The software he'd sold that day had nothing left from Sean in it.

At one point, he'd wanted to give Sean something, but then he'd had a talk with Ryder. Sean had met with Ryder the day before and had talked about suing Liam for the full amount. He claimed Liam had swindled the business out from under him and that he had proof.

Ryder suggested that any sort of payment to Sean would appear like a payoff after the fact. So, he'd stopped answering Sean's calls and when a lawyer did come calling, he'd hired his own.

The first two years of his life with wealth had been spent fighting to prove to others that he deserved to keep it.

When the case had finally closed in his favor, he'd relaxed. Losing a friendship over money was hard, especially since he'd thought of Sean as a brother.

Ryder had felt that loss too, as he'd stood by Liam's side during the entire process. Sean had left a few nasty messages accusing Liam of paying Ryder off by purchasing the gym.

In truth, he'd loaned Ryder the money, which his friend had paid back in full in less than a year. Ryder had even insisted on paying interest, but Liam had talked him into spending the money on a new boxing ring instead and giving him a lifetime membership.

Even though there was a state-of-the-art gym in the basement of his house, Liam still dropped by the gym at least once a week to box or play basketball with Ryder.

By the time he was done showering and dressing, his phone inbox was full of vulgar messages and there were more than a hundred text messages from various phone numbers. In the past when he'd had the police look into it, the messages were usually from burner phones.

Taking a moment to block the phone numbers, he used the house phone to call Detective Evans.

"Hey, Mack, it's Liam. I've got a new group of messages to send you," he said when the man answered.

Mack sighed. "Well, shit, that's a new record, I think. What's it been? A month?"

"Yeah, about that." He nodded as he forwarded the bulk of messages. "I've blocked these, but I'll be changing the number again when I hang up."

"Sounds good. Text me your new digits. I'll add these to the file and look at them when I get a chance. There's still a chance our guy is going to get sloppy and use his own phone someday," Mack said.

"Right," Liam agreed.

"How's Morgan?" Mack asked.

"She's... staying at her parents' place," he said, not sure why he thought of that to say instead of how his wife was doing physically.

"Oh, I thought... so things are going okay between them?" Mack asked.

"She doesn't remember me," he admitted. "She remembers them. I guess it was just the easier choice."

Mack was quiet for a moment.

"Temporary memory loss is normal for accidents like that. What did the doctor say?" he asked.

"That her memory would return. It already has for some things, just nothing yet about me." Liam felt his stomach roll.

"Hang in there," Mack added. "I meant to call you."

"Oh?" Liam asked as he started down the stairs. "What about? Did you find something?"

"No, it's about Morgan's accident," Mack said, causing Liam to stop on the stairs.

"What about it?" he asked with a frown.

"SCI has some questions about the car."

"Her car?"

It was one of the newest models from IOA, Integrative Automotive Operations, a newer electric car manufacturing company. They weren't the ones who originally purchased his software, but after a few buyouts, they'd gotten their hands on it.

After he'd started working for ESP again, he'd bought one of their models for himself to tinker with. He'd fallen in love with it and each year upgraded to their latest model. He'd purchased a new custom model for Morgan last month for their anniversary. She loved that car and had even called it Bubbles because the car made her happy.

"What about her car?" he asked when Mack didn't continue.

"They wanted to set up a time for you to come into the station and answer some questions," Mack said, and Liam heard the professionalism in his tone. He'd known Mack for almost five years now. He trusted the man. They not only had a professional relationship, but Mack had also been one of his groomsmen when he'd married Morgan.

"Sure," he said. "I'll swing by tomorrow after I visit Morgan."

"Sounds good. We'll see you then. Don't forget to text me your new number," Mack added.

After hanging up with Mack, he pulled out a frozen meal their housekeeper, Lynda, had stocked his fridge with after Morgan's accident.

He sat at the bar top running his eyes over the code while he ate alone and almost shouted with joy when he found the code that had created a backdoor in his security. Finally, he was getting somewhere. Now all he had to do was figure out who had written it and how they'd been able to get it into their software.

It took almost half an hour to change his phone number, and he sent a text to Morgan to let her know, followed by Ryder and Mack and then his office.

Along with his message to Morgan, he told her that he was heading down there and would be there shortly before dinnertime. By the time he had driven halfway down the hills, he got Morgan's reply and let his car read off her message.

"Okay, see you then. I got my arm cast off today and have this fancy thing instead. I chose the color red to match all the flowers you gave me."

He smiled and when he hit the stop sign at the bottom of the hill, he pulled out his phone and looked at the image she'd sent him.

It was just an image of her left arm in a bright red thermoplastic cast.

Her next message came a few moments later.

"My mother hates it."

He chuckled and replied, "I love it and you. I miss you. I can't wait to see you. I'm half an hour away." He had the car send the message.

Fifteen minutes later, Ryder called him.

"He found you again?" Ryder said when Liam answered the call.

"Yeah," he sighed. "I've already sent this batch off to Mack."

"Oh man, I'm sorry. You still think it's Sean?" Ryder asked.

"I'm not sure. The voice is always muffled and, well... I haven't talked to Sean in years," he admitted.

"Yeah, me either," Ryder answered. "Then again, you

racked up a bunch of crazy fans after you earned your wealth and even more when you wed Morgan."

It was true. The moment he'd been listed in Forbes, the crazies had hunted him down. Most of them were women trying to date him or trap him in a relationship. One even claimed he was the father of her ten-year-old kid. The fact that he was nineteen when he'd sold the software hadn't dawned on a lot of the groupies. Then he'd married Morgan last year and some of their wedding photos had been leaked.

Images of the two of them had been on every tabloid cover for months along with speculation that Morgan was pregnant and that he'd trapped her into the marriage.

Liam believed that her mother had leaked the photos and the story, but he hadn't had proof, so he'd kept his mouth shut.

"Yeah, at least it's easy enough to change my number. I'm heading over to visit Morgan. You should stop by and see her sometime."

Ryder chuckled. "Oh, hell no. The last time I stepped foot in the Davenport's encampment, I almost didn't come out with all my skin."

He chuckled. "Thomas Davenport does hate anyone from the wrong side of the tracks."

"You're from the same side I'm from," Ryder reminded him.

Liam laughed. "And neither of her parents ever let me forget it. But I love Morgan and have to put up with it."

"Right," Ryder agreed. "When she goes home, I'll come and spend a weekend," he promised.

"It's a plan," Liam agreed.

"When will she get to go home?" Ryder asked.

Liam sighed as he pulled into the Davenport's driveway and punched the button for the gate. "Not soon enough. I'm here so I'll let you go. I'll stop by later so you can kick my ass in basketball."

"I'm boxing today," Ryder said cheerfully, causing Liam to moan.

"Okay, but this time, I'm tying one of your arms behind your back."

Ryder laughed. "Just because you're my best friend doesn't mean I'll go easy on you."

"You never do. Just no more black eyes, okay?"

"No promises. You should know by now how to duck. See you tomorrow," Ryder added, then he hung up.

When he walked into Morgan's room, the physical therapist was there again. This time, the man had his arms wrapped around Morgan's waist, as if he was hugging her.

From his vantage point, he could see no reason why the man would be hanging onto her like that.

"I hope I'm not interrupting anything," he said sharply.

# CHAPTER SEVEN

*Light thinks it travels faster than anything, but it is wrong.*
*No matter how fast light travels, it finds the darkness has*
*always got there first, and is waiting for it.*
**Terry Pratchett**

Morgan hadn't been able to contain her excitement after getting Liam's text messages. He missed her and loved her.

She didn't know how she felt about those words in her head, but they had her stomach fluttering and her pulse spiking. If she couldn't remember Liam, at least her body did.

She'd looked through the hundreds of photos on her phone, figuring it would help jog her memory. She'd started at the front and scrolled through every image in chronological order.

There were some pictures of them that were obviously from when they were dating. A few of them with her friends and a few guys she didn't know, whom she assumed were his friends. She was so excited to cut to the wedding pictures that she didn't really pay too much attention.

The wedding ceremony had been held on the lawn overlooking the ocean at her parents' country club. Her dress was straight out of all of her childhood fantasies. The satin V-neck dress was a one-of-a-kind design by one of her favorite celebrity designers. She'd pulled her long dark hair up in a simple bun at the nape of her neck and had diamonds and pearls around her neck and dangling from her ears.

She'd looked more beautiful than she'd imagined she would. And there was Liam, her prince.

Of course, her three best friends had been her bridesmaids. Even their dresses had been absolutely gorgeous. Each dress, although the same design, was a different vibrant color. Kimber wore a cheerful sunny yellow, Leanne was in emerald-green, and Reagan was in a bright pink. Together, they looked amazing and happy.

The flowers she carried had been just as bright. Her mother wore an ocean blue dress and appeared happy, but the twinkle in her eyes were missing, hinting at an inner turmoil. Her father appeared drunk at times and in each picture was busy talking with one of his club friends.

There was a video of her and Liam dancing, which melted her heart. Just seeing the way she was looking at him, and the way he was looking down at her, had her entire body vibrating. Love. It was so obviously painted on both of their faces.

She didn't know why, but the video made her eyes water, so she only watched it three times before moving on.

She was happily surprised to see several pictures of a shirtless Liam lounging by a pool or on a beach. She'd been a little shocked and turned on at the number of tattoos he had on his chest, arms, and belly.

So far, he'd always had his shirt on when visiting her. He was either dressed for work or casually, and she'd never seen a hint of tattoos on him.

Seeing the six-pack on him in the photos had her mouth watering. This man was all hers. He'd married her. She'd run her hands over that body plenty of times. It totally sucked that she couldn't remember any of it. Their first kiss. The first time he'd held her hand or touched her. The first moment he'd brought her to climax. The first time they'd made love or even the last time.

She was pretty sure they had honeymooned in French Polynesia since there were tons of pictures of them in a private bungalow floating over crystal-clear emerald-green waters. They even had their own swimming pool and a slide that they could use to get down into the water below. There was a video of him sliding down it that had her smiling.

There was a seriously ridiculous number of photos of food, which she enjoyed but found boring. She worried she'd posted them, but she couldn't remember her social media log-ins and they weren't loaded onto her new phone, so she figured she'd have to wait and ask Liam when she saw him next.

She was smiling down at her phone, thinking of calling Liam, when Grayson knocked on her opened door before stepping inside.

"Afternoon," he said cheerfully.

She'd been expecting him earlier in the day. Now, seeing him, her smile for Liam slipped a little.

"Hi," she said, setting her phone down.

"Ready for me?" he asked, setting down a large square table.

"I am." She moved to the edge of the bed and set her casted leg on the ground. She was super excited that the doctor had visited earlier that morning and had cut off the heavy cast on her left arm. He'd replaced it with a thermal one that had been molded to her arm. It wasn't removable, as Grayson had suggested, but it did allow her arm to breathe much better, and she could even shower in it, so she only had to seal up her leg cast when she showered now.

"Today we're going to try a little something different," Grayson said, stepping closer. Without asking, he lifted her casted arm and examined it. "Red?"

"My favorite color." She shrugged.

"Noted." He smiled down at her. "How are you feeling?"

"Not bad. I decided to stop taking the pain pills," she admitted, and his dark eyebrows rose.

"If you need them..." he started.

"Yeah, I know. They're there," she said, repeating her mother's words when she'd told her earlier that morning.

"Good." He nodded, then turned away and pulled a small blue ball from the bag he'd set down just inside the door. "Today we're going to work your right arm. We don't want to work your left too much just yet. We'll wait another week or so before we start there." Then he surprised her by tossing the ball at her.

She jerked her left arm to catch it but stopped herself halfway and used her right.

Grayson's eyebrows rose again. "A lefty?" he asked.

"Yes." She sighed heavily.

"Okay." He tilted his head. "Toss it back to me."

She looked down at the blue rubber ball, then did her best to toss it with her right hand. She laughed when it landed two feet away from her.

Grayson smiled and walked over to pick up the ball. "I bet you can do better," he said, moving away again and tossing it back to her. This time she was prepared and easily caught it in her right hand.

They played ball for a few moments until, finally, she threw one all the way across the room to him and he easily caught it.

"Now, for something a little more fun." He put the ball away and motioned to the crutch.

Taking the crutch, she stood up and tried to follow his instructions. He had her weave between the chairs in the room and walk over the rug and the tile in the bathroom. Then he tried to throw her off-kilter when she was standing there by nudging her shoulder.

She started to fall backwards, but he easily caught her, wrapping his arms around her waist.

"You have to be sturdier. Not everyone will get out of your way," he said, looking down at her.

Just being this close to him had her face flushing and her heart jumping. Then again, like before, maybe her heart was racing because she'd almost fallen seconds before?

"I hope I'm not interrupting anything," Liam said from the doorway. The tone of his voice had her wishing she was capable of jumping away from Grayson. Instead, she nudged herself free from him, making a point to shift her weight and stand firm, as he'd suggested.

"Just therapy," Grayson said easily. "I brought my massage table—"

"Nope," Liam said firmly. "If my wife needs a massage, she can have Victoria's massage therapist, Theresa, do it." Liam walked over and helped her sit on the edge of the bed. "I think we're done with you for the day," he told Grayson.

She wanted to be angry with Liam for being rude to

Grayson but then thought about how it must have looked when he'd walked in. Grayson's arms had been wrapped around her. Her right arm had been holding onto his shoulder as if... She closed her eyes and sighed.

"Thank you, Grayson," she said easily. "I'll see you again tomorrow."

Grayson nodded and then gathered his bag and massage table and left.

"You were rude to him," Morgan said when they were alone.

"I'm not normally a jealous person," Liam said as he sat next to her and picked up her right hand. "But seeing as you can't remember your feelings for me..." He smiled at her. "I think I'm allowed a little jealousy."

She smiled back at him. "I can get pretty jealous too. Especially if I had walked in on you with some...other woman."

"Never." He reached up and brushed her hair away from her face, then cupped her chin in his hand. "There could never be another that makes my heart beat as fast as it does when I see you smile."

She heated and melted at the same time as she looked deep within those green eyes of his.

Just then, a memory flashed in her mind. It was an image of her standing in a dark crowded room. Loud music caused her head to ache. Her feet hurt because she'd worn the sexy red heels that Kimber had talked her into spending too much money on. Still, the shoes and the skimpy black dress made her feel damn sexy.

She was about to talk her friends into leaving when she'd spotted the sexy green eyes from across the room. At that moment, it was as if everything else disappeared. Her breath caught in her lungs the first time she'd locked eyes with Liam across a crowded bar.

"Morgan?" Liam's voice broke the trance.

"We met at a bar," she said, and then realized how silly she sounded.

Liam's smile flashed, causing her heart to jump again. "Yes, we did." His hand tightened slightly. "Do you remember?"

"I... remember seeing you across the room. You were sitting next to..." She narrowed her eyes, trying to remember.

"Ryder. My best friend." He nodded. "Do you remember him? He's wanted to come visit but... He and your parents don't mix."

She frowned as she remembered the man standing across from her in boxing gloves and shorts, telling her to lift her fists. The man was smiling at her and egging her on to hit him like she was hitting her mother. "Ryder. He owns a boxing ring?"

"A gym, but yeah, he's been training you to box. We both thought it was a good thing for you to know self-defense." Liam frowned slightly and she got the hint that he was hiding something from her. "What else do you remember?"

She thought about it for a moment, but the headache had settled in like a brick behind her eyes.

"Sorry," she finally said, shaking her head. "I suppose I'm too tired now."

"It's okay," Liam said with a slight sigh. "It'll come to you. I'm pretty sure that when you come home, you'll remember the rest."

She nodded. "Does my mother really have a massage therapist?"

He chuckled. "Yes, don't you remember Theresa?"

Morgan shook her head. "I guess not."

"If you want, I can tell Victoria you want a session with her?" he offered.

"Maybe tomorrow. Right now, I think I want some dinner and rest." She thought about taking something for her headache as well.

"Here." Liam shifted and nudged her shoulders until she was facing away from him. Then his hands started moving over her shoulders and her neck, and she groaned as some of the tension started to leave her body.

When there was a knock on the door, Liam called out for them to come in.

"Evening," Ann said, carrying a tray of food. Ann was easily the nicest housekeeper her mother had ever employed. There had been a few over the years, none of whom could tolerate working with her mother. Ann had been hired shortly before Morgan's thirteenth birthday and had stuck around ever since.

The woman's red hair was always worn in a tight bun at the base of her neck. To Morgan's recollection, she'd never seen her wear her hair down.

Her thin frail frame was a deception since Morgan could remember the woman easily lifting half her weight. She was always full of energy and had never once complained about tasks or errands that her mother sent her on.

"Evening, Ann," Liam said easily. "How about we take dinner out by the pool?" he suggested, turning to Morgan. "I bet you could use some fresh air."

"Yes," she replied a little too eagerly. "I'd like that." She hadn't been outside since she was shifted from the hospital to here. Even then, it had been such a quick trip and she'd been so tired, she hadn't gotten to enjoy much.

"Very well. Will you be staying for dinner as well?" Ann asked Liam. "I can bring you a plate?"

"Yes, thank you." He got up and helped Morgan to her feet, then handed her the crutch. "Shall we?" he asked her. She nodded and they made their way down the hallway, through the living room, across all those marble floors her mother enjoyed so much, and out the arched glass doors that led out back.

Stepping out directly on the cement decking of the pool, she took a deep breath and enjoyed the warm air.

"God, I'd forgotten what outside smells like," she joked as they made their way around the lounge chairs to a table that sat under a balcony. There was a bar area as well as an outdoor kitchen that she was pretty sure her parents had never used themselves.

The pool, on the other hand, had been used a great deal when she'd lived there. Her parents had yearly parties with tons of influential people. The patio doors were usually thrown open and the entire house was decked out. Caterers and staff met all of the guests' needs. Her parents' New Year's parties had always been Morgan's favorite.

"This is nice," she said after sitting down.

"Yes." Liam smiled over at her. "The air is getting the color back in your cheeks." He smiled across from her as Ann delivered their meals.

"Let me know if you want anything else," Ann said.

"Thank you. Are my parents here?" she asked, wondering why the house was so quiet.

"No, ma'am, they had an event tonight at the country club," Ann answered.

"Where's my brother?"

"He's at his club," Ann answered.

"The country club?" she asked.

"No, his club," Ann answered.

"My brother has a club?" Morgan frowned.

"Yes, Nightshade," Ann answered easily before turning away. Morgan didn't know what she was talking about but nodded anyway.

When they were alone, Liam asked, "You don't remember your brother's club?"

"No. My brother has a club called Nightshade? Care to clue me in on when that all went down? The last I remember, Aaron had graduated high school and was thinking of moving to Paris for a year to chase skirts and sow his wild oats, as my parents had put it." She took a bite of the pasta.

"About two months ago he came up with the idea. Your parents purchased an old brick building downtown for more money than it was worth, and Aaron turned it into a swanky nightclub called Nightshade," Liam explained. "Now he spends most of his days and nights there," he added with a frown.

"My brother opened a nightclub." She shook her head in complete disbelief. It didn't sound like the Aaron she remembered. Aaron was spoiled. There was no denying it. Where she'd been ripped out of the coddling they'd received from their parents, Aaron had thrived on it. He'd eaten it up and then had demanded more.

Liam nodded. "Yes, it's..." He shrugged as he frowned down into his food. "Very high end. You know, the kind of place where there's a dress code and a bouncer keeping out the riffraff. Only the hottest of the hot get in, the richest and the famous. Think Studio 54 in downtown LA."

She frowned. "Oh god, and my parents paid for it?"

Liam nodded. "Yeah."

"How's it going?" she asked. "More importantly, did I agree to help out and how?"

"You agreed to help out with the grand opening night. Because it's your brother." He took a bite of his food.

"For the past two months, you have been spending most of your time driving back and forth to the city each day, lending a hand and organizing the main event."

"When was this event?" she asked, somehow already knowing the answer.

Liam frowned and set his fork down. He looked at his food as if it disgusted him. "It was the night of your crash," he answered quietly.

She waited, but when he didn't add more, she asked, "Why weren't you going with me?"

He swallowed and looked up at her, his green eyes looking lost, apologetic.

"I received a call about an emergency at work." He reached across the table for her hand. "I should have been there. I would have been driving. If—"

"Don't," she said, breaking in. "The past can't be changed."

He nodded slightly. "I know, but..." He shook his head and took a deep breath as he pulled his hand away from hers.

She could see the guilt in his eyes when he looked at her now. Understood why her mother was treating him the way she was. Because she blamed Liam for the accident. Blamed him for not driving or being with her that night.

Reaching out, she took his hand once more. "Liam, I don't remember what we had, but I know one thing. It's impossible to blame someone for an accident when they weren't even there. You had your reasons for not going that night. From the sounds of it, your work is important to you."

"Not as important as you are," he said firmly, his eyes searching hers. "It's not a mistake I'm going to make again. I promise you."

She smiled. "Have you been to the club?" she asked, feeling her face flush at the way Liam was looking at her.

"No. The last time I was in a nightclub, I found what I'd been looking for. You." He smiled.

"Is this how you won me over the first time?" she asked, leaning on the table, propping herself up on her red-casted arm.

He chuckled. "No, actually, you're the one who won me over. I remember seeing you across the room, and there was an instant attraction. I bought you a drink, then we found someplace quiet to talk." He chuckled. "Before your quad squad dragged you out on the dance floor. Luckily, you dragged me, and I impressed you further with my moves." He jerked his shoulders and arms back and forth in a dance move and she laughed.

"Oh, I'm impressed now," she said between laughs. "I can't wait to see what else you can do."

Liam's smile grew as his eyes heated. "Yeah, you like all my moves." He wiggled his eyebrows, and her face heated.

"Okay, so we met in a club. Then what?" she asked as they continued to eat.

"I called you the next day, and we met at a library."

"Our first official date was at a library?" she asked with a frown.

"Yes, you had to study for the class you were taking..."

"Right." She rolled her eyes. "I was going to college." She frowned. "For..." She tapped the side of her head, then held up her finger when Liam opened his mouth to tell her. "No, I'll remember." She closed her eyes and remembered sitting in class listening to a lecture about... "History?" She shook her head.

Liam smiled. "Yes, you were getting your teacher's certificate. You told me that you wanted to be a history teacher to—and I'm quoting you here—piss your mother off."

She smiled. "Sounds about right." Then she sighed and glanced towards the doors. "Did I finish school at least?"

"You did." He smiled. "Your friends had taken you out to celebrate the night we met."

"Why were you there that night? At the club?" she asked him.

He chuckled. "I was out on a double date."

## CHAPTER EIGHT

*Don't fight darkness – bring the light,*
*and darkness will disappear.*
**Maharishi Mahesh Yogi**

Spending time with Morgan sitting around the pool had him relaxing for the first time since the night of her accident. He laughed more than he had in weeks and enjoyed the way she flirted with him. It reminded him of when they'd first met.

Not that she had stopped flirting with him since they'd been married, but it was nice knowing that she wanted to flirt with him. Especially since she didn't remember him from before.

He tried not to think about the physical therapist and how Morgan's face had looked flushed around the guy. Obviously, the man had been flirting with Morgan both times he'd walked in on them.

Even with her bruises and broken bones, Morgan was beautiful, but as she'd pointed out when they'd first met, most men found her inheritance more attractive.

That was one thing they had bonded over that first night. The woman he'd been on a double date with had talked nonstop about his wealth. She'd tried to convince him to pay for her rent within the first fifteen minutes of knowing him.

When he'd declined, she'd lost all interest in him and had started flirting with a man who'd walked up to her and purchased her a drink.

He'd actually been moping at the bar, waiting for Ryder to lose interest in the woman he was flirting with when, thankfully, Morgan had walked in.

After finishing dinner, he could tell that Morgan was tired so he helped her back into the bedroom and kissed her goodnight, making a point to linger over her lips so the slight taste of her would stay in his mind until he saw her again.

"I'll see you tomorrow," he promised and left her.

She was practically asleep when he walked out. He'd brought his gym clothes and headed directly to Ryder's gym.

When he walked in, Ryder was in the boxing ring with Marty, a kid around sixteen years old, who was living in the same orphanage he and Ryder had grown up in.

That was the nice thing about his best friend. Shortly after purchasing the gym, he'd opened up free memberships to anyone living in the orphanage or a halfway house.

He'd actually talked local businesses into sponsoring the kids, even hiring some of them on. It kept them off the streets and allowed them a safe outlet.

Marty was one of the best boxers the gym had seen, according to Ryder. After watching the two of them spar for a few minutes, Liam had to agree.

By the time Ryder called the sparring session to a close,

his friend was completely covered in sweat and looked worn out.

"Hey," Ryder said, stepping over to the side of the ring.

"Hey," Liam smiled.

"I'm done boxing for the day. The kid wiped the floor with my ass." Ryder chuckled. "How about we head out and shoot some hoops instead?"

"Looks like maybe I'll finally have a chance to beat you in basketball." Liam joked.

Ryder chuckled. "That kid could easily win the championship."

Liam glanced over at the kid and nodded. "Yeah, so what's stopping him?"

Ryder turned back to him and frowned. "He turns eighteen next month." He climbed out of the ring and wiped his face with a towel.

"Eighteen? No, he just turned sixteen a few..." He stopped and thought about it. "Shit, I guess we're getting old."

Ryder chuckled. "Speak for yourself. I just held my own in the ring with a seventeen-year-old." He slapped him on the shoulder as they walked into the locker room.

Liam set his gym bag down and opened his own locker. "What's he going to do?"

"For now?" Ryder shrugged as he sat down on the bench and started pulling off his gloves. "He has a job working at the shoe place down the street."

"He's at the Wayward Home?" he asked.

"Until his birthday. They're trying to find a home for him, but placement is hard. There's another home that might take him, but it's for recovering addicts. To my knowledge, Marty has never touched drugs. He's too concerned about his health. He's a good kid."

"Yeah." Liam knew that was the truth. In the past few years, Marty had done nothing but work hard and help others in the gym. "What about you taking him in?"

Ryder frowned at him. "I've got a studio apartment upstairs." He pointed to the ceiling. "I don't even have enough privacy to bring a date over, even without having an eighteen-year-old live with me."

"Right," Liam sighed. "I live clear out of the city, and I'm trying to convince my wife, who doesn't remember me, to move back in."

Ryder chuckled. "How's that going for you?"

Liam smiled. "Good. She's up and walking on a crutch. She had her arm cast removed and one of those thermal casts put on so she can shower."

"Nice. When I broke my arm that thing was a lifesaver," Ryder said as he untaped his hands.

Liam kicked off his shoes and changed into his basketball shorts and shirt. Then he stuffed his items into his locker and waited for Ryder to pull on his basketball shoes.

As they walked out onto the basketball court, he was so deep in thought about the kid that Ryder easily kicked his ass on the court.

Not that he'd ever won against his friend, but still, losing by so much stung enough that when Ryder asked for another game, he turned him down. Besides, he wanted to get home so he could be in the office first thing in the morning. He needed to investigate just how the hack had happened.

He'd already sent the fixed code in so an update could be pushed out. Thankfully, simple updates like this were done without the car owner's knowledge.

After a quick shower, he pulled out of the parking lot of the gym and a sales sign caught his eye.

Ryder's gym was in a single-story red brick building that took up most of the block. It had been Moe's Gym prior to his friend taking ownership of it. Now, a simple backlit sign read Main Street Gym.

Main Street ran for three blocks total. At the end of it was a massive four-story building that housed Wayward Home, the orphanage they had grown up in.

Its proximity to the gym was one of the reasons they had always found themselves hanging out there. Plus, Moe had a soft spot for orphans.

There were dozens of old buildings along this row, but the one that interested him now sat directly across from the gym. It was a smaller three-story brick building that, from the outside, appeared in great shape.

He remembered at one point that it had been renovated but couldn't remember when or into what.

Pulling over to the front, he parked and got out.

"Hey, I was heading out to grab a bite to eat when I saw you pull over. Having car problems?" Ryder asked, pulling his truck up beside him.

"No," he answered quickly, then he motioned to the building. "How long has this beauty been up for sale?"

Ryder thought about it for a moment. "About a month. If you ask me, the owner wants too much for it. Last year he raised all the rents and then evicted everyone who couldn't pay. I think it's empty currently. I haven't seen anyone coming or going in a while."

Liam smiled. "Perfect. Do you think we can get in and have a look around?"

"I'll call the owner." Ryder pulled over and parked in front of him.

Liam looked up at the building, ideas swirling in his head as Ryder joined him on the sidewalk.

"He's out of town right now, but he gave me the code to get in. He says he's only got one tenant at the moment, which is why he's selling. Apparently, a couple of the units need some work done." He punched the keypad by the front doors. "At least this works." Ryder laughed as he opened the door.

When they stepped into the lobby, Liam knew instantly that the building would work for what he was thinking.

"What are we doing here, Liam?" Ryder turned to him.

"How many cold nights did we have to sleep on the streets?" He turned to his friend.

"Too many to count," Ryder answered with a shake of his head, then he groaned. "Tell me that you're not thinking what I think you're thinking."

"It's perfect. Not only is it down the street from the orphanage, but it's across the street from the gym." He motioned to the mailboxes. "Eight units." He smiled. "Not too many, but just enough for kids who deserve that chance."

"The world doesn't deserve you," Ryder said, slapping his back.

The following day, he walked into work feeling a little lighter. Even though he'd only gotten a few hours of sleep, he and Ryder had worked out the perfect plan for Second Chance Apartments.

There were only eight units in the building, and one was already occupied by a man who, as luck would have it, worked at the orphanage.

Six of the units were two bedrooms and the other two were singles. Since they couldn't get into them last night, he didn't know how much work had to be done, but he figured whatever it was would be worth the cost.

He just hoped that at least one unit would be ready before Marty turned eighteen.

"Morning," he said cheerfully to Cheryl as he started to walk past her desk on his way to his office.

"Morning." Cheryl jumped up and rushed after him. "Sir, there's someone..."

Liam had already opened the door to his office and could see Dave Leimberg sitting behind Liam's desk.

Of all the board members Liam had to deal with, Dave was by far the worst.

"Can I help you find something, Dave?" Liam asked without missing a beat. This wasn't the first time he'd walked in on the man sitting behind his desk and something told him that it wouldn't be the last.

Dave didn't even bother looking apologetic as he stood up. "I hope you don't mind. I had to make a few calls." Before Liam could respond, Dave turned to Cheryl. "Thank you, that will be all," Dave said, dismissing the woman, who obviously had more to tell Liam.

Cheryl glanced at Liam.

"Thanks, I'll ring you when I'm available. Until then, hold my calls." Liam walked over and pushed his office chair out until Dave slowly stood up. The man didn't do anything fast. He talked and walked so slowly that Liam believed it was on purpose to piss off everyone around him. He'd seen the man talk and move quickly enough, but when he wanted to make a point, he usually slowed down to do it.

Liam set his laptop case down on his desk and sat in his own chair. He motioned to the chairs across from his desk and waited until Dave settled in one of them.

"What can I help you with today, Dave?" Liam asked.

"The board isn't happy with this hacking situation," Dave said as he dusted off his tie. "Word has gotten out that it's all due to your incompetence since your attention has been divided lately."

"My..." Liam frowned. "Are you saying that the board believes that my wife's accident is hindering my work and that because of her almost dying, I allowed someone to hack our software and put a backdoor in our security code?"

Dave tilted his head and just looked at him, smugly. The man could infuriate anyone. Whereas most people allowed their words to cut, Dave allowed the silence after making a pointed comment to do the job for him.

"Right." Liam nodded. "You've stated your opinion. If you don't mind, I have work."

"It's not just my opinion," Dave added slowly.

"At this point, I don't care. If the board questions my ability to do my job, set up a meeting. Until then, I have to confirm that the update ran smoothly and double-check the code again for any more problems." He started to pull out his laptop from the case.

"I don't think you understand the gravity of this situation," Dave said while Liam logged into the network.

"Oh?" he asked, not really paying any further attention to the man.

"There's talk of replacing you," Dave answered.

"Talk?" Liam had heard this before from Dave. The man was either after his job or just straight up didn't like him, and he didn't know why.

Dave motioned slightly with his hands. "Yes, and after this latest ordeal, I'm positive the board is looking for your replacement."

"You?" Liam leaned on the desk slightly and tilted his head as he ran his eyes over the man. Middle-aged, somewhere around forty years old. He was wearing a blue Armani suit, much like the one Liam was currently wearing. He'd shaved his blonde hair down on the sides and appeared to be trying to grow it longer on the top, like Liam's style, only the man's hair on top was a whole lot thinner.

Actually, if Liam thought about it, everything Liam did, Dave had been right there, trying to take credit for it.

"If the board sees fit. Yes," Dave said with a smile.

"Why are you here?" he asked the man suddenly. "It's been obvious since the moment I returned to ESP that you can't tolerate me. Why come and warn me? Gloating?" Liam's eyes narrowed, then he shifted gears and something else became perfectly clear. "Correct me if I'm wrong, but you do have access to the network. To the software files."

"Of course. The board has requested that I quality check every change before we push out the updates," Dave answered, sounding a little shocked and offended.

"Interesting." Liam turned back to his computer without saying anything further. Let that sink in, Dave, he thought as he started to get to work.

It took two minutes before the man stood up and left without another word.

Smiling, he waited a few more minutes before buzzing Cheryl back into his office.

He took a few moments later that day to double-check Dave's credentials and scour through the logs for anything... off. After seeing that the man had not only graduated top of his class at MIT but had worked at a couple of other major software companies, he figured the man was smart enough not to leave a trail if he had been the one to sabotage the software.

To Liam's thinking, there was really only one reason why he would have done something like that. To get Liam fired.

It wasn't as if the man wasn't qualified to take over Liam's job. Hell, there were a few strong tech types that could have easily filled his shoes when he'd sold the company in the first place.

Liam's skills were... very narrow. He knew code inside and out. But then again, so did two dozen people just in this zip code.

The only thing that made Liam unique was that he was the one to originally build the backbone of ESPs software. The core of it was Liam's baby.

He'd thought about stepping down since marrying Morgan. He wanted more time to spend with her. To travel and see those places they always talked about. Maybe even to start a family.

They'd talked a lot about kids prior to her accident. They'd spent their one-year anniversary in Hawaii. An entire week lying on the beach, sipping drinks and making love as often as they could.

The topic had come up a time or two then, and they'd both agreed that after another year of traveling, they'd start trying for their own family. Three kids, to be exact.

Would she still want those three kids with him? What happened if she never regained her memories of what they had together? Could he convince her to give him another chance? Make her fall in love with him a second time?

He'd been so lucky that first time. Hell, he didn't even know what tricks he'd used to get her to walk across a crowded bar and talk to him, let alone go out on a second date.

He remembered being cautious since he'd struggled with trust issues, thanks to all the women who had pursued him for his wealth. But Morgan had been different.

The moment the media had gotten wind of their

involvement, articles in every tabloid had claimed he was after her inheritance.

They'd been labeled the pauper and the princess. Even though he'd had huge wealth thanks to the buyout, and he'd already taken the job as CEO for ESP, he'd still been labeled an average Joe, out for the heiress's wealth.

At first, he'd believed that was one of the reasons her parents hadn't liked him. After that first month together, Morgan had confessed that it wasn't the reason.

"No matter how much money you have, my parents had hoped I'd marry up. Not for wealth, but for title," she'd told him when she had been wrapped around him, naked, one night.

"Title?" he'd asked, unsure what she'd meant.

She'd laughed into his chest. "You know, there are several perfectly good bachelor princes out there."

"Seriously?" He'd laughed.

"At least a dozen." She'd mimicked her mother's tone. Morgan had leaned over and kissed him. "No one will ever be good enough for my mother. I'm sorry that's the case, but just know that you are far too good for me."

From that moment on, he'd done everything in his power to be the best man he could for her.

When he'd proposed, he'd pulled out all the most romantic things he could think of and had gotten down on his knee when they took a romantic weekend up to Napa Valley.

She'd mentioned how it had been years since she'd been there and missed just taking the long weekend drive.

He couldn't wait to do more of the same with her again.

# CHAPTER NINE



*Every moment of light and dark is a miracle.*
**Walt Whitman**

For Morgan, days bled into one another and became weeks. If it wasn't for Liam's daily visits, her three friends' weekly visits, and her physical therapy twice a week, she would have gone stir crazy.

Before she knew it, the doctor removed the cast on her wrist and talked about removing the one on her leg and giving her a boot to wear instead.

Upon hearing that news, her mother was displeased enough that she actually sent Dr. Ellis away.

"That man does not know what he's talking about. It's far too early for you to walk on your own," her mother said, fluffing Morgan's pillows.

"You seemed to think he knew what he was doing when Liam wanted to take me home instead of having me come here," Morgan pointed out. Her mother glared at her. "Besides, I wouldn't be walking on my own. I'd have a boot and crutches," she added. This caused her mother's glare to greaten.

"Seriously, I won't let any daughter of mine roam around willy-nilly wearing a ridiculous boot." Her mother turned away. "Now you just get some rest. I'll go check on lunch."

Half an hour later, instead of Ann bringing in a tray, Liam walked in with a huge smile.

"What do you say to heading out and getting some sunlight?" he asked her.

"That sounds wonderful." She'd showered earlier that morning since she knew that Dr. Ellis would be stopping by. In truth, she'd hoped the man would have a little more information about why she still couldn't remember the past two years of her life.

All of her childhood memories and even most of her college memories had returned. But still, the majority of her time with Liam hadn't returned.

She had pieced together the rest of the night they'd met. She could remember flirting with him, dancing with him, and their first kiss. This memory had her looking at his lips each time he'd visited ever since. But that was it. Everything else was locked away somewhere in her head, and she was growing desperate to get to it.

Liam continued to hint that if she'd just return home, she'd remember everything. But whenever she'd bring it up, her mother would grow angry until Morgan dropped the subject.

She wondered how her mother had let her go in the first place when she'd married Liam a year ago.

Liam took her arm and helped her stand up, then he frowned down at her left arm. "You got your cast off?"

She nodded as he ran his fingers over her skin, which sent waves of sexual awareness rushing through her.

Swallowing hard before she spoke, she finally managed to get out, "Dr. Ellis thinks I might be able to move to a boot next week instead of having this massive itchy thing holding me back." She motioned to her leg as he handed her a crutch.

"Wow, so soon?" Liam asked with a smile.

"Not if my mother has anything to do with it." She rolled her eyes.

"Speaking of which, I didn't see her when I came in," Liam said, helping her slip a sandal onto her good leg.

"She's probably in the kitchen getting lunch together."

Liam smiled and started helping her through the house. Instead of heading to the backdoor and the pool area, he turned towards the front door.

"Where are we going?" she asked.

His smile grew. "Out." She glanced over her shoulder, afraid that her mother would be there to talk her out of going, but she was desperate to get out of the house, to see something, somewhere new.

"Afraid?" Liam asked as he wiggled his eyebrows.

"No." She chuckled. "But I don't want my mother to call the police, so I'll send her a text in the car. That way she can't talk me out of it."

They stepped out the front door, and she was so concerned about making it down the steps that she didn't look at his car until he was holding the door open for her.

The moment she saw the sleek black car, a memory flashed behind her eyes so quickly, she almost doubled over.

"Hey." Liam was by her side, taking her in his arms. "What's wrong?"

"I... think I just had a flashback of the car accident." She blinked a few times.

"Really?" he asked, looking worried.

"Yes." She looked at the car again, but nothing happened this time. "It's gone now," she said with a shrug.

"Come on, let's head out. You can tell me about it while I drive." He helped her get into the car and then handed her the crutch.

As he drove down her parents' long drive, she sent a text message to her mother.

"Gone out to lunch with Liam. Don't wait up." She smiled at the message and waited for the reply as Liam pulled through the gate.

Instead of a text, her phone rang when they were almost a mile from her parents' place.

"What do you mean you've gone out? I have your lunch here. You aren't fit to leave the house yet," her mother complained the second she answered the phone.

"I'm fit," she replied. "Dr. Ellis—"

"I don't care what Dr. Ellis said. You can't even walk. You simply need to tell Liam to turn the car around and—"

"No," Morgan interrupted. "I'm perfectly capable of making my own decisions. I'm going with Liam. I'll be back later." She hung up the phone.

"There she is," Liam said with a smile. "There's my Morgan."

She narrowed her eyes at him. "What do you mean?"

"Spunk," he said with a smile. "This is the first time since your accident that I've seen it." He took a deep breath. "It's nice."

"I'm finally feeling more like myself," she admitted. "How did I ever escape the first time?"

"Your parents?" he asked, glancing over quickly.

"Yes. I mean, I assume I was still living with them when we married. That part of my life is still a blur," she admitted.

"Technically, yes. But you were at my house most nights." He reached over and took her left hand and held it lightly in his as he drove. She was sure that the move was an unconscious one, as if he did it all of the time when they rode in a car together.

"I moved in with you?" she asked him as she looked at their joined hands. Without thinking about it, she'd wrapped her fingers around his.

"Yes." He smiled at her. "You sound a little surprised at that."

She shrugged. "I guess I am. I'd always told myself that I wouldn't move in with someone before marriage."

He chuckled. "Technically, we were married when you moved in."

"Technically?" she asked, confused, as he turned off the highway.

"Yes, well…" He glanced over her. "I'd hoped you would remember this part on your own. Since it was your idea, not mine."

"I… suggested we elope?" She frowned.

"Yes. Your thought was that if we eloped, your mother couldn't talk you out of getting married." He removed his hand from hers so he could grip the wheel as he turned. "So we went down to the courthouse one day and officially married two months before the elaborate ceremony."

"At my parents' country club. I saw the photos on my phone."

They were traveling on a narrow stretch of road. To the left of the road was a steep cliff that appeared to hang over the Pacific Ocean. The right side of the road was sheer rock face.

She realized that they were out of the city for the first time.

"Yes, it was beautiful," he answered as he turned off the road into a long narrow driveway. He stopped at a large black iron gate that opened automatically for him.

"Where are we going?" she asked suddenly.

He smiled over at her. "To lunch." Her eyes narrowed and he laughed. "I know that you don't like surprises but, trust me, you'll like this one."

She frowned for a moment, then sighed and nodded.

They climbed the hill until a tall three-story building appeared on the left.

"That's the garage," Liam said, passing it. "We'll go up to the main building this time."

"We have a three-story garage?" she asked, looking at it as they passed it.

"It's also my home office and a guest house. We have another garage up at the main house, but we like parking down here most of the time."

"Right," she said, as they climbed even higher up the hill.

When the glass house came into view, she was very impressed. From the circular drive, it appeared to be a two-story U-shaped building.

Liam parked in front of massive glass doors that filled up the entire center of the U and then shut off the engine.

She sat there, looking at the home, willing any memories to come to her. Instead, she was filled with awe at the beauty of building.

Liam climbed out and rushed to help her out of the car, holding the crutch for her.

"Wow," she said, leaning on the crutch.

"Yeah, it's one of the reasons I bought the place five years ago. That and the fact that it let me be up here, alone, out of the hustle and bustle of the city." He held onto her arm and helped her walk towards the door.

"There's the other five-car garage there," he said, motioning to the right wing of the main floor. "We don't really use it to park in. We set it up as a makeshift game room." He smiled. "You beat me at pool once and never wanted me to forget it. So I got you a pool table along with a ping pong table."

She chuckled. "I'm really good at pool," she admitted.

She watched as the glass door swung open, a quarter of it inward, the rest outward, and a memory flashed in her mind.

"I... remember this." She motioned to the glass door. "Being here, seeing that before. I remember thinking how beautifully simple it was."

Liam smiled down at her. "Yes? Maybe the inside will jog some more memories."

She'd seen several photos of the inside of their home on her phone, of the splashes of color she obviously had added herself since she had before and after photos of a bunch of rooms. None of them had jogged her memory, but maybe being there would.

They stepped through the glass doors directly into the foyer. Light-colored wood crisscrossed the floor.

A unique glass and wood staircase sat slightly to the right, a sitting and television area to the left. The floors changed to marble in areas and there were brightly colored area rugs. Instantly, she could see her touches to the interior decorating.

"The kitchen is back there," Liam said, motioning past

the stairs. "But I'll show you around first." He turned to the right. "A powder room." He opened the door and she looked in. There was a bright blue rug, a blue vase with white flowers on the countertop, and bright blue towels.

"I like the blue," she said with a smile.

"You picked out everything." He stepped back and shut the door. "The dining room." He motioned to area that held a huge wood table that could easily sit twenty. A glass wall opened up to the backyard, where a beautiful rectangular swimming pool sat surrounded by green grass and white tile. They walked down a wide hallway and stopped at a doorway.

"The pantry," Liam said, opening the door. The room was big enough to step into. Custom wood shelves were filled with canned goods and neatly labeled containers. "You organized all this."

"Yeah, I can be a little... particular at times," she admitted.

He laughed. "Tell me about it." He motioned to the glass wall where another short hallway was. "The wine closet is on the other side. There's a small dumbwaiter to bring wine up from the tasting room in the basement." He motioned to the other door opposite this one. "Here is the kitchen."

They stepped into the kitchen and, once again, there were bright hints of her personality everywhere.

The white and gray marble countertops and dark gray cabinets would have been very dull if not for the bright hits of color everywhere, from colorful vases filled with flowers to placemats, rugs, and throw pillows on the sofa and chairs in the sitting room across from the kitchen bar.

"This is our television room." Liam motioned. "We spend a lot of time in here. You're a binge-watcher," he joked. "You latch onto a show, and we won't move until we've watched the last episode."

She smiled. Yeah, that was her all right.

The entire left wall was glass that led out to the pool area. Currently, she could see all the way to downtown LA and beyond. "Wow, look at that view."

"You can see the ocean from the west wing," he told her. "Our bedroom is in that wing. Come on, let's head upstairs."

They made their way back out towards the stairs, and she suddenly realized that they were shaped like a triangle. Three individual sets of staircases were set in a pattern to go up each level.

"There are three levels?" she asked, looking down and up the stairs.

"Yes, there's a basement. We'll go there first." Instead of heading towards the stairs, which she'd been afraid to use, he walked over to a set of black glass doors next to the powder room doorway. She watched him hit a button. "The elevator."

"We have an elevator?" she asked, amazed.

He chuckled. "Yes. We really don't use it often, but now it works out great for you. Those stairs would have been an issue."

She silently agreed and stepped inside. Even in here, there were hints of colors she liked. The carpet was red and blue, reminding her of a trip to Jamaica she'd taken as a teen.

When they stepped out, they rounded the corner to the left.

"The theater," he said, turning on a light. "We've crowded over a dozen people in here at once. For my birthday a couple months ago, you threw me a surprise party."

"What did we watch?" she asked.

His smile grew. "We binge-watched all the old *Gilligan's Island* episodes. Most of my friends had never seen them. You knew how much I loved them. It was perfect."

She smiled and added that piece of information about him to her growing list.

They turned left and made their way down the hallway. "The massage room." He opened the door and turned on the light. The room reminded her of her mother's massage room. "We have Marina come up once a week. Once you're back, she'll be here for you." He shut the door and opened another. "The sauna and locker room, and this is the gym." He motioned to the room at the end of the section. It was a full-fledged gym, complete with two walls of mirrors and all the standard gym equipment.

It was at that point that she realized the house was in the shape of a three-winged propeller, like a huge fidget spinner. "There are three wings to the house?"

"Yes. The west faces the ocean, the south-east overlooks the city, and the north-east faces them both on either side. The south-east wing connects with the garage on this level. Of course, we're in our basement, but if we head over to the detached garage, we'd been on its top floor." He took her hand, and they made their way down the hallway again. At the center, instead of going right, they went left. They passed another bathroom and stepped into a huge room. "This is a wine room with a service kitchen that's only used when we have catered parties."

"Do we have those often?" she asked, curious.

"Twice a year. Your birthday and New Year's Eve." He smiled. "You know how to throw a party."

She chuckled. "I learned from my mother." She rolled her eyes.

"Right. For now, let's skip the tour of the garage building. There is an elevator there, but I think we'll stick to the main building for now."

"Sure," she agreed, and they made their way back to the elevator and rode to the top floor.

This time when they stepped out, she noticed an entirely different feel to the house. Here, things felt more comfortable. More personal. Instantly, she remembered being here. It was more of feeling of home than any one memory.

"Down those two wings are two bedrooms each with their own bathrooms. Here there is a kitchenette area. We keep snacks and drinks in it, so that we don't have to run downstairs if we get a craving in the night." The kitchenette was directly beside the elevator, along with a massive linen closet that was neatly organized. Then he motioned to the left and straight ahead. "There are bedrooms in the garage building too, and when your squad comes and stays, they stay in those," he said. "Our room is here," he said, heading to the right.

Another small sitting area faced the glass walls of the stairs. Then they opened a door to another smaller sitting area and the bedroom. The entire wall was glass and Liam was right, the view of the ocean was beautiful. She stopped and just took it in for a moment. Then she turned and when she saw the white, blue, and green comforter, a full memory played in her head. She swayed as it played out.

Liam was looking at her from across the room, his eyes glued to hers as she moved closer to him. With each step, she removed an article of clothing, tossing it to the ground haphazardly.

His eyes heated as each piece of clothing disappeared. When she finally reached him, she stood before him, naked and wanting. The desire was so great, she swayed with it, desperate to feel him touching her. Feel him inside her. Then his arms wrapped around her, and she felt steadier.

"Morgan?" Liam's voice broke into her memory. Just like in her memory, Liam's arms were around her, holding her upright.

"Liam, I..." She shook her head as tears filled her eyes. Her throat ached, as did her entire body. Instead of speaking, she leaned in and placed her lips over his, pouring her feelings, the ones she'd been having in the memory, into the kiss.

# CHAPTER TEN

*The light of the day is followed by night, as a shadow follows
a body.*
**Aristotle**

There was nothing he wanted more at that moment than to be with her. It had been almost three months since her accident, and he missed her more than he cared to admit.

She was his everything. Which was the main reason he was trying to tie up some loose ends so he could be with her more.

His hands roamed over her freely as he was lost in the memory of being with her. She was home. She was his center. His family. His everything. He wanted to show her this, but when his hand moved over her and she lost her balance and leaned on him, he remembered the cast on her leg. Remembered the guilt about what had hurt her and pulled back slightly.

"I... Lynda's made us some lunch. I thought we'd sit out by the pool and enjoy the sunshine." He watched her eyes as more pain flooded them. Only this time, he knew it wasn't physical. "I want to be with you," he said softly, cupping her face. "Soon," he promised.

She swallowed and nodded. "I could eat," she said with a slight smile.

He took her back down the elevator and got her settled outside, then ran in and grabbed the plates of food out of the warmer and added some bottled water and two glasses of wine to the tray. When he stepped out, she was resting back, her sunglasses hiding her eyes.

"Feeling better?" he asked her as he set the tray down.

"Much," she sighed. "I should be recovering here," she admitted when he sat down. "I've already had a few memories. I think that if I came back, I might remember everything. If it's okay with you."

"If it's okay with me? Hell, yes. I didn't want you to go to your parents' place to begin with," he blurted out, causing her to smile. "Please, come back." His voice cracked slightly as he reached across the table for her hand. "If you feel strange about it, I'll sleep in one of the other rooms."

"No," she broke in, "you don't have to do that."

He relaxed. "Good. Now, let's have this lunch. Lynda made you her famous six-cheese grilled cheese sandwiches and French onion soup."

"Tell me about our wedding," she said after a few bites of food. "I saw the photos and some videos, but... I'd like to hear more."

He nodded. "Your mother arranged to have it at your country club. Since you liked the idea of getting married outside with the sunset as a backdrop, you agreed."

"And you? Where did you want to be married?"

He smiled. "We were married the first time where I wanted. In the courthouse."

When she smiled, his heart flipped a couple times. "That reminds me. I haven't been able to get into my social media sites." She pulled out her phone. "I can't remember the passwords." She set the phone down and pushed the phone towards him.

"We have a password app. Every password is protected. Security reasons. This way you just need to remember one password."

He picked up the phone, logged into it, then had to wait for the password app to upload since she hadn't used it since he had given her the new phone. "Here." He scooted his chair closer to her as they looked down at the phone together.

He gave her the password, which he changed once a month, then showed her how to log in and use it for each of her social media accounts, including her email.

"Wow, there's so much I have to catch up on now," she said, showing him her screen. "Thousands of comments or messages on each platform." She rolled her eyes.

"You have a lot of friends that have been worried about you." He frowned slightly. "Speaking of which, we should probably make a statement. The press has been hounding me. I'm sure they're nagging your parents as well."

"Right." She frowned down at her phone, then set it down. He could see the pain in her eyes when she looked up at him.

"It's too hot and bright out here." He reached up and flipped open the umbrella, shrouding them in shade instantly.

"I'm fine. I'm wishing I could jump in that to cool off though." She motioned to the pool.

"When does the doctor say you can get that replaced with a boot?" he asked her.

"Not soon enough," she answered with a sigh. "If my mother has anything to do with it..."

"She doesn't." He reached over and took her hand. "She can only give you her thoughts. You make your own decisions on your health. Remember?"

"Right." She smiled, then sighed and rested her head back. "I could go for a nap."

"We should let your mother know about you moving out," he suggested.

"Later." She sighed, then glanced around. "Would you help me to the lounge?" She motioned to the two lounge chairs under the shade of a few palm trees.

He helped her, then cleaned up their lunch mess before joining her to sit by the pool. While she napped, he scrolled through his phone and his own messages. Almost an hour later, Morgan began mumbling in her sleep.

Glancing over, he could see the nightmare take hold of her and rushed over to her side to gently wake her.

"Hey," he said softly, gathering her in his arms. "I'm here."

"No, I can't... They aren't working. Help me... Stop." She screamed the last word and jerked herself awake.

"I'm here," he repeated. "It was just a dream." He held onto her a little tighter when he felt her arms wrap around him.

She'd lost a lot of weight since her accident. She'd been skinny to begin with. In the months leading up to the accident, she'd dropped a few pounds working around her mother all the time. When he'd mentioned it, she'd claimed that it was all the stress her mother was putting on her.

He'd suggested she stop working and start doing something she loved instead. She'd promised that after her brother's club opened, she would.

"You're too thin," he said into her hair. "You've lost too much weight."

She sighed and then chuckled. "Just what every woman wants to hear when she wakes up."

He pulled back and looked down at her. She appeared well rested, but he could see that her cheeks were hollowed out and there were slight purple circles under her eyes.

"When will you move back?" he asked, needing her to be closer so he could protect her and make sure she was eating enough and getting good rest.

She tilted her head and blinked a few times. "I don't see why I would have to return to my parents' place at all. I mean, there are a few things you brought there, my clothes and things, but we could always go get them tomorrow."

He smiled. "I like the way you think." Then he surprised her by lifting her in his arms and carrying her inside. "It's hot out here. Let's head inside." She smiled as he carried her inside and set her gently down on the sofa. Then he handed her the remote. "Find something for us to watch. I'll get us some dessert."

"Ice cream?" she asked, turning on the television.

"You know it." He chuckled. "There's always a freezer full of mint chocolate chip for you and toffee for me."

"I like toffee too," she added as she flipped through the channels.

"I know. One scoop of each coming up."

When he returned to the sofa with two bowls of ice cream and some wafer cookies to share, she had found their Netflix list.

"It says we've watched all of these, but since I can't remember..." She looked over at him.

He motioned with the bowl. "Go ahead. Have you thought about exactly how far back your memory goes?

When it stops, I mean." He set the bowls down on the coffee table.

"No." She frowned as she took up the bowl. "I guess the best way to judge that is..." She sighed.

"You didn't remember going to college," he hinted.

"Right." She nodded. "Okay, so high school? I do remember graduation. After that... Not so much."

"You took a year off after graduation," he reminded her.

Her eyes narrowed as if she was thinking. "I traveled."

"Yes." He smiled. "Egypt first, then you spent a few months moving around Europe—England, Ireland, France, Spain—then on to Africa, where you'd done some peace work in high school."

"I did," she agreed with a smile. "I went and saw Nailah!" she exclaimed. "I remember. I'd been pen pals with her since she was five. She's eleven now..." She thought again. "Eleven."

"Fifteen now," he corrected. "And yes, you're still pen pals. You spent a month in her village, helping set up windmills and water pumps."

"She's fifteen?" Morgan frowned. "Aaron," she said. "That's why he looked so different from what I remember. I've lost four years of my life."

He wrapped an arm around her. "You'll find them. We'll find them together," he added, hating to see the lost look in her eyes. He wrapped his arm around her, and they sat back and watched reruns as they enjoyed their ice cream. When the second episode was over, she paused the set.

"Before we start the next episode, I'd better call my mother," she suggested.

"I'll leave you to it, if you want?" he said. She'd normally left his side whenever talking to her mother. Not that she was trying to hide their conversation, but she didn't want him to see her upset.

"No, you can stay." She called her mother.

"Hi, Mom." Morgan's voice changed slightly, as it always did whenever she was talking to her parents. Her tone was usually a little lower and far more professional. As if she was in a business meeting instead of talking to parents. The people who raised you. Loved you.

Then again, he'd never had parents, so he couldn't imagine how he would have acted around them. Especially with parents like Morgan's. In the two years they had been together, not once had they made him feel like part of their family. Actually, most of the time they went out of their way to exclude him.

Thankfully, Morgan had always been there to stand by his side. Up until the accident. It wasn't as if her parents hunted him down and treated him bad on purpose.

While he listened to her tell her mother about moving back home, he thought of the last time she'd told them she was moving out. That time it had taken three months before her mother would talk to her again. He wondered if that would be the case this time too.

The longer Morgan talked, the more he knew there would be problems. Victoria Davenport usually got what she wanted and if she didn't, someone was going to hear about it.

By the time Morgan hung up, he could tell she was tired again.

"That didn't go well," she said, looking at him apologetically.

"It never does. Your mother never agreed with anything in regard to us."

"How did she agree to us getting married in the first place?" she asked him.

He chuckled. "You let it slip out at one of your interviews. Then the magazine did a huge article on us and our upcoming nuptials. Your mother had no choice."

"I bet she hated that. She never did like when any member of our family was in the tabloids." She sighed and settled back down in his arms.

"She didn't talk to you for three months. Then, the month before the wedding, she jumped in with both feet and tried to take over the planning of everything."

"Tell me I didn't let her." She groaned.

"Nope." He smiled. "Morgan Taylor, who you were at the time, is nothing like Morgan Davenport. Mrs. Taylor is a strong woman who won't be bullied." He repeated her words.

"Yeah, that sounds about right." She nodded. "She is exhausting."

"Yup." He nodded in agreement. "Need more sugar?"

"No, what I need is another nap." She looked up at him with a grin and after two years, he knew that look too well.

Leaning down, he brushed his lips against hers. "Morgan?"

"Liam." Her fingers tangled in his hair. "Remind me what it's like," she said between kisses. "Please."

It was the please that did it. She'd never begged him. Only when she was near the end of her rope. He hoisted her up in his arms, thinking that, even though he'd lost count of the times they'd been together over the years, for her, this was their first. Which meant he had to do everything right. Take his time. Show her just what she meant to him.

He carried her up the stairs, cautious of the heavy cast

on her leg, and brought her to their bedroom as she trailed kisses down his neck.

"Are you sure you're up for this?" he asked, concerned, as he looked down at her leg.

Not long ago she'd been broken, almost dead. Now he was finally free to celebrate that she was alive and his once more.

"Yes," she said, brushing her fingers in his hair and pulling his mouth back down to her lips. "Remind me."

The kiss was just like their first, but it kept building, getting stronger, more powerful, like a storm brewing between them. He could feel the power of his longing and knew that if he didn't take control, the desire that had built up since their last time together would consume him and he'd lose his mind and end up hurting her.

Pulling back, he looked down into her eyes as he moved towards the bed and gently laid her down on the brightly colored comforter.

Then he knelt in front of her and removed the one shoe she had on before running his hands up her good leg. He kept his eyes locked with hers.

"Do you know how good you feel in my hands?" he asked as he touched her skin with just his fingertips.

"Oh god," she moaned and leaned back on her elbows. "You make me weak," she said softly.

"Good." He smiled. "Now you know what you do to me." He bent his head and trailed his mouth up to her knee, then traced her toned thighs with his tongue as she moaned and arched towards him.

He wanted to touch her everywhere, but the cast on her other leg only allowed him to shift between her legs. Finally, he moved her further onto the bed so he could lie between her legs.

"Morgan, look at me," he said, until she looked up and smiled at him. "You're home." He leaned down and kissed her once more. "I've missed you," he said as he ran his finger gently over her, nudging her shirt up higher until her soft skin brushed against his fingertips.

He'd always loved the way she had responded to his touch. It was as if she was coming alive, and he was right there with her.

"Liam." Morgan tugged at his shirt, and he leaned back to pull it over his head. "Wow." She smiled up at him. "I saw pictures..." She ran her fingertips over his chest. "Soon, you'll tell me what each of these designs means to you."

He smiled. "Again?"

She chuckled and nodded. "Please."

He helped her remove her shirt, which was a lot easier than removing the flowing capris that she was wearing over her cast. Once she was lying under him in a pair of sexy black underwear, he leaned down and kissed her until she reached for the clasp of his shorts.

He had to pull away now, or he'd be lost forever again. Lost in her kiss, lost in the way she felt under him. He would be unable to give her everything she needed, everything she deserved.

When he moved away, she made a disapproving sound. He smiled as he leaned over and trailed his mouth over the curve of her breasts.

"Your taste has been on my mind," he growled as he nudged the silk aside and took her nipple into his mouth.

"Liam!" She arched into him, her fingers curling tight in his hair. "I..."

Then he reached down and found her hot, wet, and ready for him. His fingers brushed the silk and lace aside and found her clit. All it took was running his finger over her before he felt her explode for him.

"My god," he growled out as he grew even harder than he'd been before. He couldn't remember it being like this before. Even their first time together. It had been all speed. A flash in the night. This was something new. Something... amazing. And he felt as if he had only begun to touch her.

This time when she reached for his shorts, he helped pull them off his hips.

"Do we... worry about protection?" she asked. "I haven't been taking a pill."

"No." He frowned slightly. "We... were trying for kids. But if you want..." He reached for the nightstand, but she stopped him. She was smiling up at him.

"No, I like kids." She pulled him back down to her.

He smiled and then he was kissing her again, and everything he was melted into her.

# CHAPTER ELEVEN



*When you light a candle, you also cast a shadow.*
**Ursula K. Le Guin**

Falling asleep in her husband's arms was a surreal thing. Her body vibrated with the afterglow of the best sex she'd ever had. Well, ever remembered, at any rate.

The pictures on her phone hadn't done Liam justice. Under the brightly colored tattoos was a body chiseled out of stone. He had a light dusting of dark hair that traveled down below his bellybutton to his sex, and she couldn't stop thinking about.

His arms and chest were strong enough that he'd had no difficulty carrying her up the stairs the night before, heavy cast and all.

There was something about the way he moved over her, in her, that had her body responding quickly.

It had only taken a simple touch last night for her to explode and now, just imagining it, her body heated at the memory.

How had she forgotten him? If everything he was saying

was true, he was the best thing that had ever happened to her.

When Liam's eyes opened, she was leaning over him, her head resting in her hands as she looked down at his face. It was an amazing face. His jaw was covered in dark stubble, which she reached up and ran her hand over as his green eyes focused on her.

"Morning," he said softly, his hands going up behind her and cupping her hip. "Did you sleep well?"

"Yes," she answered, still running her eyes over him. Then she traced the black designs on his chest. "When did you get this one?"

He glanced down and after sighed. "I was sixteen when I got my first tattoo. Some of them mean something, others don't. We got matching tattoos on our honeymoon."

"We did?" She sat up a little. "I have a tattoo?" She started frantically looking around her body, causing him to laugh.

"Here," he said, helping her roll over. Then his fingers traced a spot on her upper left hip, just above her butt cheek. Then he showed her his left bicep.

There was a simple blue rose, but instead of a normal thin line as a stem, she could easily read her name in curving letters.

"They are the same, except yours says Liam," he explained.

"My mother would love that," she said sarcastically.

"Which is why you got yours here." He ran his hand over her hip again. "Even a bathing suit hides it. For my eyes only." He winked at her. Then he leaned closer and brushed his lips over her. "I have to go into work today, but Lynda will be here shortly. If you want, I can arrange for Marina to stop by later for a massage?"

"I'd love that. My mother's massage therapist Theresa has been MIA for the last week."

"She has? Vacation?"

She shrugged. "I'm not sure. Now that I have my cast off my arm, I'll need..." She gasped, followed by a groan. "I was supposed to have therapy this morning with Grayson. I need to..." She rolled over to grab her phone, but Liam stopped her.

"You can call him after we shower." He pulled her back up against him. "We can shower after..." He kissed her deeply, and she melted against him, letting all of her worries disappear until all she could focus on was being with Liam. Her husband.

Even with the heavy cast on her leg, he found a way to make her feel cherished, sexy, and desired instead of awkward and clumsy.

She desperately wanted to wrap her legs around his hips. To hold him as close to her as she could. Instead, she wrapped her arms around his waist and dug her fingernails into his skin as he made her climax multiple times in a row.

She was so exhausted after, that she instantly fell asleep again.

This time when she woke, she was in the bed alone. Rolling over, she smiled at the note from Liam. His handwriting was crisp clean lines and looked vaguely familiar.

"I had to go in to work. I messaged your mother to have her cancel your PT. Lynda will be here at nine and have breakfast ready for you. I messaged Marina, and she'll be here at two. I'll be home around seven. If you need anything, let Lynda know or message me. I miss you already. Love, Liam"

Morgan glanced at the clock. It was a quarter past nine, which meant, there was probably breakfast downstairs.

She desperately wanted that shower Liam had mentioned but figured it would be a hard to find something to wrap around her cast. Still, she could clean up a little.

The tour yesterday hadn't extended to the bathroom or closet, so when she stepped into the room, she took a moment to appreciate the massive space. There was a huge stand-alone tub sitting in the middle of the room, a massive gray-tiled shower, complete with multiple showerheads and a long bench along the back wall. On either side of it were two closet toilets, one with feminine products in it, which she assumed was hers. The other must be Liam's.

Taking a quick moment, she used her toilet and tried to remember being there before. She'd lived in the house for over a year. This was one room she must have used a lot, but nothing was coming to her.

Across from the toilet closets were his-and-her sinks. Hers was on the same side as her toilet room. She found drawers of her makeup, hair products, and other toiletry items all neatly organized and labeled. Here she felt very much at home, even if she didn't remember it.

She stepped through an archway on her left and entered the massive closet space. There were three islands in the middle of the room, and along the walls were wood organizers filled with her things. Her shoes and dresses hung in one section, and her sweaters were all neatly orga-nized in see-through bins. Her jewelry was in one island, including several pieces she'd never seen before.

She knew she had been the one to organize everything here since it was all separated by season, designer, and then color.

When she found her favorite sweater from high school, she felt her eyes water. Pulling it on over her head, she switched out of her pants from the day before into soft cotton pants that she could easily pull on herself, thanks to a bench in the closet.

After combing her hair and applying a little makeup, she stepped out of the bedroom and was about to head down the elevator to the main floor. Instead, she detoured to poke her head in each of the guest rooms on that floor, curious to see what touches she had added to them.

Each room faced large glass walls and had a queen size bed complete with brightly colored throw pillows and rugs. Two of the guest rooms overlooked the pool area and the ocean beyond, like the main bedroom did. The other two rooms overlooked the city. They all had balconies.

Finally, she made her way back to the elevator and headed down to the kitchen. She couldn't believe they had an elevator and wondered if she'd ever used it before. She doubted it since she would have deemed the stairs a healthier choice. Still, it was lucky the house had it.

She stepped into the kitchen as an older blonde woman pulled a kettle off the stove.

"Oh, Mrs. Taylor, it's so wonderful that you're finally home," the woman said with a clipped British accent as she set the pan down and rushed over to hug her.

"Please, call me Morgan," she replied.

"Yes, ma'am, you've told me that very same thing a hundred times," Lynda said with a smile.

"Have you ever called me Morgan?" she asked.

"No ma'am." Lynda chuckled. "Come, I've got breakfast on for you and the tea you like."

"Has Liam explained that I can't remember anything, you, all this?" Morgan motioned around them.

"Yes, ma'am. I'm so sorry about your accident. I'm thankful you're okay though. You gave Mr. Taylor a bad scare." She helped Morgan to the table. "Don't you worry, until you get back on both feet, I'll be right here. Mr. Taylor says that he called Marina for you later today. Until then, I'll help you catch up on what's what around here." She set a plate of delicious-looking breakfast quiche in front of her.

"You're Lynda," she said. "Our housekeeper?"

"Yes, ma'am. Lynda Whitaker," Lynda said as she got the tea ready, and Morgan noted that she poured two cups and then sat across from her as if it was something she normally did. Yet the woman refused to call her Morgan. This made Morgan smile. The woman was obviously steeped in tradition, yet Morgan had at least broken through her rough exterior enough to make her feel comfortable taking tea with her.

"How long have you been working for us?" Morgan asked after taking a bite of the delicious food.

"Mr. Taylor, four years," Lynda answered with a smile.

"What exactly do you do around here?" Morgan asked.

Lynda smiled. "Everything the two of you don't have time to. I prepare weekly meals so all you need to do is heat them up. I shop. There's a digital list on the refrigerator's screen. I'll show you how to input items after breakfast."

Morgan glanced back and noticed that the huge double-wide refrigerator had a monitor on the front. "Okay, thanks."

"I cook, clean, and help with anything else you need. When you moved in, I helped reorganize... well..." Lynda chuckled. "Everything." Then she leaned closer. "We are both like-minded in the organization area. Mr. Taylor, he lived like a bachelor before you."

Morgan chuckled. "I think you and I are going to get along just fine."

"Oh, we do," Lynda responded with a smile and a wink.

After lunch, Lynda told her how the household ran and

showed Morgan around the other areas in the home. Morgan could see her influence here as well. There were charts in her handwriting in the pantry. All the containers were labeled and organized to Morgan's pleasure.

Once she had the lay of the land, Lynda went to work upstairs. Morgan was about to head out to the pool when a buzzer went off, signaling someone was at the gate.

Since Lynda was upstairs, Morgan made her way to the security panel and saw Grayson's face on the screen.

"Hi, you found the place," she said.

"Hi, is Morgan—" Grayson started.

"This is me. Come on up." She hit the gate release button and waited for Grayson at the front door. It took a little while, but finally his car parked directly outside.

"Wow," he said, getting out of his car as he grabbed his duffle bag.

"Welcome." She smiled. It was nice seeing a familiar face. Plus, she really didn't want her therapy to be interrupted. Each day she worked, her body felt stronger, and she felt more in control.

"Thanks," he said, throwing his bag over his shoulder. "Do you have some place we can work?"

"There's an entire gym here," she said gleefully. "It's downstairs."

Grayson frowned. "We haven't really worked on stairs yet."

"Don't worry, we have an elevator." She moved over to the door and hit the button.

"Wow," he said with a smile.

"Yeah." She smiled and stepped inside. "I'm glad you're here."

"Oh?" he asked, his eyes running over her. "Are you hurting?"

"No, just..." She sighed and relaxed her shoulders, feeling stupid. She didn't want to tell him that he was the only steady face that had been around after her accident, besides Liam and her own family. "I got my cast off," she said suddenly, holding up her left arm.

"Wow, good." He took her arm in his hands and was examining it when the doors opened.

Lynda stood just outside the elevator, looking at them. Morgan must have hit the up button instead of the down. She hadn't even realized they had traveled up instead of down.

"Oh, Lynda, this is Grayson, my physical therapist." She dropped her arm from his hold. "This is Lynda, our housekeeper."

"I heard the buzzer," Lynda supplied.

"Yes, I let him in. We were going to head down to the gym and work. I guess I hit the up button instead of the down one."

"If you need anything," Lynda said with a slight frown.

"No, thank you," Morgan added before the doors shut again.

They rode down to the bottom floor in silence.

"I may have said it too many times already, but wow," Grayson said when they stepped into the gym.

"Yeah, I'm right there with you. I saw all this for the first time yesterday."

"Oh, right, because of your memory loss." He set his bag down. "I think we have everything we need to get to work." He walked over to pick up a medicine bag.

Today for therapy he had her sitting down on a yoga mat and rolling the medicine ball back and forth like a kid playing catch. He also had her twist it in circles with her left arm, which actually made her arm hurt.

"I think that's enough for today," he said almost an hour later. He was helping her up off the mat, since the cast on her leg weighed a ton, when they heard a cough from the door.

A very short Asian woman stood just inside the gym doors.

"Sorry, I didn't mean to interrupt," the woman said.

"No, we were just finishing up." Morgan dropped her hands from Grayson's.

The woman nodded. "I heard you're having issues with your memory." She stepped in further, her eyes going between Morgan and Grayson. "I'm Marina."

"Yes." Morgan relaxed. "I figured."

"Liam messaged me that you're back and ready for a massage," Marina added with a smile.

"Yes." Morgan held in a groan, but apparently not well enough because Marina chuckled.

"I'll show myself out," Grayson said, but then Lynda appeared in the doorway.

"I'll show you out," Lynda said firmly.

"I'll see you in two days," Grayson added. "Until then, continue working on the exercises I showed you. If you want, you can lift some weights, nothing more than those two pounders there." He motioned to the wall that held racks filled with weights.

"Thanks," she said and then followed Marina into the private massage room.

"That's your physical therapist?" Marina asked when they were alone.

"Yes," Morgan answered as she sat down on the table.

"He looks familiar," Marina added with a shrug. "I've probably seen him around since he's in the business. He's dreamy." She sighed. "Clothes off," Marina said, then handed Morgan a towel. "I've seen it, so don't get shy on me," she added with a smile.

Morgan wasn't a shy person when it came to nudity, around women she knew at any rate. There wasn't any doubt that she was very comfortable with Marina.

Pulling off her shirt, she heard Marina hiss and walk over to her and touch her shoulder.

"What did you do to your beautiful body?" Marina asked as she ran her finger over her arm.

Morgan had several long scars on her left shoulder and upper arm. Most had been hidden under the cast when she'd woken up.

The day the doctor switched her to the thermal cast, she'd gotten her first look at the wounds. Actually, she still hadn't gotten a good look at everything.

She'd been avoiding looking at the rest of her body, which is why she'd missed the tattoo on her backside.

She wasn't really very vain, but from what little she did see of herself after the accident, she feared that what she couldn't see would be worse.

"It's not that bad. At least I can move my arm." She rotated her left arm slightly and winced when pain caused her to stop midway around. "A little."

"If you need more therapy, I'm always available," Marina said as Morgan started pulling off her pants and the rest of her clothes.

"Grayson's been doing fine. Thanks." She wasn't sure she could handle more than twice a week.

"I bet. The man is a hunk." Marina sighed and leaned against the table, then bent down and helped out when she noticed Morgan was having a difficult time removing her pants.

"I can see if he's single?" Morgan said, shifting to lie on

the table. She was thankful that Marina helped lift her cast onto the table for her.

"No," she said quickly. "I guess I need to come out to you a second time," she said as she lathered lotion onto her hands.

"Oh." Morgan groaned and then smiled. "Then maybe I can find someone else to hook you up with?"

"Nope, I'm happily single. For the moment. That doesn't mean I can't admire a piece of art," Marina added as she started working on Morgan's shoulders.

After her massage from Marina, Morgan sat by the pool, totally relaxed. She sipped a sweet tea and went through her many emails and social media messages.

There were so many well-wishing messages, she ended up just scrolling through most of them. She was pretty sure she didn't know anyone, but just in case, she hit like or starred every single one of them.

When she grew bored of that, she moved over to her emails and instantly gave up when there were more than a thousand unread messages. Instead, she scrolled through photos and videos on her phone.

When she came upon faces that she didn't know, she would search through her own social media to find out their names.

There were a ton of pictures of Liam's best friend, Ryder. The man was built like Liam and apparently owned a gym downtown, which explained why he was so in shape.

There were a few pictures of Ryder with one woman hanging on his arm and then later a different, which hinted at the fact that he was still single.

She instantly wondered why her three friends were still single. Had she tried to set any of them up with Ryder? If not, why? He was a very good-looking man.

There were pictures of Liam and Ryder boxing together, and Ryder had easily as many tattoos as Liam did. Maybe more.

The best picture she found of the pair was them laughing with their arms thrown over each other's shoulders after a boxing match. Liam had a red cheek and a fat lip, and Ryder had a black eye. Their gloves were still on, but the pair looked happy.

She was smiling down at the image when her phone rang.

She didn't recognize the number and there was no name attached to it, but she answered the call anyway.

"Hello?"

"It sure was a surprise that you survived. You shouldn't have. Maybe next time you won't," a deep voice said before quickly hanging up.

# CHAPTER TWELVE

*Maybe you have to know the darkness before you can appreciate the light.*
**Madeline L'Engle**

L iam wished more than anything that he could hit the gym before heading home. He had a huge desire to pummel something. The last thing he wanted to do was bring the negative mood home to Morgan.

Since he couldn't release the frustration of the day, his mood was sour as he parked in the garage and made his way into the main part of the house.

Morgan was sitting at the kitchen table, currently on the phone with someone.

When she noticed him, she quickly hung up, then rushed across the room and straight into his arms. The moment she did so, all of the negativity dissipated as his arms wrapped around her.

"Did you miss me?" he asked with a chuckle. Then she pulled back and looked up at him, and he knew something was wrong. "What happened?"

"I... got a call a couple hours ago." She pulled out her phone and showed him her phone. "They threatened me."

He tensed. "What did they say?" He looked down at the number she was showing him.

She closed her eyes, took a deep breath, and then said, "It sure was a surprise that you survived. You shouldn't have. Maybe next time you won't."

He looked into her eyes, set her phone down, and wrapped his arms around her. "It's probably just someone trying to spook you," he said against her hair.

"I know. I've told myself that a hundred times since then, but..." She sighed and he felt her relax. "It's nice that you're home. After Marina and Lynda left... I worked myself into a panic."

"I'm here now." He held onto her a little tighter, and she practically melted in his hands.

"I didn't mean to freak out," she said, pulling back a little. "Really, I didn't."

He smiled. "You can't even watch scary movies. I can only image how a phone call like that would upset you." He brushed his lips across hers. "Come on, let's have some dinner and watch something to take your mind off it."

They heated dinner together and then sat in the living room and watched reruns of an old television show that he'd watched before, but she acted as if she was seeing it for the first time.

When she fell asleep next to him, he lifted her up and carried her upstairs. Since she was wearing cotton pants and a tank top, he figured she was comfortable enough and laid the blankets over her.

He remembered he'd left his laptop case downstairs and went down to retrieve it. He had to spend a few hours working before shutting down for the night.

They had shut all the lights off downstairs while they'd been watching television and as he walked across the living foyer to get his laptop, he saw a movement out of the corner of his eye and froze.

Someone was outside the glass front doors. The security lights should have turned on, lighting up the entire circular driveway, but everything was still dark.

He watched the green lights of his security system screen next to the door turn red, signaling that someone had just shut the system down. Every fiber of his body went on guard as he looked around for something to use as a weapon. His gun safe was upstairs in the bedroom.

The front doors were on a magnetic locking system, which used a phone app as a key. Anyone wanting to break in would have to have direct access through an app, which he would have to approve and give access for.

As he stood there, frozen in place, the door lock chimed softly as the lock was disengaged. He took a fighter's stance, ready for what was about to happen.

The door swung open silently and a dark figure stepped inside the door. It was too dark to see anything other than the outline. The moment he moved towards the figure, it zoned in on him and rushed forward, knocking Liam back onto a glass table, which shattered beneath his weight.

The back of Liam's head hit the marble floor, causing him to see stars and bright lights. Still, he was in defense mode and kicked out, knocking the body off of him, throwing them across the marble flooring.

When the man gained his feet, instead of fighting, he bolted towards the door and was outside when the bell on the elevator chimed and the door opened.

The foyer was flooded in light as Morgan rushed from the elevator and turned on the lights.

"What?" She blinked and then took in the opened front door, the shattered table, and Liam.

Liam wanted to take off after the intruder, but he couldn't chance it. What if there was more than one? He wasn't going to leave Morgan alone. Not knowing that whoever had broken in had just bypassed all of his security.

Walking over to the security system, he punched in the emergency code, which would have the police arriving in less than ten minutes.

"I heard glass..." Morgan said, shaking her head.

He walked over and wrapped her in his arms. "It's okay," he said softly, his eyes still on the doorway to the darkness outside. "I scared them off."

"You... have a chunk of glass in your shoulder." She gasped when he turned slightly, and she got a better look.

He felt it then, the sharp pain in his shoulder.

By the time the police arrived, Morgan had his shirt off and most of the glass removed from his skin. He refused the ambulance ride and allowed the paramedic to bandage up the cuts.

The police went through every room in the house, checking doors and windows for signs of entry.

His security company sent someone out there to update the system and reset the locks on the doors, which meant they had to contact anyone who currently had access and let them know the system had been reset and they would have to get a code from him again.

It was past two in the morning when everything finally settled down. His evening plans of working while Morgan slept were ruined and, instead, he crawled into bed with her and instantly fell asleep with her in his arms.

He woke with his alarm and, as much as he wanted to spend the day sleeping next to Morgan, he had an early morning meeting with the board. He slipped out of the bed, showered, dressed, and grabbed some fruit as he wrote a note for Morgan. Before leaving, he sent a text message to Lynda, giving her a new access code for the door.

The moment he walked into his office, he knew it was going to be a terrible day. Dave was once again sitting at his desk, only this time both Dawn and Larry, other board members, were sitting in the chairs across from him.

"Morning," Liam said casually as he walked over, pulled out his chair, and nodded for Dave to vacate it. He wanted to say more, to punch the guy in the face, but years of training had him biting his tongue.

Dave shifted slightly and then slowly stood up. "Morning. We were wondering if you were going to show," Dave said as he moved to lean on the corner of Liam's desk.

"Don't you have an office of your own?" Liam asked.

Dave chuckled as if Liam had just said the funniest thing. "Not with this view." He motioned to the window. "Besides, we wanted to talk to you before the meeting."

"Oh?" Liam asked as he sat down and logged into his system.

"We're concerned about the security breaches," Larry chimed in.

"Which is why the board meeting has been called for today. I'll explain everything then," Liam said.

"We heard you found out something new?" Dawn asked. "We're hoping you can clue us in on what it is before the meeting."

Liam glanced around the room at the three faces and smiled. "All new information I and my security team have found out will be revealed at the meeting"—he glanced at his watch—"in an hour. Until then, I have a few loose ends to tie up." He motioned to the door. When none of them made a move to leave, he called Cheryl and suggested she show the three of them to the board room and get them some coffee so they could wait there.

That got them moving, but as they left, Dave glanced around and sneered at him.

Over the past few weeks, Liam and two other members of his team, whom he trusted completely, had combed through every inch of the security logs. They had proof of who had placed the code in the update files and proof of who had approved the update.

It hadn't been hard, really. What disturbed Liam the most was that it hadn't been who he'd thought it would be.

He'd been pretty sure Dave had something to do with it, but so far, the man was clean. Which is what Liam had been wanting to work on last night before the break-in. He wanted to go over the data once more just to make sure.

There was no way the new employee could have gotten that deep into the system to upload the backdoor program. Kevin Moore had been hired just six weeks prior to the hack. The moment Liam's team had found out it was his login that uploaded the code, the man had been walked out of the building by security.

When they discovered others who were involved, they too were escorted out. The legal department was handling any charges that might be brought against them.

Nothing Liam had found so far pointed to Dave or any of the other members on the board. He was determined to get each and every person responsible.

Maybe it was the lack of sleep or the fact that he wanted to be home spending as much time as he could with Morgan, but when he logged into his computer system, he accidently logged into the admin account on his computer system instead of his normal login account with his name and password.

He didn't realize what he'd done until he saw the screen image, which was normally a photo of Morgan on the beach during their honeymoon. Now it was just the standard blue screen.

He was about to log out and log back in under his user ID when he noticed a folder labeled "working" on the desktop.

He didn't really use the office system for anything other than emails, as his laptop was more secure and mobile.

He clicked into the folder and was shocked to find a copy of the firmware file that included the hack. How did it get on his computer? Why? He spent the next thirty minutes trying to answer that question.

He was slightly shocked to find out when the file had been created on his desktop. The exact night of Morgan's accident. The more he looked at it, the more he began to wonder if this was the original file. There were some slight differences from the copy they had found on Kevin Moore's system.

Putting a copy of the file onto a thumb drive, he removed it from his computer and then changed the admin password and even his own password on the system.

After the first time he'd caught Dave in his office, he'd thought about installing a hidden camera. Now he wished he had and made a point to stop by the security office to see if they had something. If not, he'd make a run to an electronics store and buy something himself.

He needed proof and needed to know who had written or planted the file on his PC. He thought about the board meeting, about telling them about the file, but figured it was best to hold back. After all, wouldn't they accuse him of creating the code in the first place.

He wondered how many other computers in the firm had the file hidden on them and what other hacks were on the systems in the building?

He had less than twenty minutes before the meeting and decided to head down to the IT department for a quick meeting first.

Normally, the four employees that made up the department were running around the building. Luckily, when he walked into their office, all four of the team were there standing around a box of donuts, drinking coffee. It was obvious they had just gotten into the office.

After a brief meeting with them, he found out that they were about to touch each system for an update and told them to keep an eye out for the program files. He gave them strict instructions to let Liam know which systems were affected and to clean them up, and then he headed up to the meeting.

When he walked in, everyone else was just filing into the room as well. He shook hands and tried to be cordial with everyone.

Seeing Dave at the head of the table had Liam's temperature boiling. The man acted as if he was the head of the board when, in fact, each of the ten members were all equals.

"Thank you," Dave broke into the chatter, and everyone settled down.

Thankfully, at that moment, Christina Newton, the official recorder, called the meeting to order and started taking roll and running through the agenda.

When it was his turn to have the floor, he ran through what information he had, how many employees had been fired, and what had been turned over to the investigating and legal teams.

All in all, it was very quick, and he only spoke for about ten minutes. Then, to his and the board's total surprise, Dave stood up and, out of the blue, suggested that every employee's computer and laptop be searched.

"We can't take the chance that someone else who was involved in this fiasco has slipped through the cracks," Dave said, his face going a little red. Then he slammed his fist on the table. "Already, this business has cost the company not only our reputation, but so many manhours."

Liam could tell what Dave was expecting. The man honestly thought he was going to catch Liam. Somehow, Dave knew about the file on Liam's computer.

Thankfully, one of the first things he'd talked to the IT department about was installing a security camera in his office. Rebecca, the head of IT, said she would take care of it personally and text him the login information so he could view the footage himself. Since they had security cameras on all of the server rooms, it wasn't unusual.

"I couldn't agree with you more," Liam said. "I've already coordinated with the IT team. As we speak, they've started going through everyone's computers."

"They have?" Dave asked, looking a little shocked.

"Yes. Of course, they had already gone through the programmers' computers, but we hadn't thought to go through everyone else's. The accounting department, marketing, and even everyone in this room," he added. "I've requested they start at the top and go down."

"Including yours?" Dave motioned to his laptop case sitting next to him on the table.

"They've gone through this one and are checking my PC in my office now. They will check log-ins and run complete scans. They're also updating our virus protection at the moment. I expect they will be done by late tomorrow," Liam answered. He saw a smug look cross Dave's face.

What he didn't tell them is that he'd talked to Rebecca about the file he'd found on his system. He'd known Rebecca since before he'd been bought out. Actually, when he returned as CEO, he was the one who had hired her.

She'd helped him with some programming back when she'd worked at the local library while she'd been going to college.

"Good," Dave said, sitting back down. "Good."

"They'll need access to your laptops." Liam motioned to a few people who had their laptops sitting in front of them. "Rebecca has sent out an email letting all employees know that they're doing a virus update. We'd like to keep the search under wraps. For now."

Just then, there was a knock on the conference room door. Christina stood up and opened it and, after speaking with someone, stood back.

Rebecca walked directly over to him and leaned down and whispered, "We may have a problem."

# CHAPTER THIRTEEN

*There's a light, where the darkness ends, touch me now and let me see again.*
**Elton John**

The last thing she expected when she woke up the morning after the break-in was to see her mother in the kitchen along with her friends.

Thankfully, she'd taken some time to get dressed and do her hair and makeup before coming downstairs.

Her mother was sipping a drink at the bar, while her friends and Lynda were all rushing around cooking breakfast or making drinks. Kimber was dicing fruit, and Leanne was stirring some eggs on the stove. Reagan was opening a bottle of champagne.

"What's all this?" she asked, setting her crutch down and sitting at the bar top.

"You're awake," Kimber said cheerfully. "We thought you deserved a welcome-home party."

Reagan walked over and handed her a glass filled with what she suspected was a mimosa.

"It's just orange juice. I know you're on some serious meds right now." Reagan winked at her.

"I stopped taking the pain pills," she admitted.

"In that case." Reagan took the glass out of her fingers and replaced it with another. "Bottoms up."

"You stopped taking the pills?" her mother asked in a concerned tone, and Morgan inwardly groaned.

If her mother hadn't been there, she would have thoroughly enjoyed the breakfast. As it was, even the cheerfulness of her friends couldn't drown out her mother's disdain.

Finally, almost an hour after they'd moved out onto the patio after breakfast, her mother received a call and left the four friends alone. The moment after her mother left, her friends put on their suits and jumped into the pool.

It was strange—they appeared more comfortable around the home than Morgan did at the moment.

She sat at the edge of the pool, dangling her left leg in the water while her casted leg sat on the edge of the pool.

"When do you get that thing off?" Kimber asked.

"Not soon enough," she moaned. "Actually, Dr. Ellis said he could give me one of those boots."

"Why haven't you let him?" Reagan asked.

"My mother," she said, rolling her eyes.

"How's the memory?" Leanne asked. "Still fuzzy?"

"Liam and I figured out that I'm missing the last four years."

"Four years?" Her friends all gasped. "Then you don't remember our trip to Cabo or... your year off when you went traveling?" Reagan asked.

"Nope. I've forgotten that and other little things like... oh right, meeting and falling in love with my husband. My wedding or honeymoon." She shrugged.

"Being around here should help," Kimber said.

"It does. I've had a few moments where I remember things like…" She looked around. "I remember picking out those throw pillows."

Leanne laughed. "You remember throw pillows but not the man you promised to spend the rest of your life with?"

She nodded and shrugged.

"How's that working out, by the way. Is Liam sleeping in a guest room?" Kimber asked.

"No." She smiled, remembering the other night.

"Ohhhh," all three of her friends said at the same time.

"Do tell us all. We liked the guy from the start the first time. If you tell me that man has made you fall for him a second time, then I might just have to kill you and take him for myself," Leanne joked.

Which had Morgan instantly remembering the previous night.

"Someone broke in last night," she blurted out.

"What?" Leanne gasped. "Here?"

"Yes. They hacked into the security system and unlocked the door. Liam had gone down to get his laptop, and he scared the guy off after a brief fight. In the shuffle of things, the front table was broken."

"I wondered why it was missing," Kimber said. "Was Liam hurt?"

"A large piece of glass was embedded in his shoulder. Other than that, a few cuts and bruises." Morgan remembered cleaning him up and falling asleep in his arms, feeling safe once more. Liam had assured her that the changes the security company had made to their system would safeguard against another break-in.

"Where were you?" Kimber asked.

"Upstairs. I'd fallen asleep watching television down

here." She motioned to the glass wall behind them. "Liam had carried me upstairs."

All three of her friends sighed and she smiled. She couldn't remember ever being treated so gently before by a man. Liam not only knew how to treat her, but he also knew all the ways to make her come alive. There was no doubt in her mind after being with him the other night that he'd spent the last two years learning just how to please her.

It was as if all he had to do was smile at her now for her body to react. Muscle memory. She'd doubted it was a real thing until Liam walked in the door and her entire body, inside and out, turned to jelly and warmed for him.

"So, things are going good between you? I mean, with your memory loss and all?" Kimber asked.

"Yes." She smiled. "I can see why I fell for him the first time." She sighed. "He's... perfect."

"I need a man." Leanne groaned.

"We all do," Kimber added.

"Do you know the last time I was laid?" Reagan groaned. "Two weeks ago."

"That long?" Leanne joked, earning a nudge from Reagan.

"Why haven't I set any of you up with Liam's friend Ryder?" Morgan asked.

"You have." Leanne groaned and climbed out of the pool to sit on the side by Morgan.

"Is something wrong with Ryder?" Morgan asked, concerned.

"No, he's dreamy." Reagan sighed, then took a sip of her drink as she hung onto the side of the pool. "But he hasn't shown any interest in any of us."

"Yet," Kimber added.

"Oh?" Morgan smiled. "I feel a need to throw a party coming on."

"No!" all three friends said at the same time.

"No offense, but every time you've tried, Ryder seems to have the best defense," Kimber said as she floated closer to Morgan.

"Last time he brought a date that trash-talked the three of us all night. Then Ryder heard about it and left with the girl," Leanne said.

She wanted to ask more about her husband's best friend but was cautious.

She'd been concerned that she wouldn't like the guy when she met him. But so far, each picture or video she'd seen of him and her, they had appeared friendly enough. They'd been laughing and joking with one another freely.

"What's that look for?" Kimber asked, shifting off the float and coming to stand next to Morgan.

"What look?" she asked, innocently.

"That look." Kimber pointed at her face. "Worry doesn't look good on you."

Morgan sighed. "How am I with Ryder?"

Kimber's eyebrows shot up. "You two are best mates," she answered snidely.

"Something tells me that if Ryder hadn't liked you so much, Liam wouldn't have popped the question in the first place," Leanne answered.

She smiled at that and then frowned when she realized that she didn't know the story of how Liam proposed to her.

"How did he pop the question?" she asked her friends.

"Oh, I like this story." Reagan leaned on the side of the pool with a smile.

She listened while her three friends filled her in on how Liam had planned a long weekend in Napa Valley and had gotten down on one knee right there in the vineyard at sunset. He'd proposed and given her the most beautiful ring.

"Where is your ring?" Reagan asked, motioning to Morgan's left hand.

She looked down at it with a frown. "I... don't know."

"I'm sure Liam has it. The hospital probably removed it because your fingers were swollen," Kimber said.

"Everything of mine was swollen." She looked down at her fingers. "Still is." She showed them her hands.

"How is therapy going?" Kimber asked.

"Great." She held up her left hand. "Look at what I can do now." She moved her left wrist, twisting it slightly from side to side.

"And that is good?" Kimber asked.

"It's much better than I could do last week," she answered happily.

"Last week you had a cast on," Kimber said dryly.

"Yes, so it's a lot of improvement," she joked.

"How much therapy will you need once that's off?" Leanne asked, motioning to the cast on Morgan's leg.

Looking down at it, she wondered that herself. "I'm not sure. My leg was broken in three places, so..." She shrugged. "I would think a lot."

"Did that sexy therapist follow you up the hill?" Leanne asked, then made a growling sound.

"Grayson? Yes, he was here yesterday." Morgan pulled her good leg out of the water. She desperately wanted to jump in, wanted a shower, but instead had had to settle with washing herself down that morning with a washcloth and shampooing her hair in the sink.

She couldn't wait to get the cast off. Her leg itched and the more she thought about the hair growing on her leg, the more grossed out she was. She thought about the possibility of taking a shower or a bath and held in a groan.

"I think I'll call the doctor and see if he can come up here and take this thing off today," she said, pulling out her phone. Did she even have Dr. Ellis's number?

Searching through her contacts, she found his number and sent a text message.

"He is my doctor, after all." She looked between her friends.

"Hell yes," Leanne chimed in.

Kimber's phone rang and, shortly after that, her friends had to pack up and leave. She had hoped they would stay longer, but it had been a long night, and she was feeling a little tired and wanted to lie down.

Leaving Lynda in the kitchen cleaning up, she headed upstairs and fell face-first into bed. She woke sometime later when her phone chimed with a new message from Dr. Ellis.

"I can't make it today, but I'll be there first thing in the morning."

Smiling, she rolled over and decided to explore the house a little more since she was fully awake. She had yet to make it out to the garage area. Maybe she'd head out there?

After taking a moment in the bathroom, she was heading out when she spotted something off in the closet. There was a hook that was twisted horizontally at the very end of the long closet. She made her way across to it and twisted it back and almost fell backwards on her butt when the entire wall popped open.

A light turned on inside the small room, and she instantly knew it was a safe room. There were blankets and pillows, medical supplies, and screens that showed scenes from the cameras outside of the house. The room was no bigger than the shower in their bathroom, but it was big enough for them to hide in until the police came.

Shutting the wall, she watched the hook return to its normal position. She turned the hook a few times and each time, the wall slid open silently.

What other wonders did this house have that she didn't know about?

She used the elevator to go all the way to the bottom floor. Liam had said that there was a hallway that led to the garage from that level.

In the basement, she took a right out of the elevator and passed the wine room and the massive laundry room, where Lynda was currently folding clothes.

"Can I help you with something?" she asked as Morgan passed by.

"No, just exploring. I thought I'd go see the garage," Morgan answered.

"Oh, okay, have fun." Lynda turned back to her tasks.

Past the laundry area was a set of straight stairs that led up into the pantry area behind the main kitchen upstairs. When Morgan stepped into the service kitchen, which was the same size as the living space upstairs, she looked around a little better than she had on their first tour.

It was a lot like the kitchen above, only instead of the nice wood cabinets and marble countertops, it had stainless steel cabinets and countertops. A proper kitchen equal to any restaurant kitchen.

Behind the back wall there was a door, and she opened it and stepped into a short breezeway with glass walls. She'd expected to be underground but found she was at ground level.

Beyond a smaller kitchen, the building split in two, with the elevator in the middle. To the right was a hallway that led to a bedroom with a bathroom. It reminded her of a hotel suite. The room to the left matched it exactly, down to the cream-colored comforter. Bright orange pillows and rugs highlighted the right room and bright yellow on the left. The view wasn't as good as from the house above, but it was nice enough.

She took the elevator to the next floor down and stepped out. There were stairs to the right of the elevator and two rooms directly across from it.

As with the rooms above, these had their own bathrooms, albeit smaller. They were decorated in bright blue and a bright green.

She really enjoyed the hits of color everywhere. Each room had unique paintings that matched the themes of the rooms. Taking the elevator once more, she stepped out into the garage and was hit with a memory so strong, it almost brought her to her knees.

"What do you mean you can't go?" Morgan was saying to Liam. Even though Liam had his tuxedo on, he was standing by the car, looking down at his phone.

"It's important," Liam said, not looking up at her.

"So is this. Do you know how long I've worked on this? Aaron..." She stopped talking when Liam glared up at her. "Do it for me. You're the one who wanted me to do something for myself. You encouraged me," she added, her voice sounding a little whiney.

"I know, but... I can't just ignore this." He held up his phone. "I'm CEO."

"Well, maybe you shouldn't be," she said angrily. Then she climbed into her car and slammed the door behind her. Tears stung her eyes as she peeled out of the garage and headed down the hill.

# CHAPTER FOURTEEN

*Though the light shines on things unclean,*
*yet it is not thereby defiled.*
**Augustine**

Something was off that evening when Liam returned home. Morgan was quieter than normal, which usually meant something was up.

They ate dinner on the back patio. The grilled salmon was one of her favorite meals, yet she barely touched her plate.

"What's wrong?" he asked finally when his plate was finished.

"Nothing," she said immediately.

"Morgan, you may not remember the past two years, but I do. I know you." He reached over and took her hand. "Something's wrong. Talk to me."

He watched her close her eyes and take a deep breath. Then, to his horror, tears rolled down her cheeks.

"I... we fought," she said with a slight stutter.

"When?" He frowned and wished more than anything that he could wrap his arms around her and assure her.

"That night. Before my accident." She reached up and wiped her tears away.

"No, we didn't." He was frowning even more now.

"Yes, I... remembered. I walked around the garage and... remembered leaving that night for Aaron's club opening. I know that you were planning on coming, you had on your tux, but then you got a call and..." She broke off.

"You were upset. I shouldn't have let you go, but we didn't fight." He lifted her hand to his lips. "We have never fought about anything." He smiled. "Trust me, I remember."

Her lips curved slightly and, thankfully, she looked a little happier. "I was upset," she said with a sigh. "I said some things."

"Water under the bridge," he assured her. "As I said, the accident was my fault. I shouldn't have cancelled. At least I shouldn't have let you drive away upset. I've felt responsible from the moment I found out."

She shook her head quickly as more tears rolled down her face. "No, it was an accident. Neither of us could have avoided it." She moved closer to him and laid a hand on his face. "I feared that..." She shook her head, her eyes moving down to his lips. "I didn't know what kind of relationship we had before... My parents... my mother runs the house. My father spends most of his time at the country club. For years—well, what I can remember—I've always believed that he's had someone on the side."

"Monica." Liam nodded and sighed. "Yeah, you found out right before our wedding." She closed her eyes, and he could see the pain of the discovery all over again. "Sorry, I should have—"

"No, it's okay," she broke in. "Does my mother know?"

He nodded, remembering the fight. How her mother had lived in the guest rooms in the garage for almost a month before lifting her chin and deciding it was Thomas that should move out of their house instead of her. Thomas had moved in with Monica for less than a week before he came crawling back to Victoria.

"It's over now. Things were bad for a few months, but now, they're good," he said with a smile.

Morgan's eyebrows shot up. "He's not cheating anymore?"

"Not with Monica at least," he answered dryly. "You had more suspicions but no proof."

"Right," she sighed.

"Victoria is determined not to let it ruin her reputation or that of the Davenports." He shrugged. "So your dad still spends most of his time at the club." He air-quoted. "And your mother smiles and pretends as if nothing is wrong. She does have a massage therapist come in every now and then. One that is not Marina. If you get my drift."

Morgan moaned. "Right. Okay, enough about them. I don't want a marriage like that."

"No." He took both of her hands in his. "Never. We promised each other on the day we got married, the first time," he added with a smile, "to be open and honest with one another no matter what." He pulled her into his lap, which took a little doing with the cast, and then just held onto her. "You are my one. When I thought I'd lost you..." He shook his head and closed his eyes, burying his face into her hair and enjoying the scent of her. "I almost lost my mind. You are my heart." He pulled back and looked into her eyes. "My everything." He'd poured his heart out to her so many times over the past two years, but this time, it was different. This time, he knew that to her it was all new.

"Liam, I—"

He stopped her by placing his lips over hers softly.

"Morgan, until you remember what we had, how you feel, I don't want you saying the words." He rested his forehead against hers. "Let's head upstairs. I'm terribly tired."

She chuckled. "It's only six in the evening."

He smiled. "I think there are a few things we can do to entertain ourselves for the rest of the evening."

She chuckled and then gasped when he stood up, taking her with him.

"The dishes," she said as he walked inside.

"They'll be okay until tomorrow morning." He stepped inside, shutting and locking the glass door behind him.

"You can put me down," she suggested when he had to shift her slightly to turn on the alarm.

"You weigh nothing, and I like carrying you. If you had your memory, you'd remember this." He smiled. "It's just one more thing that I will just have to prove to you." He kissed her before heading to the stairs.

Her fingers dug into his hair, pulling him back down to her lips. He stopped mid-step and wondered if he was going to make it all the way up to their bedroom.

"Liam, I need you now," she said softly against his heated skin.

"God, you make me crazy," he groaned and took the next few steps two at a time.

"Don't be gentle with me. I won't break." She pulled him back down to her once he set her on the edge of the bed.

"Morgan," he warned, but she was yanking his buttons open and pulling his shirt off his shoulders.

"No." She stopped for a moment and looked up at him. "My leg is the only thing still broken on me. I'm not fragile."

"You are," he warned, running his eyes over her. Then he brushed her hair aside and leaned down to kiss her.

"Liam, before the accident, did you treat me like I was going to break all of the time?" she asked.

He smiled. "No."

"Then don't treat me that way now." She unzipped his pants and pushed them down his hips.

When she took him in her hands, he groaned and teetered slightly. Then she took him into her mouth, and every muscle in his body tensed. His hands dipped into her dark hair, tangled in her long curls, and willed her to never stop.

When he felt as if he was on the edge of losing his control, he leaned back and stepped out of his pants. Then without thinking, he pulled her clothes off her quickly, not caring if he ripped anything.

She'd made him forget just how fragile she was. Made him remember how demanding of a lover she could be. He yanked her panties aside and embedded himself in her quickly. She cried out as her nails dug into his skin.

"Is this what you wanted?" he growled as he pounded into her.

"Yes!" she cried out, wrapping her good leg around his hip. "More."

He laughed loudly and gave her what she wanted. What he needed. All the while convincing himself that what he was doing was for her. Somewhere in the back of his mind, the truth registered. He'd needed this. Needed to know that she still wanted him.

That even though she'd lost her memories of him, she still wanted him. That she was still his.

When he felt her on the brink of coming, he reached down and ran a thumb over her clit, sending her into waves of convulsions underneath him. His own climax took over his body at the same time.

"I love you," he softly said into her ear after he'd collapsed on top of her.

"Mmm," she purred back, and he smiled.

Morgan's cell phone woke them shortly after four in the morning.

"Who?" She groaned and searched around for the source of the ringing. Liam found it first and after seeing her mother's number on the screen, handed it to her.

"Mom?" Morgan answered, then quickly sat up. "What?"

Liam reached over and turned on a light while Morgan listened.

"I..." Morgan glanced at him. "We're on our way."

"What?" he asked after she'd hung up.

"It's Ann. Someone... broke in and..." Morgan shook her head.

"What?" he asked, taking her into his arms. She'd turned very pale and looked as if she was about to throw up.

"She's dead," Morgan said against his chest. "Someone broke into her room and killed her."

"What?" He tensed. "In your parents' house?"

Morgan nodded. "Yes, I..." She shook her head. "My mother sounded so... lost."

"Come on, we'll get dressed and head down there." He held onto her for a moment more.

Morgan nodded and he heard her sniffle.

"Ann was like my mother's best friend, even though my mother would never admit it. She's been there for so long. Why?" Morgan leaned back and looked up at him. "Why would they do that?"

"Maybe it was a robbery? Maybe..." He shook his head

and shrugged. "I don't know. Let's head down there and see what the police have to say."

The drive into town to her parents' place was a quiet one. They got there shortly after three in the morning and when they pulled up, there were still two patrol cars in front of the house with their lights still on.

He helped Morgan out of the car and up the stairs into the house.

Her parents were sitting in the living room talking to a female officer while a very large male officer, who looked slightly familiar to Liam, stood in the corner with his arms crossed.

The moment the man spotted them, the guy's entire demeaner changed.

"Liam?" The man smiled as he walked across the room and held his hand out. "It's me, Roy, from Wayward."

Liam recognized the man now. He'd lived with him for a few years, until he'd been adopted at age eleven.

"Roy?" Liam shook the man's hand. "Wow, Roy. You've... changed."

Roy laughed. "Yeah, I used to be a skinny kid," he explained to Morgan. "You must be the daughter?" he asked, sobering up.

"Yes," Morgan said. She moved over to sit with her parents.

"What happened here?" Liam asked softy.

"Let's head out." Roy nodded towards the door.

He followed Roy out the front door back into the cool early morning air.

"On the surface it appears like a standard break-in," Roy said.

"On the surface?" Liam asked.

"Yeah, a broken window for entrance, a few items were

taken, but underneath..." He shook his head. "It appears more like a hit."

"A..." Liam's took a deep breath. "What have you told the family?"

"Nothing yet. We'll have to take everyone downtown for questioning. Becca's trying to persuade them to come in now," Roy added. Then he smiled. "You did all right for yourself, I hear. You and Ryder. I hit his gym three times a week."

"I've never seen you there," Liam said.

"I'm an early morning kind of guy. I get off shift around six and hit the gym on the way home," Roy explained.

"Married?" Liam asked.

Roy laughed. "Haven't found the right woman yet." He nodded to the front door. "I heard about your wife's accident. I was actually one of the first on the scene. I guess I didn't place that the Davenports were your in-laws until I saw you walk in." Roy shook his head. "I must be tired. This was a pretty bad one."

"Ann?" Liam shook his head. "How?"

"She was beaten to death. The crazy thing is, if her room had been part of the main house, someone would have heard it. There's not even security out there." Roy shook his head. "All these security measures for the main building..." He motioned to the cameras hanging in plain sight and the alarm system at the doorway.

Liam was confused. "I guess I didn't even know Ann lived here."

Roy nodded. "In a small building at the back of the lot."

"How did someone discover her then?" Liam asked.

"Mrs. Davenport called out there just before four to arrange the breakfast schedule," Roy answered.

"At four in the morning?" Liam shook his head. He

knew that Victoria was a real diva when it came to things around her house. Every time he'd seen Ann, the woman had been running crazy to keep up with all of Victoria's demands.

"Yeah, I guess Mrs. Davenport is a very early riser." He shrugged. "Anyway, when the maid didn't answer… she sent her husband out there to check up on the woman."

"Right." Liam glanced towards the door again. "I'd better…" He motioned inside.

"Right." Roy held out his hand.

"It was good to see you. We should stay in touch," Liam suggested.

Roy pulled out a business card from his shirt pocket and handed it to him. "Give me a call."

"Will do," Liam answered with a smile. "I'd love to catch up with you."

"Maybe Ryder, Sean, you, and I could hang sometime?" Roy suggested.

Liam wanted to let him in on the fact that he hadn't seen or talked to Sean in years, but he just nodded and followed the man back inside.

Morgan was sitting across from her parents, talking to the female officer. He could tell that she'd been crying, but her mother's eyes were red but dry and her father appeared very angry.

He sat next to Morgan and took her hand in his. It was cold, so he started rubbing it absently in his own as she answered questions.

He noticed that the questions were more to calm Morgan down than anything.

By the time the questions stopped, the sun was up, and he knew that he had to be in the office soon. Thankfully, he'd dressed for work when they'd left, and Morgan had agreed to spend the day with her mother. She had an appointment with Dr. Ellis that morning to remove her cast and before he left for work, he texted the doctor that she was at her parents' place.

She was looking forward to having a little freedom and showering without putting a trash bag over her cast. He had cautioned her that she still wouldn't be able to put weight on that leg until she'd gotten the approval from the doctor.

Aaron walked in the front door the same time Liam was leaving. The man looked happy and far more than a little tipsy. He hadn't pegged Aaron as someone who dallied in drugs, but the guy's pupils were beyond dilated, and he was walking like a man who was flying.

The drive into work was short, but it took almost twice as long as normal thanks to traffic. He stopped and grabbed a muffin and coffee less than a block from work and walked in half an hour later than he'd hoped to be in.

Thankfully, his office was empty this morning. He'd half expected to see Dave sitting in his chair again. Maybe the man had gotten wind that he'd installed hidden cameras in there?

At any rate, he was thankful that he didn't have to deal with the guy this morning. After getting just a few hours of sleep and with the murder looming over him, he was in a foul mood.

If he played his cards right, he could take the man down before stepping down. Whatever happened to the company he'd started years ago, he didn't want Dave to get his grubby hands on it. He felt it in every fiber of his being. Something told him that the man would run it into the ground while lifting his own wealth up.

Almost two hours after he'd arrived at work, his office line rang, which was unusual. Most people in the office messaged him or emailed since chances were good he wouldn't be in the office.

When he picked up, the voice was so muffled, he had to block his other ear just to hear what the person was saying.

"I'm sorry," he started as he pressed the phone to his ear. He heard someone say his name but then there was a loud bang, and he yanked the receiver away as his ear rang. "Hello?" he said several times before the line went dead.

He set the phone down and was about to go back to work when a chill swept over him, rushing up his spine and making the hair on his arms stand up.

Pulling out his cell phone, he called Morgan. When her cell phone went to voice mail, he began to panic and dialed her mother's number, which went to voice mail as well. Her father's number didn't even ring before it went to a message, which told him it was off. He tried the house number, but knew they never answered it.

He left a message and rushed out of the office in full panic mode. He pulled Roy's business card out of his pocket and called the man in hopes that he'd beat him to the house.

# CHAPTER FIFTEEN

*It matters not how fast light may travel, darkness shall
always be there awaiting its arrival.*
**Mark W Boyer**

S pending the morning with both of her parents after
finding out about Ann was like putting gas on a fire.
Her parents had never really fought when she was growing
up. They were too refined for such normalcies.

However, both of them had sharp tongues so no one
walked away uncut. Especially after something like Ann's
murder.

"We're ruined," her mother complained as she tried to
turn on the coffee maker. When the machine wouldn't turn
on, she grew frustrated and wiggled the machine, as if that
would somehow make the coffee grinds and filters fall into
place.

"Mom, let me," Morgan said. She stood up and pulled
out the coffee that Ann kept in the pantry and placed a filter
in the machine. Her mother willingly stepped aside and sat
down where Morgan had just been sitting.

"How are we ruined?" her father asked, sounding more bored than upset.

"It will be all over the news about the…" At this point her mother dropped her voice as if someone was listening to them. "Murder," she finished.

"So?" Morgan asked, turning around and leaning on the countertop. "Ann's murder should be in the papers. If someone knows something…" Then she got an idea. "We should put out a reward for information."

Both of her parents looked at her as if she'd just grown an extra head.

"Oh really," her mother finally said as she rolled her eyes. "I doubt the police are that desperate."

"Mom, Ann was more than your maid and your housekeeper. She was your friend," Morgan said calmly.

"Now who is going to make breakfast?" her mother asked.

"Oh, I…" Morgan started to suggest she do it, but then remembered her leg. And Morgan remembered how much her mother had relied on her one summer when Ann had taken off work to have a minor surgery. Her mother had easily replaced Ann with Morgan to the point that Morgan's summer had been swallowed up by running errands that her mother was too lazy to do herself.

She doubted at this point that her mother even knew how to cook an egg.

"You can hire someone else," Morgan suggested.

"Don't say that. You know Ann is the only one we would let into our home," her mother said in a shocked tone.

The fact was, her parents let plenty of people into their home. Besides Ann, there was Theresa, her mother's massage therapist who came in at least twice a week. Theresa was younger than Morgan had expected, roughly her own age. She had short blonde hair and looked like a young Marilyn Monroe. But Theresa had acted as if she knew Morgan, which somehow made Morgan feel uncomfortable around the woman.

Then there were the maids, who came in three times a week. A pool company had a handful of people letting themselves into the yard every other day. The yard maintenance team had even more people walking around the grounds every week.

If her mother was hosting any sort of social event, there were a slew of caterers running around, after which a cleaning crew was brought it.

But as far as personal contact with her parents, it was limited to Ann and Theresa. The rest were just like worker ants that she doubted her mother even acknowledged.

"Then you'll just have to get used to doing things for yourself around here," Morgan suggested, earning her another glare from her mother.

The fact that they were avoiding talking about the murder and who might have done it didn't go unnoticed by Morgan. She wanted to bring up the topic, to ask her own questions about Ann, but didn't want to chance upsetting her mother again.

She didn't even know much about the woman. Had she been seeing someone? Did she have family? Where was she even from? Morgan remembered her having a slight accent when Morgan was younger, and but over time it had disappeared.

Why would someone break into that part of the property? All that was back there was a small building that held two bedrooms and a shared bathroom. Ann had moved into the building long ago after her mother complained about the woman getting stuck in traffic one morning.

Her mother always got her way, no matter what. She couldn't imagine her mother getting over Ann's death anytime soon.

Morgan wished for the first time since her accident that she could drive. She wanted to go home, back to Angel Bluff, to spend her day going through the rest of her emails and messages. She'd posted a picture of her and Liam last night on social media and thanked everyone for their well wishes.

Liam had helped her post the update on her health and even shared her post on his accounts as well.

When her stomach growled, she poured herself another cup of coffee.

Her mother watched her, and when Morgan was done pouring herself a cup, she held out her own cup.

"I can't walk and carry a cup," she pointed out to her mother.

Just then, Kimber, Leanne, and Reagan walked in. Her father immediately stood up and left the room, but not before glaring in her friends' direction. Her dad usually didn't stick around when her friends were there. Morgan figured it was because he'd had enough of the friends over the years.

"We came over the moment we heard," Leanne said, walking over and hugging Morgan. Then Reagan wrapped her arms around them, followed by Kimber.

"How are you doing?" Leanne asked.

Morgan had thought that she'd cried enough. Now, as her eyes filled again, she realized it was nice to have her friends there.

"I'm okay," she said softly.

"We brought muffins," Leanne said, squeezing her arm.

"Perfect." Morgan's mother took one for herself.

Reagan grabbed Morgan a plate and put a chocolate chip muffin on it for her. "Here," she said with a slight smile. "You can eat this while you tell us what happened."

While Morgan filled her friends in on what she knew, her mother sat at the bar silently listening.

"What now?" Kimber asked when she was done filling them in. "Where's Liam?"

"At work. I'll stick around here today," Morgan said with a sigh. "Dr. Ellis will be here shortly to remove this cast." She motioned to her leg.

"Oh, right." Her mother sighed. "I'd forgotten about that." Her mother walked over and poured herself a cup of coffee and then glanced out the window as if she was bored.

Aaron walked into the kitchen at that moment, and Morgan could instantly tell that he was stoned. If it had just been marijuana, she wouldn't have said anything, but Aaron was obviously hyped up on something much stronger. Her brother was bouncing around the kitchen as if he were a two-year-old after a sugar-filled birthday party. Kimber seemed very interested in her brother's story and was the only one asking him questions.

Her other friends had pulled out their phones and were acting as if Aaron wasn't there at all.

Aaron was so busy talking about himself and the night he'd had at the club that no one had even gotten a chance to tell him about Ann yet.

"Oh, do settle down," her mother finally groaned as she pushed her fingers into the sides of her temple. "You're giving me a headache."

Aaron either didn't hear or didn't care since he continued to babble on.

"We're so happy for your conquests," Morgan said dryly when he talked about the hot woman he was banging.

Morgan noticed that he didn't use a name, maybe because he didn't know it. "While you were out partying, someone broke in and murdered Ann."

"Ann who?" Aaron said, pouring a spoonful of sugar into his coffee.

"Ann." Morgan was appalled by her brother. "Our Ann." She motioned around the kitchen.

"Oh." Aaron glanced around. "So, this is it for breakfast? Stale muffins?"

If Morgan's leg hadn't been in a cast and hurting, thanks to standing on it too long, she would have kicked her brother in the shins.

Her mother chose that moment to leave the room instead of berating her son.

"Seriously?" Morgan asked Aaron.

"What? It wasn't as if she was related to us." Aaron shrugged. "She worked for us. Two nights ago, one of my bouncers got stabbed. You don't see me crying over it," Aaron said with a chuckle.

"We'd better..." Leanne stood up and motioned to the others, then walked out of the room.

"Yeah, we'll see you later." Reagan grabbed Kimber's arm and pulled her out of the room.

Aaron pulled a jug of orange juice from the fridge and drank directly from it.

"Gross." Morgan groaned. "Who raised you?"

Aaron smiled over his shoulder. "Two demons on a pathway to hell."

The joke was old and honestly Morgan couldn't remember when or why her brother had started saying it. Still, it made her smile.

"Why haven't you moved out of the hell house yet?" she asked, running her eyes over her brother. He had changed from her memories. The last she could picture him, he'd still been a little chubby. His blond hair had been shorter and less stylish than it was now.

She'd gotten her father's darker skin, brown eyes, and darker hair while Aaron took after their mother, with pale skin, blond hair, and lighter blue eyes. Morgan had always been jealous of her brother's good looks. Not that she was ugly, but she was far mousier than she liked

"Why would I?" Aaron asked, leaning on the counter. His eyes went to her cast. For a moment, he looked sad, but then he shrugged and looked away. "I have free rent and food and can be completely ignored all I want. You're their golden child, remember? You get all the attention."

Morgan frowned. What was this about? She'd never heard her brother talk like this before. Normally, they'd gotten along great. It had always been the two of them against their parents. Sure, Aaron was a little spoiled, but he'd never been mean to her. Not that she could remember, at any rate.

Then to her surprise, he pulled out a little baggie of white powder, dipped his pinkie in, and sniffed it right in front of her.

"Was that coke?" she asked, shocked.

"Who are you? My mother?" Aaron rolled his eyes at her.

"You shouldn't do drugs," she said, concerned.

"Fuck off." Aaron jerked around to face her. His face turned a beet red, something she'd never seen before in her life. "I can do whatever the hell I want." His voice had risen so much that she was sure their father would rush into the room and tell Aaron to stop yelling. Instead, Aaron continued to yell. "You think just because you're the golden child, just because everything you do turns out perfectly, that you can come back in here and tell me what to do?" He took a step closer to her and, for the first time, she was afraid of her younger brother. "Why don't you just go back to your castle on the hill and stay the fuck out of my life." He spun around and stormed out of the room, leaving Morgan shaking and a little breathless.

It took her a few moments to settle down after that. She sat in the chair, watching the leaves on the tree outside sway with the light wind. She missed the view from Angel Bluff, missed seeing the vastness of the ocean beyond or the city in the distance. Her parents' place was surrounded by palm trees and fences, making her feel trapped, imprisoned.

Since she couldn't carry a coffee cup and walk with a crutch, she left the mug of lukewarm coffee and headed outside to sit in the sun.

After taking several deep breaths, she felt steadier as she relaxed on a lounge chair. She must have fallen asleep because she jumped when someone touched her shoulder.

"Sorry," Dr. Ellis said calmly. "I called out for you, but you were fast asleep."

"I..." She stretched her arms over her head. "Yes, I guess the sun felt so wonderful, I dozed off." She blinked a few times.

"I heard about Ann," Dr. Ellis said, sitting across from her on the other lounge chair. "How are you doing?"

Morgan sighed. "I'm okay. It's all a shock. I think my mother is in denial." She glanced towards the house.

"I've prescribed her a sedative. She seemed to need it. You?" he asked her.

"No." She smiled weakly. "As demonstrated by my deep slumber in broad daylight."

Dr. Ellis chuckled. "How's the leg?" He motioned to her cast.

"Hot. Sweaty. And, I have no doubt, very, very hairy."

He chuckled again. "Well, I can help you with that. Let's head inside, and I'll cut the thing off you. I brought my saw."

"You don't need an X-ray?"

"For you, no. You can have a boot, but promise me no walking on it until you come in and we get some shots of it first."

"Agreed." She sighed.

Dr. Ellis helped her stand and handed her the crutch. "How is therapy going?"

"Good," she said, and then she cringed. "Grayson was supposed to stop by today. I'll have to text him that I'm stuck here until Liam gets off work."

"You're still doing PT twice a week?" Dr. Ellis asked as she followed him into her mother's massage room. His bag and saw were already set up in there.

"Yes, should I be seeing him more?" she asked, concerned.

"No, not until you can start walking on this leg. How hard you'll have to work will depend on how much nerve and muscle damage you end up having."

She hadn't thought about that. Sure, her left arm felt basically like a child's. It was weak and she could barely hold a pen for more than a minute. But at least she could move it around freely.

She'd been hoping to do the same with her leg, but as Dr. Ellis used a small circular saw to cut the thick cast off, she realized just how silly she'd been. She wasn't going to be able to use her leg like she could use her arm. She would be able to shower and maybe swim or at least float in the pool, but walking? Even with the black leg boot sitting next to her, she knew that putting any weight on it wouldn't be wise at this point.

Once the cast was off her leg and Dr. Ellis removed the gauze that had caused her leg to itch in so many places, she looked down at her hideous leg and laughed.

"That's not the usual response." Dr. Ellis smiled at her.

"It's ugly." She smiled up at him.

"It's still there." He patted her arm. "You're lucky."

She frowned. "Was it that close?"

He sighed. "When I saw pictures of your accident..." He shook his head. "I don't know how you made it through that wreck alive."

She hadn't seen pictures of the wreck. Hadn't even known there were any. She remembered her friends talking about it being in all the papers but hadn't thought to look them up herself.

"Thank you." She patted the old man's hand.

"Here, I'll let you clean up first. If you have any questions on how to use the boot..."

"I think I can manage," she said as he started cleaning up the mess. She stopped him from throwing the cast away. Her friends had signed it, and she wanted to keep it for some strange reason. Maybe to prove to her future self that she'd overcome something so terrible.

"Your mother has offered me some tea. I'll be just outside if you need me. Remember, it's only replacing the cast. You're not to put any weight on it. Use your crutch," he warned. Then he took his bag and stepped out of the room.

Using her crutch, she hobbled over to the shower, pulled off her clothes, and sat on the bench. She let the hot water wash away the grime on her leg. Chunks of plaster were embedded in her long leg hair. Thankfully, there was a disposable razor she could use. It took almost half an hour to get every last long hair.

She noticed a slight dip in her calf muscle and when she ran her fingers over it, she winced with pain. She thought she'd be able to feel the broken bones in her leg, but instead, what she could feel felt smooth and strong.

She stepped out of the shower and was reaching for a towel when her good foot slipped on the wet tile. Her instinct was to protect her broken leg so when she landed, she fell hard on her left hip and left shoulder. The side of her head smacked the tile floor hard.

Dazed and breathless, she took a moment to collect herself. Seeing her cell phone, she reached out and blindly called for Liam.

She could hear his voice before the phone slipped from her fingers as she blacked out.

# CHAPTER SIXTEEN

After darkness comes the light
**Nepos**

Liam broke every speed limit on his way to the Davenport's place. Just as he was pulling into the drive, his phone rang.

Seeing Morgan's face on the screen, he answered it.

"Are you okay?" he asked.

"Yes," she said quickly. "I'm fine."

"I'm just pulling in." He parked behind a black pickup truck.

"Roy is here," she said. Her voice sounded slightly off. "I'm okay. I feel so embarrassed."

"What happened" he asked, getting out of the car and rushing to the front door.

"I showered." She groaned. "I guess..."

He stepped inside and saw her sitting on the sofa, wrapped in a white terry robe. When she saw him, she hung up her phone.

He rushed to her and wrapped his arms around her. She looked pale and, as he held her, she was shaking.

"I guess I passed out," she said into his shoulder.

"You took a shower alone?" He leaned back and looked at her. Instantly, he noticed her cast was gone. Her right leg was propped up on the sofa. It looked thinner than the other one and extremely pale. He worried that she may have injured it.

"How's your leg? Did you fall on it?"

"No, I fell on my hip and shoulder. I must have banged my head." She reached up and touched the back of her head. He ran his fingers over it gently and noticed a small bump. She winced slightly.

"The gate was open," Roy said. "When I banged on the front door, no one answered, so I let myself in to do a wellness check. I found Morgan crumpled on the floor inside that bathroom." He motioned to the massage area.

Liam looked around. "Where in god's name are your parents?" he growled out. "You could have been seriously injured."

"I..." Morgan started, but just then her mother walked out, laughing up at a very young man wearing only swimming trunks. When she noticed the three of them watching her and saw Morgan in a robe, she dropped her hand from the man's arm. "Oh, I didn't realize you were back," she said to Liam, then she frowned at Roy. "Do I know you?"

"Officer Roy Marcus. I was here earlier with my partner Becca," Roy supplied.

Liam watched Victoria's face drop as she took a step away from the younger man.

"What's happened?" she asked, sounding concerned.

"Morgan fell and knocked herself out. She was out so long that I was able to drive all the way here from work. I called Roy to rush over and do a wellness check when I couldn't reach you or Thomas." His arm tightened slightly around Morgan. "You should have been here," he added, his eyes going to the young man, who quickly left.

Victoria walked closer. "Are you okay?" she asked Morgan.

"Yes, I..." she started, but Liam jumped in.

"She could have seriously injured her leg now that her cast is off," he said, feeling his anger grow. "Where is Thomas?"

"He's at the country club," Victoria answered.

"Liam, really, I'm fine," Morgan said, touching his hand.

"I trusted them. I left you here," he said, brushing a strand of her wet hair aside. "If you had been home, Lynda would have been there for you. I'm taking you back home."

Morgan smiled and nodded. "I'll go get dressed and put on my boot." She motioned to her leg then glanced around. "I'll need my crutch."

Liam stood up, lifted her in his arms, and carried her back into the bathroom attached to the massage area.

"Are you okay?" he asked her once they were alone.

"I am. I'm just really embarrassed that your friend saw me naked." She rolled her eyes.

"I trust Roy," he said with a smile. "I'll have to gouge his eyes out and maybe break his nose, but I'm just thankful he was there." He leaned in and brushed his lips across hers. "Your leg looks good." He had sat her on the massage table and took a moment to run his hand gently over her leg. He noticed a slight dip in her calf. She didn't wince with pain when he examined her leg. "I'd better go send Roy off and have a talk with your mother."

"Don't..." Morgan started, but when he looked at her

with raised eyebrows, she stopped. "Just be kind," she finished.

He smiled and kissed her again. "Always."

When he stepped back out into the living room, Roy was standing where he'd left him. Victoria was sitting where Morgan had just been, talking on her cell phone.

Ignoring Victoria, he walked over and shook Roy's hand.

"Thanks for coming so quickly," Liam told the man.

"Any time." Roy sighed. "I didn't look," he said quickly. "Just... not sure if you're the type to..."

Liam chuckled. "I am normally, but when my wife's life is on the line..." He nodded again. "Thanks, man."

Roy smiled. "Let me know when you and the guys want to meet up." He walked towards the door. When they stood outside, Roy added, "Even though I'm not here on official business, that was some pretty messed up behavior right after her personal assistant of twenty years was brutally murdered. Don't you think?"

Liam glanced back inside where Victoria was berating her husband on the phone for not being there for their daughter.

"It's par for the course around here. It's one of the reasons we haven't seen them very often since the wedding," he admitted.

"I'm thankful I was lucky enough to have Carla and Diego adopt me. You can't choose your family, but if I could, I would have totally picked them. Diego's a retired detective. He's the reason I'm working towards my own badge," Roy said with a smile. "Did you and the guys ever get adopted?"

"No." Liam shook his head. "Morgan is my family now," he added with a smile. "Ryder and I hang about three times a week still. We haven't seen Sean in years."

"Oh? Oh, that's right. I'd read somewhere that he'd left your business right before you hit it big. I guess he must have been upset," Roy said.

"Yeah, something like that. We'll catch up soon." Liam held out his hand again. "Thanks again."

"I'm just thankful Morgan's okay." He shook Liam's hand.

"Me too." He watched the man leave before returning inside. Morgan had yet to come out, and Victoria was off the phone, sitting on the sofa and reading a magazine.

"I know what you're going to say," she said, without looking up. "As far as I knew, she was in the room, resting."

"You had one job," he said to her. "She was here less than two hours."

"Oh, get off your high horse." Victoria stood up and walked towards him. "She almost died under your watch."

Just then Morgan stepped out on crutches with a new black boot on her leg.

"Mother!" Morgan exclaimed.

"What? Everyone's thinking it. We've even had the police look into whether he tampered somehow with your car, after one of the officers mentioned there weren't any skid marks," Victoria spat back.

"What?" Morgan exclaimed. "You think Liam had something to do with my accident?"

"It's crossed our minds. He does stand to inherit—"

"I won't stand here and listen to this any longer," Morgan broke in. "Liam is worth thirty times what you and daddy have given me."

"Yes, that's what the detective told us," she said dryly.

"Liam, let's go." Morgan walked over and took his hand briefly. "I'm tired."

After helping her back into his car, he started to drive towards their place.

"You don't think I had anything to do with your accident, do you?" he asked after a long stretch of silence.

"No," she answered quickly. "I've told you—"

"I mean, what your mother said," he asked, glancing over at her.

"My mother is a child lashing out because she was caught shagging the pool boy," Morgan answered with a sigh. "She wanted the attention off of her and onto anyone else."

"That's who that was?" he asked her.

Morgan glanced over at him and then laughed. "I think." She shrugged. "I can't remember."

He smiled at her, then took her hand in his and brushed his lips across her knuckles. "Are you sure you're okay?"

"Sore, embarrassed, and pissed at my family, but yes. I'm okay." She smiled back at him. "I would have thought that my parents would have mourned Ann for at least a day before returning to their normal lives."

"Yeah, Roy questioned that as well. Ann worked for your parents for over twenty years. You would have thought that..." He stopped himself and sighed. "Then again, I suppose we should have expected it."

"Right. Aaron wasn't even upset." Morgan shook her head and then added. "He's doing coke."

"What?" Liam frowned. "Are you sure?"

"Pretty sure. He did it right in front of me. He didn't even try to hide it. Almost as if..." She rolled her shoulders. "He wanted me to know. Maybe I already knew?" she asked.

"You would have told me before. This is the first I'm hearing of it."

"Right. I'm hungry. Can we stop somewhere?"

He smiled. "You read my mind." He had already taken the exit and was heading to her favorite restaurant. "Are you sure you're up for it?" he asked, parking in the parking lot of Mastro's.

"Oh, I love this place," she said, leaning forward and looking at the building.

Liam chuckled. "I know. We eat here at least once a week."

The boot made it a lot easier for Morgan to get around. She had no problem walking through the restaurant to a table out on the covered patio.

"Mrs. Taylor!" Rose, one of the staff there said excitedly when she saw them. "You're back." She rushed forward and hugged Morgan.

"I am." Morgan looked at him with question in her eyes.

"Rose," he mouthed.

"Rose," she said easily. "It's good to be back."

"Oh, I have to run and tell the others." The young woman started to turn, but then glanced back at them. "Your usuals?"

"Yes, please, Rose," Liam answered with a smile.

"Just what are our usuals?" Morgan asked when they were alone.

He chuckled. "You'll see," he said with a sigh. "You'll be busy greeting the entire staff soon. Just go with it. They really like you. Especially after you coordinated the fun run to help pay for Roger's medical bills after he was involved in a hit and run."

"Oh, that does sound..." She didn't get any further because four other staff members all rushed towards their table.

It felt good, watching her chatting with what he thought

of as their friends. Morgan was a natural socialite. He supposed it was all thanks to Victoria and how Morgan had been raised.

Whatever the reason, he enjoyed how relaxed she was in awkward situations.

He doubted that anyone she talked to during their entire meal knew that she couldn't remember them.

Thankfully, no one asked her about the accident and before their desserts were delivered, someone had run and gotten her a bouquet of wildflowers with a card that was signed by everyone on staff at the moment.

"Wow," Morgan said as he drove the rest of the way home. "Is this normal?" she asked, holding the vase of flowers.

He laughed. "Not really. I mean, yes, the staff there loves you." He smiled as he turned up their long drive. "But normally they don't give you flowers. Except on your birthday."

"It's nice living closer to Mastro's," she said with a sigh. "I'd only been able to go there a few times before with my friends," Morgan said.

"It was where we went our second date," he admitted.

"Really?" she asked as he parked in the garage.

"Yeah, I was already living here and had fallen in love with the place. It was purely coincidental. You later told me it was one of the reasons you fell in love with me." He smiled as he turned off the car and turned towards her. "Fate, you said. I had not only taken you to your favorite restaurant on our second date, but I knew several of the staff members' names..."

"You did, even back then?"

He shrugged. "It's the best restaurant within ten miles of my house. I was a bachelor back then, and Lynda had only been working for me part time. Since I was single and worked nonstop, there wasn't a lot to do around the place."

"You hired her full time after we married?" she asked.

"When you moved in with me," he answered. "Then you found Marina."

"Where did I find her, by the way? She's far better than Theresa," Morgan said as he helped her from the car.

They made their way inside, and Lynda met them at the door. "You're home early," she said, holding a laundry basket full of folded towels.

"Morgan had a spill at her parents' place," Liam answered as his cell phone rang. "Why don't you go up and rest?" he suggested to Morgan. "I'll be up after I get some work done."

"Sure," Morgan said, and she headed towards the elevator.

"Hello?" he answered the call from an unknown number.

"Liam, it's Roy," Roy said. "I just heard a bit of news I thought you'd want to know."

"What's up?" he asked, moving into the dining room and setting his laptop case down.

"It's about Theresa Smith," Roy said.

"Theresa... Victoria's massage therapist?" he asked, sitting down.

"Yes, I thought you and Morgan would want to know before you saw it on the news. After the break-in and murder, we had officers go and talk to everyone that had access to the Davenport property. Mrs. Davenport claimed that her massage therapist had been on vacation for the past week or so. When officers dropped by her apartment..."

"What?" he asked when Roy paused.

"They found her dead. She'd apparently been so for a while," Roy answered.

"What?" Liam stood up and glanced upstairs. "That's... two people that worked for..."

"I know, which is why I called you the moment I found out," Roy interjected. "I also heard about your break-in last night. I suggest you get some private security for a while. The Davenports are being notified right now."

"Thanks," Liam said, taking the stairs two at a time.

"I'll let you know anything I find out. You may get a visit from a detective later today."

"Thanks," Liam said quickly. "I'll talk to you later." He hung up and made a note to add the man's number into his phone when he had a moment.

Liam rushed into the bedroom, expecting to see Morgan asleep on the bed, but it was empty. His heart skipped a few beats before he heard her moving around in the bathroom.

"Morgan?" he called out.

"Just a moment," she answered, and he heard the toilet flush in her private bathroom.

When she stepped out, he took her in his arms.

"What is it?" she asked, concerned.

"They found Theresa Smith's body in her apartment." He felt her tense in his arms.

"What?" she gasped and looked up at him.

"Come on, let's sit down." He motioned to the bed.

"Liam." She shook her head, and her face turned pale. "I don't know how much more I can take today."

He sighed and held her again. "I know, baby." He kissed the top of her head. "Come on, let's shut down for a while." He carried her back to the bed. "How's the leg?" he asked when she rubbed it as he was laying her down.

"I think I bumped it during the fall," she admitted.

He hit the button that closed the electronic blinds, sinking the room into darkness, then he pulled her into his arms.

"I can get you a pain pill?" he suggested.

"No, just hold me," she answered with a sigh, and he felt her fall asleep.

## CHAPTER SEVENTEEN

I saw the light, I saw the light, no more darkness, no more
night
Roy Acuff

Morgan woke when she felt Liam leave the bed. For a moment, she was disoriented and couldn't remember where she was. Then it was as if a light switch had turned on and she remembered... everything. At least for a split second.

The moment she opened her eyes, the memories all slipped away, just out of her mind's reach.

"Sorry," he said, leaning down and kissing her. "Lynda says there's someone here to talk to me. Go back to sleep."

"No, I'm awake now. I'll come down soon. We can have something to eat." She yawned and then smiled as she lifted her right leg. "I love this boot." She sighed as Liam chuckled.

"See you down there," he added before leaving her alone.

She took her time and cleaned up, even changed her

clothes into a pair of yoga pants, which she could easily get on now thanks to the boot. She still wasn't comfortable enough to try heading down the stairs, so she took the elevator down. When she stepped out of the elevator, she saw two cops standing in the entry talking to Liam, and she tensed. One was a large bald man, and the other was a skinny black man.

"Here she is now," Liam said with a tense smile. "You can ask her yourself. Why don't we head somewhere my wife can sit?" he suggested.

After they stepped into the formal sitting area, she sat on the sofa while the two officers stood.

"I'm Detective Rhodes, this is Detective Carson," the larger man said.

"Is this about Theresa and Ann?" Morgan asked.

"Yes," Detective Carson answered. "We just had a few questions."

Morgan nodded. "Okay."

"When was the last time you saw Theresa?" Detective Carson asked.

"Um..." She thought back. "It was about a week and a half ago. She came to my parents' house and gave me a massage. I'm sure my mother has the exact date."

Detective Carson nodded to her boot. "I suppose you can't drive with that thing?"

"No." She glanced down at her boot. "My leg is broken in three places. I'm not allowed to put any pressure on it just yet."

"Right," he said, writing something in a notepad he had pulled out. Then he glanced over at Liam. "We've already talked to your husband about his whereabouts. We'll be sure to check with your office." They started to leave.

"I have a few questions," Morgan said, and they stopped.

"We may not be able to answer," Detective Carson started.

"How did Theresa die?" Morgan asked.

The man looked towards Liam. "I'd like to know as well." He took Morgan's hand in his. "We heard about Ann," he assured the man.

"At this point, we can only let you know that the two instances appear connected," the detective answered. "We'll be in touch." He turned to go. Liam jumped up and walked the men out, then came back a few moments later.

"How about I make you a sandwich and then we go for a swim?" Liam asked.

"That sounds absolutely wonderful." She followed him into the kitchen and sat at the bar while he made them some turkey breast sandwiches. He made two plates and even added a pitcher of tea and an entire bag of chips.

"I wish I could help you carry it all out there," she said, hobbling out the glass door that he held open for her.

"Don't, I can make two trips," he said with a smile. "Go, sit. I'll get the rest."

Her phone started ringing in the side pocket of her yoga pants before she could reach the chair. When she answered it, she was so concerned that she'd miss the call that she didn't even look at the caller ID.

"Hello?" she said a little breathless.

"I hope you're happy. I did this all for you." Then the line went dead.

She was still holding the phone when Liam walked out. He took one look at her face and dropped the plates with the sandwiches and rushed to her side.

"What is it?" he asked, concerned.

"I..." She closed her eyes and willed her hands to stop shaking.

"My god, you're freezing. It must be ninety degrees out and you're shivering. What?" Liam begged. "Tell me."

She handed him her phone. "I... the killer." She motioned to the phone. "He said that he killed them for me. That Ann and Theresa are dead because of me."

"My god." Liam pulled her into his arms. He was so warm, and she felt so safe in his arms that she released on him. Tears poured out of her eyes, soaking his T-shirt. Her body still shook, but only because she was sobbing.

When the tears dried up, her head ached so bad that just being outside in the sunlight hurt.

As if he'd read her mind, Liam lifted her in his arms and carried her inside.

"You dropped the sandwiches," she said as he stepped over the broken plates.

"I can make more. Maybe some soup and hot tea as well," he suggested. "I'm calling the detectives back here." He set her down on the sofa and shut the blinds before handing her a blanket.

"Why is it so cold all of a sudden?" she asked absently.

"You're in shock," Liam said, wrapping his arms around her again.

"No, I..." She closed her eyes and took several deep breaths. "I'm okay now." When she opened her eyes, Liam was watching her face closely.

"Will you be, okay?" Liam asked her. "I'll just call the detective back. Maybe get Roy up here too."

She nodded slowly. "I could use some tea."

"I'll make it while I call." He leaned closer and brushed his lips across her forehead.

Tucking the blanket tighter around her, she listened to

Liam talk to Detective Carson and then to Roy. When he handed her a mug of hot tea and set a bowl of chips down in front of her, she took a couple chips and instantly felt a little steadier. She hadn't realized just how hungry she had been.

"It might hold you over until I can make the soup and sandwiches. I've called Lynda to see if she can come back for a few hours," Liam said.

She froze. "Lynda. Oh my god. What if..." Her stomach turned.

"Hey, nothing is going to happen to her," Liam said calmly. "I've suggested that it was a good idea for her to stay here on the grounds. At least until we know more. Roy even offered to stick around here for a couple days too. If that's okay with you?"

"Yes." She smiled at him. "If you trust him, I do."

He nodded. "They'll both stay in rooms in the garage building. At least for a week," he told her as she grabbed another chip. "The detectives are on their way here. They suggested that while it's fresh in your mind, you write down exactly what the person said to you, everything you can remember about the call." He reached over and took a pen and notepaper from a drawer in one of the side tables. "Here." He handed her the pen. "Write what you know. If you can remember anything from that first phone call, add it as well."

"You think that had something to do with this?" she asked, feeling even more light-headed.

"I'm not sure, but might as well add it."

She started writing while Liam returned to the kitchen. She wrote down every detail she could remember from the last phone call, word for word. The first one she had to think back to and was only able to jot down a few different versions of what might have been said.

When she was done, Liam was back with turkey sandwiches and a cup of potato soup.

By the time they were finished eating, Lynda was there, making some more tea while Liam filled her in on the phone calls. Roy showed up half an hour later, followed by the two detectives.

Morgan relayed every word the caller had said several times until she felt almost light-headed. Her headache turned into a full-blown migraine and, an hour before sunset, she took the elevator back upstairs and pulled the blankets over her head while Liam continued talking to the officers and Roy.

The next time she woke, her face was plastered against Liam's bare chest. Even his warmth soothed her, along with his steady breathing.

She lost track of how long she lay there, listening to his heartbeat and searching her mind for why someone would want her dead and would be willing to kill two innocent people over her.

The moment she thought of Ann and Theresa, tears started leaking from her eyes.

"Hey." Liam started to move. "What's all this about?" He looked down into her eyes.

"They're dead because of me." She sniffled.

He shifted until she was lying across him and his arms were tight around her. "No," he said softly. "They're dead because some psycho wants you to think that. He wants to blame you."

"I know." She lifted her head to look down at him. Her eyes ran over his face and, even though most of her memoires weren't back yet, she realized just how familiar he was to her. How much she'd come to care for him in such a short time. "Take my mind off of it all." She leaned down and brushed her lips against his.

Liam's hands started slowly moving up her hips as she felt him grow hard underneath her, which excited her even more.

Since the boot allowed her to move around a lot more freely than the cast, she leaned up until she straddled his hips. She rode him through his shorts until the urge to feel him inside her grew almost painful.

"Morgan," Liam groaned, "you're killing me."

She smiled down at him as he tossed off his shorts and she wiggled out of her own clothes.

Instead of returning to leaning over him, he nudged her back onto the bed and covered her body with his own.

Even this felt right and slightly familiar. There was the excitement of being with someone new, but knowing they'd been with one another for two years somehow made it even more special. She silently hoped that it would always be like this as he slipped deep inside her.

Her heart swelled when he whispered those three words into her ear as stars exploded behind her eyes and her entire body convulsed with the release.

"What are we going to do today?" Liam asked her once her body cooled off.

"Don't you have work?" she asked, looking up at the ceiling.

"No, I took the day off." He took her hand in his.

She thought for a moment. "How about a swim?"

"Okay, then what?"

"Breakfast," she answered, rolling over.

"Followed by?"

She smiled. "More of this."

"A lazy day filled with debauchery. I like it," he joked.

"And swimming and food," she added with a chuckle.

"Right." He lifted his hand and brushed a strand of her hair away from her face.

In that moment, memories of him doing the exact same move flooded her mind. He'd done the same thing so many times that they all seemed to blend into one another.

"Hey." Liam's voice broke into her thoughts. The pain of the memories had caused her to close her eyes and double over. "What's wrong?"

"I... remember you," she said, rubbing her temples.

"And this caused you pain?" he asked with a frown.

"Yes and no," she answered with a chuckle. "It was like fast-forwarding a movie. I guess it just knocked the wind out of me." She sighed. "I'm okay."

"Are you sure?" he asked, concerned.

"Yes. I'm hungry now, so maybe food first then a dip?"

He nodded, his eyes scanning her face closely. "Okay, food first." He rolled her over and kissed her until she melted once more under his hands.

Almost two hours later, she lay on a float in the pool, looking up at the perfect blue sky. An iced tea was in her hands as she enjoyed the cool water and even cooler drink as the heat of the sun beat down on her.

She knew that the pale skin on her broken leg was probably burning, but it felt so good, she didn't care.

Liam had made breakfast for them himself. Even with Lynda there, he moved around the kitchen as if he enjoyed cooking. The omelets had been so good, that it was obvious that he made them all of the time.

While they floated in the pool, Roy sat just inside the glass doors, working on a laptop or talking on the phone. Lynda was in the house somewhere, most likely cleaning.

"We should have Ryder over," Morgan said out of the blue.

Liam glanced up at her from where he lay on another float next to hers. "Yeah?" he asked.

"Sure, I mean, it would be nice to meet him again." She shrugged.

Liam chuckled. "He's been wanting to come over. I can give him a call?" he suggested.

"I'd like that."

"It's..." He thought for a moment. "Thursday. He might be able to get the evening off. Head up here for dinner. We can grill out," Liam said, thinking out loud.

"Do we do that often? I mean, I would think that he's been out here before." She bit her lip.

"Yes," Liam answered smoothly. "Ryder usually comes up here at least once a month to hang. You were taking boxing with him twice a week."

"Right, you mentioned that." She frowned. "I wish I could remember more. I thought coming home would jog my memories loose."

"You've already remembered a lot." Liam pushed himself towards the side of the pool. "It'll come to you." He jumped off the float and grabbed his phone, then looked at her. "If not, we'll just have to make new ones," he added with a wink.

She listened to Liam talk to Ryder, who obviously agreed to come out for the night. Instantly, she could tell that the two of them were more than friends. They were as close as brothers. Which somehow made her feel more nervous to meet Ryder than before.

Her friends had mentioned that she and Ryder had gotten along before her accident. But things had changed. Right? She'd changed. Hadn't she?

When Liam got off the phone and rejoined her in the middle of the pool, she asked him, "Have I changed?"

"In what way?" he asked, shifting to lay on his front so that he could look at her.

"I don't know. Do I act the same as I did before my accident?" she asked, suddenly feeling stupid.

Liam was silent for a moment before answering. "You're less stressed."

"I was stressed?" she asked. "About what?"

"You were working a lot with your mother," he answered with a sigh. "With Aaron's nightclub opening and a few other projects... I don't think you were happy, but your mother had talked you into it and, as much as I tried, I couldn't talk you out." He moved until he could hold onto her float.

"I wasn't here a lot. I should have been."

"You weren't?" she asked.

"No." His eyes locked with hers. "I allowed my work to get between us," he said with a sigh. "Even now, the stresses of the hack..."

"What hack?" Morgan asked him.

Liam shook his head. "It doesn't matter. What does is that I've been thinking of stepping down."

"You have?" she asked, wondering what he would do if he did.

"Yes." He ran his hand gently over her broken leg, as if testing it. It felt good, having her skin touched softly, like an itch being scratched. "I've been moving towards stepping down since your accident." His eyes returned to hers. "Soon," he said with a smile. Just seeing that smile had her heart fluttering in her chest.

"Were we always this... close?" she asked.

"No." His smile slipped. "Not that we fought. It was

more an absence of communication. Again, my fault. I allowed myself to be too focused on my job."

"Which is why I turned to my mother," she filled in, knowing already why she would have ever agreed to help her mother out. If she'd been lonely, her mother had a way of getting under her defenses.

"Right. I'm sorry."

She smiled. "I'm sure that if I could remember, I'd appreciate the apology."

He chuckled. "I really am. I can promise you that once you're back to your normal self, you won't have a reason to help Victoria out ever again."

"I'd appreciate that," she said with a sigh. "Okay, I'm almost ready for that nap," she said with a yawn. "Plus, if I let this raw chicken leg roast in the sun any longer, you'll have to slather burn cream all over it for me."

He chuckled. "Okay." He slid into the water and helped her get back to the edge of the pool where she dried her leg off before slipping it into the boot again.

"Mr. Taylor." Lynda stepped outside. "Detective Evans is here to see you."

They both turned and looked inside. Roy was standing inside, talking to an older man who was thick and balding.

Morgan vaguely remembered seeing the man before.

"Who's that?" she asked Liam.

"He's..." Liam looked at her and then sighed. "I'll tell you later. Why don't you head upstairs and rest while I talk to the detective?" He took her hands and helped her stand up. "I promise, I'll tell you later. After you rest." He kissed her. "I'll be up soon."

As they stepped inside, the older man nodded to her. When she stepped into the elevator, she closed her eyes and willed any memories of the man to come to her.

When the memory did come, she instantly wished it hadn't.

Liam stood, his fists balled tight next to him. He was wearing a tuxedo. There were Christmas lights and decorations everywhere in the house. A massive Christmas tree sat in the corner of the living room by the fireplace.

"I don't give a damn," Liam shouted. "You find this bastard before he ends up killing one of us." She'd never seen Liam so angry before. She couldn't remember what or who he was talking about, only that he'd been so angry he'd shaken with it.

# CHAPTER EIGHTEEN

*Each of us bears this light everyday of our lives, even when
the darkness looms so large that we feel sure the light will be
extinguished.*
**Joyce Rupp**

L iam pulled on a dry shirt and then shook Mack's
hand. "I suspect you two know one another?" he said
when the men chuckled at something.

"Yeah. I didn't know you were working with Mack,"
Roy said.

"For about six years," Mack answered for him. "Liam's
been getting harassed. It got a little worse after he married."
Mack motioned towards the elevator where Morgan had
just disappeared.

"Harassed?" Roy frowned. "By whom?"

"Wish I knew," Liam said with a sigh. "I wouldn't have
to change our phone numbers so often."

"Anything serious?" Roy asked.

"Threats." Liam shrugged and offered the men seats.
"Want a drink?" he asked Mack.

"I won't say no to some of Lynda's tea," Mack said with a wink towards Lynda.

Since he'd known Mack, the man had flirted shamelessly with Lynda. Liam had never asked the detective about his personal life. He didn't know if the man was single or married, though he didn't wear a wedding band.

Lynda, for her part, seemed to enjoy the attention and always blushed around the man.

"What brings you out here?" Liam asked after Lynda left the room.

"I had some news. After the last message, I went and visited Sean myself," Mack said.

"Sean?" Roy questioned. "Sean Wilson?"

"Yes," Mack answered for him.

"And?" Liam asked, somehow already knowing the answer.

"Not much different. A whole lot of denying. But there was something." Mack pulled out a piece of newspaper from a file.

Liam took the news article. It was the piece from the local paper that had come out the morning after Morgan been found at the bottom of the cliff, not far from the house. Seeing the red smiley face inked over the image of Morgan's destroyed car had Liam's anger growing so fast that he saw red.

"What the..." Roy took the news article from his hands. "Sean had this?"

"Yes. Based on this, I was able to bring him in for questioning," Mack told them.

"And?" Roy asked.

Mack sighed. "Nothing came of it. He had an alibi for the night of the accident and there aren't any phone records or proof that he is the one making the phone calls."

"The new ones?" Roy asked.

"New ones?" Mack asked.

While Roy filled Mack in on the latest calls Morgan had received, he read through the article. He'd been far too worried about Morgan to read it back then.

"Who wrote this?" Liam asked, breaking into Roy and Mack's discussion.

"What?" Mack asked.

"This article." He slid the paper across the table. "Who wrote it? It's just a clipping. Not even the full article. Who wrote it? Do you know?"

Mack frowned down at the paper. "No, why?"

"There are details in here that I didn't even know," he said, pointing at the article. "They claim Morgan was forced off the road."

"Yeah," Mack said. "And?"

"She was forced off the road?" Liam almost yelled it. "Forced? Not an accident?"

"It was suspected at first—" Mack started.

"And I wasn't notified?" Liam stood up slowly.

"You were. Well, I assumed. You were questioned," Mack answered.

"Questioned as to what happened. I never heard that she was forced off the road." Liam felt his back teeth grind.

"That's probably because whoever worked the case wanted to keep you in the dark to find out if you knew anything," Mack answered. "It's just a theory that she was forced off the road."

"Theory? Was it ever proven?" Liam asked.

"Honestly, I don't know." Mack shrugged.

"I can find out," Roy suggested.

"Do so," Liam said quickly.

Roy nodded, then stood up and left the room as he pulled out his cell phone.

"I thought you knew," Mack said quietly.

"It's okay." He sat back down. "I'd like to read the rest of the article."

"It's probably online," Mack suggested.

Liam pulled out his own cell phone and searched. There were so many articles about Morgan's accident, it was difficult to wade through. There were hundreds of articles about their marriage and their relationship, several claiming it was on the rocks. He noticed those were all published long before her accident, most of them shortly after they'd started dating. There were even photos of them on their first date.

It took some doing, but finally, he found the article after he adjusted his search. He read through it several times so he didn't miss a thing.

The article was written by S.M. Knight. When he searched that name, only a handful of articles came up, all of which were about him or Morgan and her family. Each article he scanned had a definite pattern.

If the story was about him or Morgan, they were negative in mood. If it was about Aaron or his nightclub, a positive twist was put on the details.

There was only one article about Victoria and Thomas, which was downright vulgar and borderline harassing. He read that one very carefully. S.M. Knight claimed that Thomas had raped a thirteen-year-old girl while Victoria had been passed out in the next room after a huge orgy.

Liam showed Mack the article. "Has this been looked into?"

He waited until Mack read through the article.

"I can check." Mack pulled out his phone.

Roy returned to the room with a frown on his face.

"Well?" Liam asked him.

"The short answer is, they still don't know if Morgan was forced off the road." Roy sat down.

"How could they not know? Wouldn't there be..." He shrugged as he remembered every crime show he'd ever watched. "Paint chips or... tire marks."

Roy sighed. "Your wife's car was a heap of twisted metal at the base of an eighty-foot cliff, half in the water and half out. She was lucky to survive."

"I agree. And there isn't a moment that goes by that I'm not thankful for it. But if someone tried to murder her... I need to know." He thought about it for a second. "Have you checked the car's computer system?"

"For?" Roy asked.

"Morgan drove an IOA One. The car was one of the first with my ESP system in it. If it was still functional, I could log into it and check the system myself. But it's been over three months. I doubt the battery is charged or even connected still. Where did they tow the car?" he asked.

"It's still in impound," Roy answered.

"Can I have access?" Liam asked.

Roy shook his head. "I doubt it."

"How about my team? They could help determine if Morgan was forced off the road or not," Liam suggested.

"I might be able to convince the captain to let someone from your team look at it. But they'd have to be approved," he warned.

"Thanks." Liam relaxed slightly. Just then Mack stepped back into the room and sat down before.

"There has never been a police report filed against Thomas Davenport," Mack said.

"In regard to the article?" Liam asked.

"Ever," Mack answered. "He has had a few bumps in the road, but any charges against him have been dropped over the years. He obviously has powerful friends."

"Charges?" Liam asked.

Mack glanced down at his notepad. "Two DUIs, an assault charge, and a domestic disturbance. All within the past five years."

"What?" Liam asked. Why hadn't Morgan told him about these? Had she even known?

"Nothing about a rape of a thirteen-year-old," Mack added.

Liam glanced at the time and asked Mack if he'd stick around for some lunch.

"I can't. I've got a few things in an hour. I'll look further into what we found out and keep in touch."

"What about Sean?" Liam asked.

"He's out for now. I'll keep an eye out, like usual." Mack shook Roy's hand and then Liam's.

Lynda appeared suddenly and walked the man out of the house.

"Are you going to tell me what happened between you and Sean?" Roy asked when they were alone.

"Maybe when we have some sandwiches," he answered. "I'm going to head up and check on Morgan." He motioned to the pool. "Feel free to cool off. We'll be down for lunch."

"I'll take you up on that offer." Roy chuckled. "I've been wanting to jump in since this morning."

As he made his way up the stairs, he tried to figure out the best way to approach the subject of Thomas and the news he'd just found out.

When he stepped into their bedroom, Morgan was sitting in the middle of the bed, crying. Huge tears were streaming down her face as she hugged her knees to her chest.

"What is it?" He rushed towards her and gathered her in his arms. Her tears continued and her breath hitched as she tried to tell him something.

He couldn't understand a word of what she was saying but held onto her as she cried. Finally, when she stopped, he asked her.

"What happened? I tried to understand what you said, but..." He shrugged.

"I remembered," she answered with a sigh.

"Remembered what?"

"Everything." She looked up at him. "Everything."

"You did?" He grew excited, but the look in her eyes had him frowning. "What is it?"

"I didn't just have an accident," she answered, and he tensed.

"What happened?" he asked, brushing a tear from her cheek.

"My car... it shut off," she answered with a slight shake in her head.

"What?" he asked, disbelief in his tone.

"The power. Everything just... Poof. I'd just reached the last turn, the one before the turnoff to head downtown, when everything went dark. I had no brakes, no steering, nothing. The car wouldn't respond, and I was heading right for the cliff. I remember thinking of you. How much I would miss you." She reached up and touched his cheek. "How much I loved you."

He swallowed, hard. "What else do you remember?"

She smiled. "Everything. How we met, our first kiss, the first time... our first time together. How you proposed and our weddings. Both of them," she added with a chuckle.

He pulled her into his arms and held on, tears burning his own eyes. "My god, I've missed you."

"I'm right here. I've been right here. You were so patient waiting for me," she said as more tears rolled down her cheeks.

"I love you," he said with a smile.

"And I love you. I remember just how much I love you." She kissed him. "How much I trust you. How much I wanted to start a family with you." Her frown was back. "But you were so busy with work, so I decided to busy myself. You're right, I allowed my mother to strong-arm me into helping her out." She closed her eyes. "She and my dad were... having difficulties, and she decided to focus her attention on me since Aaron was busy with his club. I didn't know Aaron was doing drugs until recently though," she said suddenly.

He asked. "Do you remember anything else about the accident?"

"No, other than we disagreed right before I left. I was upset..." she said, but he stopped her by shaking his head.

"I shouldn't have let work get in the way. I should have been the one driving that night."

"So we both would have been hurt? Maybe even worse?" She shook her head. "There was nothing you could have done to stop it. The car died. The system just shut down."

"I wrote the system. The security system at least. I could have—"

"Liam, the car was dead. It was as if someone turned it off remotely."

He stilled, and his heartbeat felt like it stopped for a full ten seconds. "Son of a bitch!" he growled. He jumped up from the bed to go grab his laptop.

"What?" Morgan scooted to the edge of the bed, grabbed a crutch, and followed him to the sitting area. "What?" she said again as she sat next to him.

"The kill codes," he said, feeling stupid for overlooking the obvious. "It wasn't for the entire system, it was for specific cars," he said, working on his system.

"Liam?" she said, getting his attention.

He turned to her, knowing without a doubt that her accident was his fault. He had been so busy back then that he'd overlooked the hack. He'd allowed someone to break into his system and target him and his wife. And there was only one person he knew of that had anything to gain if he was out of the way.

# CHAPTER NINETEEN

*You can't discover light, by analyzing the dark.*
**Wayne Dyer**

Morgan had been crying about the last thing she'd said to Liam before the accident. She remembered telling him that maybe they should just take a break.

The look in his eyes haunted her as she woke from the dream. She was afraid she'd lose the memories again when she woke, like she had the last time, but she didn't. Instead, Liam's arms had wrapped around her and everything else she'd forgotten was just... there. Within her reach again.

So many good memories with Liam and her friends. She remembered Ryder. Not only how well she got along with the guy, but how much she appreciated his and Liam's relationship. They were brothers in every sense, which meant that she had already loved him. Especially after Liam had told her all of the stories of how he and Ryder had survived living on the streets together.

When Liam talked about Sean betraying them, she'd been heartbroken. She'd never met the man before but had seen the aftermath of the friend's treachery, how it had left a scar in both Liam's and Ryder's hearts.

She remembered how her parents had treated Liam from the moment they'd met him, like he was nothing more than a temporary distraction for her. As if she was banging the help.

Even after they had seen his wealth, they had treated him like he was poor. Yet she knew that he was so much wealthier than they were.

She'd never been more embarrassed of her family than after the first time Liam had invited them up to dinner at the house. Even Aaron had snubbed Liam. This was long before he'd thought of opening the club.

Her friends, on the other hand, had liked Liam instantly. Maybe it was because she'd confided in them that she'd fallen in love that first night in the club. Maybe it was because they were her friends. Either way, she had at least been thankful for their support. They'd been the ones to encourage her to move in with Liam after he'd asked.

When she and Liam had returned downstairs, Roy had just been climbing out of the swimming pool. There were sandwiches, chips, and fruit already set out on the table outside, along with cold drinks.

She nibbled on the food and listened to Liam talk to Roy about codes and hacking. She tried to keep up with their conversation, but they were talking so fast, almost finishing each other's sentences. From what she could understand, she surmised that someone had broken into his software and placed a code in it that could potentially shut down individual cars. Like hers.

Almost an hour after she'd returned downstairs, Lynda appeared.

"Mrs. Taylor, Mr. Moore is here for your therapy session," Lynda said as she poured Liam some more tea.

Morgan glanced over at Liam. A crease formed between his eyebrows. Still, he gave her a quick nod. "Go on." He leaned over and gave her a kiss.

Taking the elevator, she made her way down to the gym where Grayson was already setting up a mat and some small weights.

"You look rested," Grayson said with a smile.

"I have my memories back," she said, then she instantly felt stupid. The man was her physical therapist, not her doctor.

"That's good," he said after the slightest of hesitation. "Ready to get started?"

"Yes," she answered quickly.

For the next hour, he ran her through drills on both arms and hands. They even moved out to the staircase where he had her climbing and descending the stairs with her crutches.

She had grown tired and let her guard down for the slightest moment and almost toppled down the stairs. Thankfully, Grayson was there to catch her.

When his powerful arms wrapped around her waist, she realized that she should have felt something. The man was a knockout, easily as handsome as Liam. But instead, she only felt grateful for not nose-planting and hurting herself.

It was, of course, at that moment that Liam came down the stairs.

Instantly, Morgan dropped her hold on Grayson, which caused her to almost tumble again.

"Liam," she said, feeling a need to explain. Only her husband surprised her by moving to her side.

"Everything okay?" he asked her. "Did you hurt your-self falling?"

"No, Grayson was there," she explained.

"Good." Liam nodded as Grayson dropped his hold on her, and Liam helped her over to a chair. "If you're done for the day, Ryder's upstairs."

"He is?" she asked, excited to see Liam's best friend.

Liam nodded.

She glanced down at herself and realized that she'd worked up a sweat. "I'll head upstairs and shower and change first."

Liam nodded in agreement and helped her to the elevator.

She didn't want to leave the two men alone, but at the same time, didn't want to be around the awkwardness, which was making the air stale.

It felt so good to step under the hot spray in the shower. Having the boot instead of the plaster cast was a life changer.

She knew from her newly refreshed memories that Liam wasn't a jealous man, but she remembered him punching a guy once who'd been too grabby at a nightclub. In fairness, she'd warned the guy several times that she didn't want him touching her. She'd even kicked him in the shins to get her point across, but the man had been so focused on her. Thankfully, Liam had stepped in, and the man had had to be carted out.

It wasn't as if things like that had happened to her a lot over the years. It seemed that the moment she'd met and fallen for Liam, the press had been more focused on her than they had her entire life.

There hadn't been a month without her face or Liam's on the cover of a magazine or newspaper. At first, it had appeared everyone was rooting for their relationship, and she'd liked the attention.

But then the articles had turned darker, as if someone was driving the relationship to ruin for a purpose. It wasn't just one journalist or author. Instead, there were several that she could remember stalking them.

At one point, she'd thought to ask Liam to look into it or to hire someone to, but then she realized just how stupid that sounded. Because of those articles, any event she'd done was an instant hit.

Besides, the articles didn't seem to bother Liam, and she didn't want to seem petty.

She'd been in the shower so long that the glass had fogged up. Seeing movement on the other side, she called out. "Do you have time to join me?"

When Liam didn't answer, she swiped at the glass.

Seeing the unfamiliar dark figure moving closer to her, she screamed as she jerked away. Her good foot slipped on the wet tile. She tried to reach out for something to hold onto and used her right leg to steady herself as a knee-jerk reaction. The instant pain shooting up her leg was like being hit by a bolt of lightning, and she screamed even more.

She landed on the tile, thankfully, on the soft part of her butt. Still, her elbow smacked the tile seat. All this while, her eyes remained glued to the dark figure moving on the other side of the fogged glass.

She didn't stop screaming until the figure disappeared. Only then did she crawl towards the door and glance outside to ensure that she was now alone. She grabbed the towel from the hook and wrapped it around herself as she crawled over to her cell phone and called Liam.

"Hey, I was going to come up and check up on you," he answered cheerfully.

"Someone was just in here," she cried out.

"Where?" She could hear Liam run as he asked.

"In the bathroom. I saw... I fell."

"I'm on my way up. Lock the place down. Someone's here," he said to someone else.

When Liam rushed into the bathroom, she was still on the floor, the towel covering up most of her. Her broken leg was straight out in front of her, throbbing enough that she was having to breathe through the pain.

"Are you hurt?" he asked her, lifting her in his arms.

"I... used my leg to catch myself from the fall." She grabbed another towel when he walked by the hooks.

Liam set her gently on the bed. "Did you see who it was?"

"No, all I saw was a dark figure. I knew instantly it wasn't you."

"How?" he asked, handing her a robe. She scooted to the edge of the bed and wrapped it around herself.

"I..." She thought about it and then shook her head. "I just knew."

"Okay, did you notice anything? Clothes? Hair?" he asked her.

She thought back and shook her head with a sigh. "No, just... it was a dark figure."

"Are you okay here? I'm going to go check the room. Make sure..." Liam motioned.

She felt her heart skip and gripped the robe closer to her chest as she nodded slowly. "Do you think he's still here?"

"I'm going to help them search." He leaned in and kissed her. "I'll be back."

While she waited, she crawled under the blankets to

warm herself. She'd taken a hot shower, but now, after the scare, she was shivering. Her leg throbbed, and she thought about taking a pain pill to ease the ache.

Instead of Liam returning moments later, Ryder walked in.

"Hey," he said with a smile. "Liam's okay, he's just checking a few things. Roy is driving down the driveway to check things out." He moved over to sit next to her on the bed. "Liam told me you have your memories back…"

She pulled him into a hug. "I do." She couldn't explain it, but she'd missed him. Missed him like he was her own brother. Maybe even more than she'd missed Aaron, since it was obvious that her brother was too involved in his own life to be bothered with her or even care. Aaron had seemed annoyed and put out that she'd been injured instead of worried.

"I came to the hospital a few times," Ryder said, leaning back. "You were out. Then Liam mentioned you'd lost your memories and… I had a run-in with your dad."

She groaned. "He's not really racist." Ryder gave her a look. "Okay, he is a little, but he doesn't hate you because you're black. He hates you because you're important to Liam and to me."

"Are you hurt?" he asked, and she knew that he was changing the subject.

"I fell on my leg." She motioned. "I left my boot in the bathroom."

"I'll get it." He stood up and disappeared. When he returned, he had her boot and the bottle of her pain pills. "You look like you could use this." He handed her the bottle.

"Thanks," she said, taking a pill and swallowing it dry.

"I could have gotten you some water," Ryder said with a chuckle.

"I'm good," she said, putting on her boot. "Did you find anything?"

"No," Ryder answered as he grabbed her crutches from the bathroom and brought them to her. "Liam's checking the security footage now. Want to come on down?"

"Yeah, I'll just pull on something." She nodded to the closet.

"I'll be right outside the door."

"Thanks," she said, touching his hand. "Ryder, it's good you're here. I'm glad I remember how much you mean to us."

"I don't know what we would have done if we'd lost you," he responded before stepping outside.

She pulled on some yoga pants and a T-shirt, then combed through her wet hair and tried to braid it. Her left hand refused to cooperate with the simple task, but she finally managed a knotted braid and stepped out of the bedroom.

Ryder was sitting on the sofa in the small sitting area, watching sports on the television there.

"Ready?" he asked.

"Yes." She made her way to the elevator.

"It's really a good thing your house has an elevator."

"I know, right? I doubt I'd be able to go anywhere except the main floor without it. That or Liam would have to carry me everywhere."

They stepped into the elevator and talked about her injuries and her recovery as they made their way downstairs.

There were so many memories of Ryder being around.

He'd been Liam's best man and the only other one who had stood by him in their lavish wedding.

When they stepped into the living room, Liam was on his laptop and phone, yelling at someone.

Morgan made her way over to sit next to him. The food on the table sat untouched. The pain pills were supposed to be eaten with food, so she leaned over and took a burger.

"Are you okay?" Liam mouthed between yelling at whoever was on the other side of the call.

She nodded quickly and sipped the drink that was set in front of her by Lynda.

When Roy returned, he too grabbed a burger and started eating while everyone waited for Liam to get off the call. She figured out that he was talking to the security company and wasn't very happy with them.

"Well?" Ryder asked when Liam was off the phone. "What did they say?"

"They said that it was a planned outage for maintenance." Liam took a burger and took a big bite out of it. He hadn't even bothered to put condiments on it.

As he talked, she ran through what she'd remembered. How he liked his foods, what his favorite drinks, desserts, movies, and music were. Every little detail flooded her mind as she remembered as many details as she could about her husband.

She remembered just how much she loved about the man. The way he smelled and felt first thing in the morning. His warm breath on her neck after they'd made love. Her new memories mixed with the old, and she felt warmth spread in her gut.

Memories of their first time together mixed with their first time together after her accident. She couldn't help comparing the two times and how different yet wonderful both were. Throughout everything that had happened, new and old, Liam was there. Solid like a rock.

"I think the pain pill finally took hold," Ryder said, interrupting her thoughts.

"Hm?" she asked, blinking to focus. Then she realized that he was right. She was sitting at the dining table, after only taking two bites of her burger, daydreaming about making love to her husband after someone had just broken into her bathroom. "Yes." She sighed. "I'm sorry. I..."

"Hey," Ryder and Liam said at the same time.

Liam smiled and took her hand. "It's okay. How's the leg?"

"Better now," she said.

"Do you want to go lie down?" Liam asked.

She glanced upstairs and shook her head.

"You can lay on the sofa?" Liam suggested.

She thought about that and nodded. "I should have a few more bites first." She ate as much of the burger as she could while trying to focus on what the men were talking about.

This was the reason she'd stopped taking the pain pills in the first place. They made her fuzzy. It was difficult to focus, and they caused her to sleep too much.

When half of the burger was gone, she moved to the sofa and covered up with a throw pillow to watch the television until she fell asleep.

When Liam woke her sometime later, it was dark outside, and the television was turned off.

"How are you feeling?" he asked her, rubbing her shoulder.

"Tired." She groaned. "I hate taking those pills."

"I know. You must have been hurting to take them. I

should have called the doctor to have him come check on you."

"No, I'm fine. I just slipped and used my leg to try and catch myself." She sat up a little. "I'm not much of a hostess." She glanced around.

"It's okay, they understand," Liam said.

"Did you have a good time catching up at least?" she asked with a yawn, already feeling herself grow tired again. But her stomach growled, reminding her that she hadn't eaten as much as she should have earlier.

"Yeah." Liam smiled. "It was good. Ryder and Roy caught up."

"And you?"

"I was too worried about my wife." He smiled and then leaned in and kissed her. "Come on, you must be hungry."

"I am."

Liam leaned away and returned with a plate that had been sitting on the coffee table. A huge slice of chocolate cake filled the entire plate.

"Wow," she said, taking the fork from him.

"You're lucky Ryder left you a slice," Liam joked.

"This is a slice?" She laughed. "More like a quarter of the cake."

Liam smiled. "Yeah, that's about right."

"It's nice having your friends here," she added.

"The three of us were as close as brothers once," Liam said with a sigh. "Before Roy found his family."

"You at least still have Ryder. Aaron and I are strangers now," she said with a frown.

Liam reached over and took her hand.

"What did the security company say?" she asked as she took a bite.

"The system was down. All of the cameras, everything.

They claim it was maintenance and that they'd sent out emails and phone notices."

She could still hear the disgust in his voice.

"So, no videos of who it was?" she asked.

"No."

"Roy questioned whether you hadn't imagined it," Liam said.

"I didn't." She almost dropped her fork.

"No, of course not," he assured her with a smile. "Still, he's a cop and that's what they do. Question everything."

"Right." She relaxed and took another bite of the cake. "Who do you think it was?"

He was silent for a moment. "I walked your therapist out myself," he finally said with a slight sigh, "but it's possible he doubled back..."

"What?" This time she did drop her fork. "You think Grayson broke into my room?"

"He was just here," Liam said with a shrug.

"That doesn't mean he'd break back in and sneak up to our bathroom."

"The way he looks at you..." Liam started, but she stopped him by placing her hand on his cheek.

"He's my physical therapist. Nothing more."

"I know." He smiled. "I can see what you think of him in your eyes. He's there to help you, that's all. But the man looks at you differently."

"He's a man." She smiled. "It's not the first time a man has looked at me and it won't be the last."

"I know. I'm thankful I married a hot wife."

Morgan laughed. "And I'm thankful I married a hot husband," she joked back. "Now that we've established just how hot we are, any other ideas of who would break in?"

"Yeah." Liam's smile fell away. "My other brother."

# CHAPTER TWENTY

*Darkness cannot drive out darkness:*
*only light can do that.*
*Hate cannot drive out hate:*
*only love can do that.*
**Martin Luther King Jr**

It ate at him for a few days that whoever had broken into the place had done so while the three of them had been sitting out back by the pool chatting away. They'd snuck right past them, up the stairs, and into the bathroom where Morgan had been naked and vulnerable.

And they'd done so in the half-hour window that the security system had been down. Had it been coincidence? Impossible. He, Roy, and Ryder all agreed on that fact.

Roy promised that he'd look into the company personally. Still, that night after Morgan had fallen asleep, he'd started looking into the company himself and switched their service to another one that was even more reputable.

The following day, he met with the company and began the switch over to their system.

Morgan slept most of that day. Her leg was really bothering her, so she'd taken another pill in the morning, which had caused her to be groggy again.

He wanted to call Dr. Ellis over to check on her, but she'd turned him down and claimed that she just needed the rest.

The following day, the new security system was installed and running, and Morgan was back to normal. As normal as she could be.

They had also gone into town to attend both Ann's and Theresa's very somber funerals that week. Neither her parents nor her brother attended either service, he noticed. It had shocked Morgan but not Liam. After all, they were only the help, and he knew just what her family thought of their status. He was sure they hadn't wanted to appear weak in any way. Morgan, however, cried at each service.

Each time that the therapist arrived for Morgan's sessions, Liam worked out in the gym while the man worked with Morgan in the room. Even though he tried to act casual, he caught himself looking in the mirror, watching the man carefully.

The man was your typical jock has-been. Liam was pretty sure the man had been captain of whatever sport he'd played. An All-American type. Rugged good looks, cleanly shaven. Even though he was dressed in black scrubs, Liam just bet that he spent a lot on his wardrobe to impress the women.

Not that Liam didn't own a few nice suits himself, but his job required it, as did his private life. If it was his choice, he'd wear basketball shorts and T-shirts all the time.

This guy was probably the type that enjoyed showing off in every way possible. He'd seen the new Jag the guy drove. Physical therapy must pay pretty well to afford that expensive of a car.

Each time the man touched Morgan, Liam realized he was grinding his back teeth and not counting his reps.

In all the time he'd been with Morgan, not once had he displayed an ounce of jealousy. Nor had he needed to.

This, however, was different. He'd been truthful with her. He could see clearly that she had no interest in the man. Yet something about the guy bothered Liam. Maybe it was jealousy, he thought as the man's hand slipped lower on Morgan's hip as he guided her over a bench he'd set up as a makeshift obstacle course.

"I think that's enough for today," he broke in as he set his weights back on the rack.

"Yes," Morgan said with a chuckle. "I've had enough. Besides, Marina's going to be here soon." Morgan sat down on the bench.

Liam noticed then that she looked tired and was thankful he'd interrupted the session.

"I'll walk you out," Liam said to the other man. This time, he'd make sure the guy left, watching him through the new system until the gate shut behind him.

When the man drove through the gate, Marina was just coming in and had to get out of the way of the man's car. Liam waited at the door for Marina.

"Was that the physical therapist?" Marina asked as he let her inside.

"Yeah," Liam answered, and started walking with her down the stairs.

"How's Morgan doing?" Marina asked.

"She has all her memories back," he answered.

"That's good." Marina smiled as they stepped into the massage room. Morgan was sitting on the table, a towel wrapped around her. "Hey." Marina smiled and set her bag down. "I heard you can remember who you are," she joked.

Morgan chuckled. "I can't believe that I'd forgotten how funny you are."

"I'll get out of your way," Liam said, stepping out of the room. Since he was still worked up, he detoured back to the gym and this time focused on his workout.

He lost track of time as he burned through his frustrations about his job, the possibility of someone being after Morgan, and the security issues at his own home.

He didn't spot Morgan standing next to the bench watching him until he moved over and set the weights back.

"Hey," he said, turning towards her. "How was your massage?"

Instead of answering, she walked over and pulled him down and placed her lips over his. The kiss was fast, hard, and raw, reminding him of how they used to be together, before. The passion she gave to him almost made him forget that she was still broken and fragile.

"No, don't," she said, biting his bottom lip. "Don't pull back. Give me everything." She reached into his shorts and wrapped her fingers around him as she yanked the shorts off his hips. "I need you."

"I need you," he replied, hoisting her up. She wrapped her good leg around his hip as he stepped to the mirror and pinned her back against it, covering her mouth with his. Devouring, taking what he needed.

All he could smell was the scented lotion used during her massage. The scent was somehow driving him crazy.

He shoved her shirt up and her bra aside until he could take her nipple into his mouth. She cried out as her nails dug into his skin. He let her body slip down his until he was able to wiggle her out of her yoga pants. His fingers dipped inside her and found her, hot and wet. She wrapped her good leg around him again, and he plunged into her heat, groaning as she convulsed around his fingers.

"Yes, ride me," he said when her hips jerked. "Take what you need." He groaned as her fingers moved up and down him. If he didn't plunge into her soon, he'd come in her hand.

He pressed her body against the glass and his own body and settled between her legs. He lifted her good leg and held onto her as he glided into her, settling there, the one place in his life where he knew he belonged and was needed.

This time when they peaked together, Morgan cried out those three words with him and, finally, after months, he knew everything was going to be okay.

"Are you okay?" Morgan asked him moments later, after he'd pulled them down onto the mats together.

"Yes, you?" he asked, not even opening his eyes. She was running her fingers slowly over his chest.

"Perfect." She practically purred it, causing his eyes to open just a sliver.

"I remember what each tattoo means to you now," she said, smiling down at him.

"This one"—she traced the blue rose whose twin sat high on her hip—"I talked you into."

"You claimed you wanted as many tattoos as I have." He chuckled. "And almost passed out the first time the needle touched your skin."

"Hey, I made it through it though." She playfully slapped his chest.

"You did." He tightened his hold on her. "And I'm thankful you didn't want any more after. Not that I don't like a tattooed woman, but you have all this perfect skin."

His hands moved up and down her body. When he heard her moan with pleasure, he rolled over and settled between her legs.

"Liam," she sighed as he slipped slowly into her.

"Tell me how this makes you feel?" he said next to her ear.

"Loved," she whispered back.

The following day, Liam sat in the conference room once again, looking into the faces of the board of directors. This time, however, Rebecca sat next to him. He had every intention of giving her the floor, only Dave demanded attention first.

"I've done a little of my own investigation into the matter at hand," Dave said loudly. "I've found a number of computer systems, including several personal laptops, have all been infected with this file. Mine included."

There were several whispers around the room. Dave held up his hand to stop the gossip. "I have a list here of which systems I checked and which ones were affected."

At this point, Rebecca stood up. "I'm sorry to interrupt," she said, getting everyone's attention. "Thank you, Dave, for your concern. However, legally, you aren't allowed to go around logging into other people's systems. That will have to stop immediately. My team has conducted a proper investigation and have been working with the authorities."

At this point, Dave tried to interrupt, but Liam cleared his throat and had him sitting back down. Liam looked up at Rebecca and motioned for her to continue.

"There were eighteen systems that had the dot slash file on it." She paused. "That's what we're calling the hack," she explained. "The file was included in the update batch that was sent out to every one of the IOA One models." She glanced down at him.

"The dot slash hack enabled remote access to shut down select model Ones. We're still working on finding out which cars were hit and thus far only two have been known to be affected," he added.

"Two?" Regina asked. "I thought there was only one known case?"

"The second case has been confirmed as of earlier this morning. My wife's accident technically is the first instance of the hack," Liam said. He felt his anger and frustration boil, but he tempered it. This time the whispers were so loud, Rebecca had to whistle to get everyone's attention again.

"Thanks to Liam catching this in time and sending out the correction, we are one hundred percent sure that the dot slash hack has been eradicated," Rebecca said.

"Legal has looked over our findings and have agreed that we are in the clear, for now. They, however, have requested the termination of a handful of employees, many of which are, as we meet, being escorted off the premises. A few others, due to legal...reasons, will be allowed to resign." Liam's eyes landed on Dave, then moved over to Dawn, Dave's right-hand woman.

Regina gasped. "I hope it's not anyone on this board."

Both Liam and Rebecca remained quiet for a moment.

"If we're through, I have a meeting with my own team that I need to get to," Rebecca said to him.

"Yes, thank you." Liam nodded and the room remained silent until she left. As prearranged, Roy and Mack walked through the door as Rebecca left.

"What the hell is going on?" Dave demanded loudly. "What are they doing here? This is a board meeting."

"First, as I mentioned, you and Dawn will both be given the opportunity to step down. Legal has assured me that if found innocent of all charges, you will both be allowed to keep your pensions. Second, due to other reasons, Dave will be prosecuted as a co-conspirator in the hack."

"What?" Dave jumped up. "This is preposterous."

At this point, Roy, wearing his full uniform, pulled out his handcuffs while Mack guarded the door.

Liam had tried to assure Mack that Dave wasn't a runner, but Mack wasn't going to take any chances. He'd joked about getting in his laps at the gym not the office.

Without incident, Roy slapped the cuffs on Dave.

"Am I going to be arrested?" Dawn asked in a small voice.

"Not at this time. Legal does, however, want you to agree to come in for questioning," Liam answered. During this entire time, the rest of the board members sat silently by, watching everything unfold. "You will, however, be escorted off the premises. You'll be allowed to gather your personal things, excluding your work laptop."

For the next few minutes, everyone watched as Dave and Dawn were walked out of the room. When the door shut behind them, everyone turned to Liam.

"What now?" Regina asked.

"Now we get to work mending our reputation and trying to assure our clients that something like this won't happen again," he answered. With Dave gone, he instantly felt as if a burden had been removed from his chest. With the new security measures Rebecca and her team had put in place for each system and upload batch, he was assured that something like this would never happen again.

Things were finally going better for the first time since Morgan's accident. Sure, there was still a murderer on the loose, but everything else was looking up.

Now that he felt like things were getting back under

control at work, he was closer to stepping aside. Especially with Dave out of the running.

He was on such an emotional high that when he pulled up at the house and saw Morgan's parents' car in the driveway, it didn't even bother him.

"Evening," he said, when he found her, her parents, and Aaron sitting out on the back patio. Morgan had a worried look on her face, but that was her normal look when she was around her family. Leaning down, he gave Morgan a kiss before sitting next to her. "Did I forget we were doing dinner?" he asked casually.

"No, my parents and Aaron just stopped by to talk... about Ann's and Theresa's case. They've just been to the station to answer some questions." Morgan kept her eyes on her parents.

"Oh?" Liam asked with a slight frown. "And they came all this way to tell you about it?"

"No, they came here to ask me—"

"To stand with her family," Thomas said firmly.

"To lie to the police," Morgan countered.

"Lie?" Liam frowned, turning his attention to Thomas. "Lie about what?"

"This doesn't concern you," Thomas growled out.

"Seeing as you're in my home, asking my wife to lie to the police—which, by the way, is a felony—then yes, I'd say it does concern me," Liam replied quickly.

"We're not asking her to lie," Victoria added quickly. "We're just... getting our stories straight."

"About?" Liam's patience was wearing thin.

"When I left the house," Morgan answered. "Apparently, they are under the assumption I left the evening Ann was murdered," Morgan answered.

"You didn't, it was a couple days before," Liam replied.

"I know." Morgan nodded. "But apparently, things will be better for"—she lifted her hands and air-quoted—"the family if I agree that I did."

"How so?" Liam asked Thomas.

"It looks bad for Morgan," he answered. Liam took a moment and then started laughing.

"How in god's name does it look bad for my wife to leave the house where a murder happened a few days before it actually happened?" Liam asked between laughs.

"You wouldn't understand." Aaron spoke up for the first time.

"Oh, he does speak," Liam joked. "I suppose now you care you have a sister?"

"Fuck off." Aaron stood up and stormed inside.

Morgan touched Liam's hand. "They believe the press will use this to blame one of them. If I, as an invalid, agree that they were with me, caring for me while poor Ann was being murdered..." She dropped off with a wave of her hand while he filled in the rest.

"No, sorry," Liam said firmly. He glanced down at Morgan, who nodded in agreement.

"I won't lie," she told her parents firmly.

"You have to. At this point, we've already told the detective..." her mother started.

"What?" Morgan asked, anger lacing her voice.

"That you were still at home," her mother finished. "So, you see, you simply have to go along with our story or... well, as Liam pointed out..."

"It's not like your husband doesn't have a pocketful of lawyers who can bail him out and make this disappear," Liam added dryly.

"This is different. This is a big deal. It's murder," Thomas said between clenched teeth.

Liam wanted to point out that several DUIs and supposedly raping a teenager was a big deal too, but he held his tongue.

"I've heard enough. Morgan has made up her mind." Liam stood up. "Now, if you don't mind, I'll walk you out."

## CHAPTER TWENTY-ONE

*I would rather walk with a friend in the dark, than alone in the light.*
**Helen Keller**

The day after her parents' visit, Liam called her shortly after leaving for work that morning to tell her what the police had found out from her car's computer system.

It had taken some time for her to register that she hadn't been a specific target but just a random victim in someone's larger scheme.

That knowledge somehow put a damper on her mood for the day and by the time Grayson showed up for her therapy, she was achy and just wanted to be alone. She did not feel like chatting with the hunk.

"You're in a mood today," Grayson said when she tossed the ball down after getting frustrated that she couldn't spin it the way he'd requested.

"I'm fine," she lied.

"Problems?" he asked. He glanced around. "Marriage problems?"

"No," she answered, not really wanting to go into detail with the man. After all, even though he'd been her physical therapist for the past few months, she still didn't know him well enough to lay her problems on him.

Grayson moved closer and took her left hand in his and started rubbing her wrists. It wasn't as if he'd never done just that before. Her therapy called for him to examine her progress. But this time, she focused on it and felt slightly uncomfortable.

"You know, part of healing includes opening up to people," he said softly, his eyes slowly running over her face.

She felt a tightness in her chest and wished to pull away. Then she felt silly because it was probably all due to the mood that she was in. What she wanted to do was kick something, or better yet, punch something.

Ryder had been working with her in the boxing ring before her accident. She remembered she'd been damn good at it too and had enjoyed boxing more than any other activity she'd ever tried before.

"Thanks, but no thanks. I guess it's just the rain," she said with a shrug. When she'd woken, the sky had been gray and light rain had soaked everything outside.

She'd always enjoyed the sound of rain, but now it was putting her on edge for some reason.

Grayson's hands moved up to her elbow as he continued to rub her sore muscles. It felt good, but at the same time, she wished he'd stop. She didn't want to be touched at the moment. Not by him, at any rate.

"You're really tense. Maybe your massage therapist isn't doing a good enough job. If you want..." He leaned even closer, his hands going to her upper arm. The back of his fingers brushed her breast slightly.

She couldn't help it—she jumped and leaned back.

"Thanks, but I'm good." She noticed that his hands hadn't released her.

"Morgan, I wouldn't lie to you," he said, his eyes locked on hers.

"Okay," she said slowly. In all the time he'd worked with her, they'd only had a handful of personal conversations.

"So don't lie to me." His hands tightened slightly around her arm. Not uncomfortably so, but enough for her to notice.

"I'm not," she said cautiously.

He leaned ever so slightly towards her, enough that she could feel his breath on her face. She counted her heartbeats, prepared to jerk back if she needed.

Then the moment passed. He leaned back and said, "You're not doing your exercises."

She released the breath she'd been holding and groaned. "Okay, so I forgot this past week."

Almost an hour after Grayson left, detectives Rhodes and Carson knocked on their door.

Since Liam was at work, she was left to handle the two officers on her own. She'd made up her mind to tell them the truth, no matter what.

"If you don't mind, we can sit in here." She showed them into the lounge. "Can I have Lynda get you something to drink?" she asked them both.

"I won't say no to a water," Detective Carson answered. "I forgot my bottle at the office." Lynda disappeared quickly to get them some water.

"I think you know why we're here," Detective Rhodes started. "We had your parents in for questioning yesterday about Miss Phillips's and Miss Smith's murders."

"Yes, they stopped by after they left your office," she answered.

"Right." Rhodes nodded. "It's just a formality, but can we confirm with you that you were on the premises the night in question?"

"I wasn't," Morgan said firmly.

"I'm sorry?" Rhodes frowned. "You... weren't what?"

"On the premises. I returned home here two days before Ann was murdered," she clarified.

The two officers were quiet. "Your husband can confirm this?" Rhodes asked.

"He doesn't need to," Lynda said as she stepped back into the room. "I was here. I will confirm it. Mrs. Taylor returned home on the tenth, as she's just told you."

Rhodes jotted something down in his notepad. "Your parents claimed..."

"Yes, I'm well aware of what they've told you," Morgan said with a sigh. "However, they were mistaken."

"Right." Rhodes nodded. "Do you, by any chance, know where your father was on the night of the twelfth?"

"No, if he wasn't at home, I would assume he was at the country club," she answered dryly.

"And your brother Aaron?" Carson asked.

"Before nine at night?" She shrugged. "After, most likely at his club."

"Right." Rhodes wrote something else down. "Just to confirm, you were not at your parents' house on the night of the twelfth, nor were you with your father or brother during these times?"

"Correct," she answered with a frown. "What about my mother?"

"Your mother was having dinner with a friend," Carson answered. "We've confirmed with the friend already."

"A friend? Who, if I may ask?" Morgan said.

Rhodes flipped a couple pages on his notepad. "Kimber

Lafyette." Morgan felt her entire face heat. "Is there a problem?" Rhodes asked.

"No," Morgan lied. "I'm just... tired. I had physical therapy earlier today. I'm due for a pain pill and rest." She stood up, relying heavily on her crutch as she walked the two detectives to the door.

"We appreciate your time," Rhodes said as he stepped outside. "If we have any further questions—"

"You know where to find me," she interjected.

The two officers nodded and then left.

"Are you okay, Miss?" Lynda asked.

"Yes, I'm going to head up and rest." She headed for the elevator.

Once upstairs, she pulled off her shoes, removed her boot, and lay down on the bed.

How could her parents put her in such a position? Why would they even need to lie about where they'd been while Ann had been murdered?

They had told her that following morning that they'd all been home. Well, except Aaron. Morgan remembered him coming in the house, high. She'd assumed he'd been at the nightclub all night.

At this point, she didn't even know what time Ann had been murdered. Was it before Aaron had left to go to the club? Before her father came home from the country club?

Obviously, it was during the time her mother had been supposedly having dinner with Morgan's best friend. Why hadn't Kimber told her this earlier that day when she'd been on the phone with her?

What in the hell was going on? The only person in her life that she could trust completely was Liam. Which is why she'd fallen for him so early on. He'd been honest with her, probably the first person who had been.

Sure, her three besties were great and all, but Morgan had learned in the past few years that the moment she turned her back, none of them would think twice about stabbing her. Which is why she'd enjoyed moving out of town to Liam's place when they started dating, far from the craziness that was her family and close circle of friends.

At that point in her life, she had been so tired of the moronic merry-go-round. Liam was the welcomed reprieve. The savior she'd needed. Not only had he been the knight in shining armor, but he'd also been a breath of fresh air after a long journey under the sea.

Being told the truth and learning to trust someone hadn't come easy. Yet, he'd broken through the labyrinth of traps that she'd carefully built up over the years.

Gaining her memories back had only shown her just how far she'd grown in the past two years. Back then, she would have easily allowed her family and friends to manipulate her. If Liam hadn't come into her life, she would have done what her parents had asked of her and actually lied to the police for them. She'd been blind back then to the crazy lives they lived and hid from prying eyes.

She knew for a fact that her father had multiple lovers and that, as of last year, so did her mother. And while she hadn't technically known if Aaron was doing drugs, she'd had her suspicions. She'd warned him about opening a nightclub. Not that it wasn't a sound investment of his inheritance, but she knew that being around that sort of scene wouldn't be good for someone with his... character.

She'd also remembered that Kimber had hooked up a couple times with her brother. She didn't know if they knew that she was on to them, but she'd seen Kimber coming out of Aaron's room one morning and had kept that knowledge to herself. After all, she didn't think it was worth ruining her friendship over. Besides, Kimber could take care of herself.

She was still lying down when Liam came home from work. He'd woken her up when he sat on the side of the bed and ran his hands over her shoulder, rubbing some of the tension away with a simple touch.

"Hey, how are you feeling?" he whispered.

"Much better now that I've had a nap."

"Lynda told me that the police were here." Liam shifted a little closer to her.

"Hm." She nodded. "I stuck with the truth."

"Of course, you did," he said easily. "Asking you to lie for them was wrong."

She smiled up at him. "I wish they had a moral compass like yours."

He chuckled. "The rain cleared up. How about we head downstairs and watch the sunset while we eat dinner? Maybe take a dip after?"

"Sounds good." She put her boot back on, and he helped her get up.

They sat out on the back patio, watching the sunset as they ate lasagna. Liam filled her in on what had happened at work and how the board took the news.

She remembered that Liam hadn't liked Dave from the moment Liam had gone back to work at ESP. She knew that the man being involved with the hack was like a bow on top of the best present Liam could have asked for.

He practically laughed all the way through dinner as he retold the story.

"You really didn't like this guy, huh?" she asked him when he was done retelling how the man had reacted.

"The man had a knack for getting under my skin," Liam admitted. "You know the type. No matter how hard you try to get along with them..." He shook his head. "There's just always something they do that bugs you."

She thought about Grayson for some reason. Even though the man was drop-dead gorgeous and her first impressions of him had been good... the longer she worked with him, the more something about him just didn't sit right. It was obvious he was helping her—she could now move her left arm more than she could when she'd gotten her cast removed.

"Yeah, I know the type. So what happens now?" she asked.

"Now the specialty team works with the cops and comes up with the proof to prosecute Dave and the rest."

"The rest?"

"There were eight other employees that had the file on their systems and were involved in the hack," Liam answered.

"Eight?" she balked. "Why? Why would anyone put their career on the line for something like that?"

Liam looked at her as if he hadn't thought to ask that question himself.

"I should have had you helping out a lot earlier." He pulled out his phone and she waited as he sent off a text.

"What's going on?" she asked when he continued typing to someone.

"I'm having Roy look into the personal finances of the eight people involved." He glanced up at her and smiled. "To find an answer to your question."

"You think it was for money?" she asked.

He shrugged. "Why else?"

She tucked her left leg up and rested her elbow on it as she looked out over the sky as the sun cast bright colors over the Pacific. "Well, threats against one's family or to expose personal secrets are always reasons on those cop shows you like to watch."

"Right." He nodded and sent another text. "What else?"

"Power. The promise of it."

"That might have been Dave's motive," Liam nodded as he typed again.

"Then there's just ego and crazy people," she said with a shrug.

"True. You're really good at this."

She chuckled. "I'm remembering how much I like to make lists and organize things."

Liam glanced up and smiled at her. "I love that about you."

"It worked out between us because you're a neat freak too."

"I'm a minimalist," he corrected with a smile.

"I remember. You had a sofa and a bed when I moved in here," she joked.

"I had more than that," he replied with a laugh. "Still, you did a wonderful job turning this place into a home."

"We did," she corrected.

"Now we just need to fill it." He took her hand in his. "In case you don't remember, you wanted to fill all four bedrooms in the main house."

She felt her heart flutter and her body heat. "I remember."

"We could always head upstairs. You know, to get started on that goal."

"Or" she said, as she slid into his lap, "we could just…" She reached down and started rubbing him, enjoying the way he grew hard against her palm. "Start right here," she purred as she kissed him.

# CHAPTER TWENTY-TWO

*The issue is now clear. It is between light and darkness, and
everyone must choose his side.*
**G.K. Chesterton**

Work seemed to go more smoothly after Dave was removed from the office. Since there wasn't an immediate threat looming over him, Liam returned to only going into the office twice a week. He spent the other three days working in his home office.

Rebecca updated him occasionally on what the legal team had found but, for the most part, there hadn't been anything new.

Of course, the news of the breach had been leaked to the press, which meant that he'd been called in to do several interviews.

In most of them, he'd been asked not only about the hack but about Morgan and her recovery. When he was asked to comment on the connection between the hack and Morgan's car accident, he knew that someone on the board or the IT team had leaked the details. He doubted the police would give away such details on an open investigation.

Thanks to Morgan's idea, Roy and the other detectives were looking into every detail of the lives of the eight people involved—financial, personal, and professional. One way or another, the police were going to get to the bottom of why and how the hack had happened.

It was actually strange. On days Liam went into the office, he half expected to walk in on Dave sitting behind his desk. Whenever he remembered where the man was, he smiled at the irony. The man had wanted to be CEO and now he would never work at ESP again.

Since Dave's removal, everyone else around the office seemed to be in better spirits. No one was worried the man was going to jump down their throats or threaten their careers for the smallest infraction.

Dave had always used his position on the board to get what he wanted. If rumors could be believed, he'd pressured certain women in the office to sleep with him.

Those rumors were flowing now that Dave was out of the picture. More and more of the hell the man had caused around the workplace was coming to light.

Several employees had even visited HR and filed official complaints. There were rumors that some of the women just wanted money, but still, each case was handled as if the allegations were true.

With his career going more smoothly and his personal life at an all-time high, the last thing he'd expected was to receive a call that would change everything.

He'd been working in his home office after having spent a wonderful lunch with Morgan out by the pool. Even though it was showering outside, they'd sat under the covered porch and enjoyed the warm weather and the smell of everything being washed cleaned by the rain.

He'd returned to work and had been answering a few emails when his phone rang.

"Is this Liam Taylor?" a woman's voice asked.

"Yes, this is Liam."

"Oh, I hadn't expected to get you..." she said quickly. "I... um... My name is Laura, Laura Taylor."

Liam froze and his hand shook. He'd seen that name once before on a document that he'd found when he, Ryder, and Sean had snuck into the main office at the orphanage and had looked into their files.

"Do you know who I am?" she asked when he didn't say anything.

"Yes," he said softly.

"Good." The woman sighed. "I... was able to track you down after reading the recent news article. I knew who you were the moment I saw the picture on the cover."

"What do you want?" he asked, his temper somehow sneaking into his tone.

"I thought..." Laura said, not seeming to notice his anger. "That maybe we could meet?"

"No," he answered quickly. How many times had he asked himself what he would do if he ever came face to face with either of his parents? How many childhood dreams had him running into the waiting arms of parents who loved him and somehow had just... misplaced him? In those dreams, it had never been their fault that they had given him up. There had always been some unforeseen force, some villain who had taken him away from them. But then he'd grown up.

"No?" she asked, and he heard a sniffle.

"No," he repeated clearly. "I'm not open to that idea."

"Oh, I... guess... I thought..."

"What? That I would welcome someone into my life that threw me away as a helpless child?" he asked, standing up. He felt the need to pace and walked back and forth between his desk and the door. "I don't need the toxic relationship that I know will come from meeting you."

"I... I'm dying," she said, and he couldn't tell if it was the truth or just a manipulation tactic.

"We all are. It's called life," he said and, before she could respond, he hung up.

He felt like throwing the phone, but instead tucked it back into his pocket. There was more than two hours' worth of work left to do that day, but instead, he sent a message to Cheryl telling her he was clocking out and that something personal had come up.

She instantly replied that she hoped everything was okay and would redirect his calls to the answering service.

Since he didn't want the negativity to influence Morgan, he sent her a message telling her he was heading to the gym to spar with Ryder.

He'd tell her about the call later. But for now, it was his to own. His to work out. His to punch out of something or someone.

Morgan sent a message a few moments after he'd loaded his gym bag into the car.

"Okay, have fun. The squad is coming over tonight anyway."

He texted back, "Have fun. I'll be back late."

She sent him a smile emoji followed by a funny cat GIF, which had him smiling and then laughing. Damn, even when he was pissed at the world, she could still get him to smile.

As he drove into town, he played over the conversation

with Laura, and the desire to punch something surfaced again.

When he stepped into the gym, he knew just who to punch. Seeing Sean yelling at Ryder almost sent him into a rage.

First off, he hadn't seen the man in almost five years. Second, he was yelling at Ryder.

Dumping his bag, he flew across the room and had Sean by the shirt and pinned up against the wall in less than ten seconds.

"Don't kill him," Ryder was yelling in his ear as he tried to peel Liam's fingers from Sean's shirt.

"Why the hell shouldn't I?" Liam growled. "Give me one goddamned reason why I shouldn't."

"Because I asked him to stop by," Ryder answered.

"So?" Liam asked, not taking his eyes off Sean, who was glaring at Liam.

Liam had always been taller and broader than Sean. Not that Sean was a wimp, but it was extremely obvious that in the past few years, Sean hadn't hit the gym or exercised regularly at all. The man was downright stalky.

"So, if you kill him, my insurance rates are going to go through the roof," Ryder joked. "Besides, he was just leaving. Weren't you, Sean?"

"Yeah, right," Sean hissed, jerking Liam's hands from his shirt.

Liam stepped back as he dropped his arms to his side. "Don't come back here. Invited or not," he warned.

"What the fuck did I ever do to you?" Sean spat back.

"You know damned well what," Liam hissed. He pointed towards the door.

Sean was thankfully smart enough to leave without another word.

"Wanna tell me what that was all about?" Ryder asked, turning towards him.

"You first. Why would you invite him here? How did you even get ahold of him?" Liam asked.

Ryder sighed and then motioned towards the boxing ring. "Step into my office."

"Sure," Liam answered. He walked over to pick up his bag.

Ten minutes later, the pair of them were dancing around one another in the ring.

"So?" he asked after Ryder got in the first punch.

"So, I got a call yesterday," Ryder said as Liam ducked and dodged the next punch.

"From?" he asked.

"My mother," Ryder said just as he swung out. Liam was so shocked that he forgot to dodge the blow and took the hit right to the jaw, sending him sprawling onto his ass in the middle of the ring.

It took almost a full minute for Liam to get his senses back. When he did, Ryder was kneeling in front of him holding up what appeared to be two fingers.

"How many?" Ryder asked.

"Did you say your mother?" he asked, instead of answering him.

"Yeah." Ryder sighed as he rested on his knees.

"I just got a call from someone claiming to be *my* mother. Laura Taylor," he replied. Somehow just saying the name out loud had his temper growing.

"Yeah, I thought so." Ryder held out his hand and helped Liam to his feet. "Before you go seeing red again, I don't think the woman who claimed to be Amahle Tripp was my real mother."

"You don't?" Liam frowned. "What makes you say

that?"

"Because the woman may have had the right name, but her story was all wrong." Ryder sighed.

"I'm not following you." Liam walked over and grabbed his bottled water and took a long sip.

"It's sort of complicated." Ryder leaned on the ropes. "Remember back when we were ten or eleven…" He tilted his head. "When we broke into the office and read through our files?"

"Yeah." Liam nodded.

"Well, I didn't tell you or Sean then, but the details of my parents abandoning me were wrong in my file." Ryder shrugged.

"They were?" Liam tried to remember his friend's story but couldn't. Hell, he hadn't even remembered that Ryder's mother's name was Amahle.

"Yeah. In my file, it said that I'd been abandoned at the train station." Ryder looked off over the gym.

"And?" Liam asked.

"It was a bus station." He turned to Liam. "I remember it because my mother and I had taken the bus there, and she didn't have enough money for two tickets to Chicago. She told me to sit there and wait while she ran to the bathroom. Only, I watched her get on the bus and leave me."

"Holy shit." Liam sighed.

"Yeah. I was five. What kind of woman leaves a five-year-old at a bus station?"

Ryder shrugged. "A bastard of a woman." He slapped his friend's shoulder.

"Yeah, right. Well, when this woman called, after she told me who she was, she said she was so sorry for leaving me at the train station." Ryder nodded.

"So, you knew she was a fake. I guess I didn't even ask

Laura—or the woman claiming to be her, at any rate—any questions. Then again, I was only a few weeks old when I was found, so I wouldn't have remembered shit anyway."

"Right, and since I know your memory is shit... No offense."

"None taken." Liam smiled. "What's your name again?"

Ryder pushed his shoulder and chuckled.

"I knew that the only other person who had seen that bullshit story had a photographic memory," Ryder added.

"Shit," Liam groaned. "Sean."

Ryder nodded. "Yup. So I hunted down his number and called to confront him. Only he shows up claiming he got a call from his dear old mother too. Only he met the bitch."

"And?" Liam asked.

"She gave him the whole sob story. Told him she was sorry. Then he claims he gave her ten grand, and she promised to pay him back. Only, the number she called from isn't working any longer," Ryder said.

"You think he got scammed too?" Liam asked.

"Hell no. I think Sean is playing a long game. I think his broke ass came up with a way to get back at us and make a little dough while he was at it. I'd bet you the gym that if you met the woman claiming to be your mother, that it would be a hell of a lot more than ten grand."

"Yeah, I bet you're right," Liam agreed.

"So, we both dodged that bullet." Ryder chuckled.

"I should have knocked his head right off his shoulders," Liam added.

Ryder laughed again. "You can't even dodge a right hook."

Liam laughed. "I can when I'm not distracted."

Ryder's eyebrow rose. "Oh yeah? Care to put a friendly wager on it?"

"Hell yes. Our usual?" Liam asked, slapping his gloves to Ryder's.

"You're going to owe me a Coke," Ryder warned.

"Not if I win," Liam teased back as they started circling each other in the ring again.

Liam's mood was vastly improved as he pulled back into his garage shortly after midnight. After losing to Ryder, again, they'd gone out for drinks. Their idea of a good time was sodas and a few rounds of pool at the bar down the street from the gym.

He hadn't meant to stay out so late, but Morgan had sent him a text that the squad was staying the night since they'd opened a few bottles of wine.

When he made his way into the house, he spotted a leg —not Morgan's—flung over the back of the sofa in the living room.

Seeing the empty wine bottles, he chuckled as he tip-toed through the dark house. Whoever was passed out on the sofa wasn't the only one who'd fallen asleep outside of a bedroom.

He assumed it was Kimber who was face-planted on the sofa by the stairs, and Morgan was half lying, half sitting on the stairs with her head leaning against the railing.

The fact that his wife was lightly snoring had him smiling. Setting his gym bag down, he lifted her easily into his arms and chuckled when she said. "Oh, my handsome husband is finally home."

"I am indeed," he said softly. He placed a kiss on her forehead. "Did you have fun?"

"Mmm-hmm," she said, and then she started snoring again. But when he laid her down in the bed, her eyes popped opened and focused on his face. "You have a black eye." She reached up and touched his cheek. "Who punched you?"

"Don't worry, I punched back," he answered with a chuckle.

"Good." She sighed. "My friends think you're sexy," she said with a giggle.

"Yeah, I've heard that before." He chuckled as he kicked off his shoes and pulled off his clothes. When Morgan sighed loudly, he glanced at her.

"I think you're sexy," she said with a smile.

"Oh?" He sat on the edge of the bed and ran his hands over her hips. He was just about to peel the things off her when the house alarm started going off. They both jumped.

"Stay here," he warned as he pulled his pants back on and rushed downstairs. He heard Morgan calling after him, but he didn't stop until he reached the front door, which was wide open.

"Sorry," Kimber said, as she stood in the doorway. "I was sneaking out for a smoke." She held up her hands and he saw the cigarette and lighter.

"It's okay." He walked over to punch in the security code, then answered the call from the company and told them everything was fine, giving them the security password.

"Sorry again," Kimber said, as she lit the cigarette just outside the front door. Liam noticed that she was swaying slightly.

"Is everything okay?" Morgan called down from the stair railing.

"Yes, Kimber needed a smoke," he replied.

"Classic Kimber," Morgan called down. Kimber giggled until she almost fell over.

"I'll be up soon," he called back to Morgan. "I'll lock up once she's done."

"M-kay," Morgan answered.

"I'm really sorry." Kimber sighed, and he watched her run her eyes over his chest. "I hope I didn't... interrupt anything."

"No." He leaned against the door frame, crossing his arms over his chest. He'd been half-naked around Morgan's friends plenty of times. After all, they'd had loads of pool parties at the house. He knew that, out of all of her friends, Kimber was the one that held her liquor the best. For her to be swaying this much, she must be really blitzed.

"Oh good," she said, almost falling over and reaching out to hold onto his arm. "I'd hate for you to go..." Her hand snaked down and, before he could stop her, she grabbed his cock. "Un-fulfilled."

This wasn't the first time a drunk Kimber had hit on him. Normally, he and Morgan blew it off since they knew that's how she was. She didn't really mean anything by it. At least that's what they told themselves.

He jerked her arm away and stepped back. "I think you're done for the night." He took the cigarette from her and tossed it into the rocks. Then he took her arm and helped her back inside. "You can find your own way to your room." He locked up and turned the security system back on.

"Oh, boo," she said with a slight whine. "I was just trying to have some fun."

"Have it with someone who's interested." He started walking towards the stairs, and she followed him. He stepped aside so she could go up them first. When they reached the top, he expected Kimber to head off to one of the guest rooms, but at the top of the stairs, Kimber made a move towards him. Once again, he easily sidestepped her.

"Come on," she purred. "You've thought about what it would be like, being with me."

"Not even once," he told her truthfully.

He turned and was almost across the sitting room just outside his bedroom when one of the glass vases that sat on a small table shattered at his feet.

"Fuck off," Kimber said, then she rushed down the hallway towards a guest room.

Thankfully, the noise didn't wake anyone up, especially Morgan, who was fast asleep when he returned to their room after cleaning up the glass.

When he climbed into bed next to Morgan, he pulled her into his arms, careful not to jostle her broken leg, and buried his face into her hair. This was home. This is where he wanted to be. Always.

# CHAPTER TWENTY-THREE

*I will love the light for it shows me the way, yet I will endure
the darkness because
it shows me the stars.*
**Og Mandino**

Morgan woke with a classic too-much-wine-last-night headache. Still, feeling Liam's strong arms wrapped around her made everything feel better.

"There she is," he said with a slight yawn. "How are you feeling? Headache?"

She nodded, not wanting to speak.

"How about I make your favorite for breakfast?" he asked.

Banana pancakes with whipped cream and caramel sauce. Just the thought of them had her stomach growling.

Liam chuckled. "I'll take that as a yes."

She nodded but stopped him from moving. "One more minute." She sighed.

"Okay. Oh, before you hear it from her, Kimber hit on me last night."

"Did you let her down gracefully?" Morgan asked.

"Like always."

Morgan reached up and ran her hand over his chest. "Did you know that Kimber and my brother had a thing?"

"That is a surprise," he admitted. "Is it serious?"

"She denied it, but I've known for a while," Morgan said, still running her hands over him.

"Well, we both know how she gets when she's drunk," Liam said.

"Yeah." Her stomach growled again. She wanted to spend the morning in bed with him but knew that he would have to go to work in his home office soon and desperately wanted those pancakes. "Okay," she told her stomach, "I'm getting up."

Liam chuckled and rolled out of bed.

"I'm going to shower first." She grabbed her crutch.

"Meet you downstairs," he called out after he pulled on his pants and a shirt.

She took a quick shower, then stepped into her closet to find something to wear. Since it was supposed to be hot later, she pulled on a pair of shorts and a tank top over a swimsuit.

She was just about to leave the closet when she noticed the door to the panic room was slightly opened.

It hadn't been the last time she'd been in the closet, she was sure of it. Walking over, she opened it, glanced inside, and seeing nothing out of place, shut it, thinking that Liam must have needed something inside.

When she walked into the kitchen and sat at the bar, her friends were already sitting there, watching Liam cook. Each of them had a drink in hand.

"Mimosa?" Liam asked her.

"Hair of the dog," Reagan groaned, then she took a sip of her drink.

"Please," she answered.

"We're enjoying watching your husband cook," Leanne added.

"If only he would cook nude," Kimber joked.

"Speaking of which." Morgan nodded as Liam set a drink down in front of her. "I heard you got a handful of my man's junk last night."

Kimber groaned. "Sorry, man," she said to Liam, who chuckled as he shrugged.

"You are the one who walked into a nest of drunk women. You should have known better, being all sexy like you are," Leanne said. "I'm surprised Kimber didn't stuff a few dollars down your pants."

"No, but she did set off our security alarm," Liam added as he flipped a pancake, much to the delight of her friends, who probably would have cheered if they all weren't suffering the same effects as Morgan was.

Liam was used to being teased by the quad squad. From the moment they'd started dating, her friends had been relentless. At first, Liam had seemed embarrassed, but after a while, he had relaxed and even started joking back with them.

He set a plate of pancakes down in front of her, and she felt her entire body melt with the first taste.

"Delicious, as always," she told him. Liam smiled back at her.

"Like you." He leaned in and kissed her.

Her friends groaned. "Get a room," Leanne teased.

"What are your plans for the day?" Liam asked as he turned back to the stove to make more for her friends.

"As little as possible," Morgan answered. "I was thinking of taking a morning swim."

Kimber groaned.

"What?" Morgan asked her.

"Friends don't let friends become recluses. Let's go shopping downtown today. I need a new dress for a party this weekend," Kimber whined.

"Yes, that's a great idea," Reagan chimed in.

"Don't worry, we'll take perfect care of you," Leanne added. "We can even stop at the salon and have Marcus do something with your hair."

"What's wrong with my hair?" Morgan asked, reaching up and touching the long ponytail.

Her three friends glanced at one another. "Nothing," they all said sarcastically at the same time.

Morgan rolled her eyes. "Fine." To be honest, a day out did actually sound good. Since she'd been home, the only place she had gone to was Mastro's that first day. "I'll head up and get dressed after breakfast."

Her friends cheered. The talk turned to the scandal that had rocked Liam's work. The interviews he'd done for several of the papers and news stations were practically on a loop.

She'd enjoyed seeing her husband on the set but what they'd gone through to get him there hadn't been so much fun. Every time she stopped to think about the cause of her accident, her heart started racing.

Liam had told her that the only other person who had been affected by the hack was a woman in her mid-sixties, who apparently had nothing to do with either business. She hadn't been so lucky and had died from her injuries when her car stopped on the freeway right in front of a semi.

It had to be random. She kept telling herself that as she applied makeup and pulled on a blouse and a skirt.

She had to admit, this was the first time since her accident that she had put in the effort for her looks. She'd forgotten how nice it felt to look in the mirror and see herself not looking broken and bruised.

"Wow," Leanne said as she stepped out of the elevator. "You look amazing."

Her friends were all sitting in the living room waiting for her. They had all changed and looked like models, like they normally did. Each of them wore expensive designer clothes. Morgan had a closet full of clothes just like it, but today she'd chosen a simple medium-length flower skirt with a white blouse. Since she only could wear one shoe, she'd gone with a flat sandal.

"Thanks, you guys look... hot," she said, looking at all of them.

Leanne was wearing a pair of silk shorts with a Gucci belt, a matching silk top, and a large white jacket. Together with her Gucci bag, sunglasses, and spiky heeled boots, she could have just stepped off the runway.

Reagan was in a very chic tight white jumper. One of her arms was in a long sleeve while the other shoulder was fully exposed. There was a sleek cut over the breast, allowing the material to twist. She had paired it with her Dolce and Gabbana gold chain belt and heels. Just seeing her friend in the outfit made Morgan feel small and unsexy.

Then there was Kimber. Her Louis Vuitton sleeveless silk skirt and her Dolce and Gabbana thigh-high boots would make any man's or woman's mouth water.

"I should go change..." She started to head back to the elevator.

"No," her friends all said at once, rushing to stop her.

"You're perfect," Leanne said, taking her arm.

"No, I'm not. Compared to you three, I'm... homey." She looked down at the large black boot on her leg.

"You're perfect." Reagan repeated Leanne's words. "Besides needing some work on your hair, I love this outfit."

She allowed them to shuffle her outside and into Kimber's new Porsche Cayenne. They even let her sit in the passenger seat so she didn't have to try to get in the back.

Their first stop was the salon, where she spent over two hours in Marcus's chair. Normally, she would have enjoyed the attention, but all everyone in the salon wanted to hear about was her accident and the IOA hack. By the time she walked out of the salon, with a new style and a few inches less hair, she was starving and tired of talking.

"Let's hit Sudomo's for lunch," Kimber suggested.

"Yes, please," Leanne groaned. "Eating carbs for breakfast always makes me starved for sushi."

"You had half a pancake," Reagan pointed out.

"That's a quarter more than you had," Leanne returned.

Morgan realized she'd eaten three whole pancakes herself. At one point, she'd been like her friends—dressing in designer clothes, watching what she ate, spending most of her time thumbing through social media for the latest trends.

Now, however, she just couldn't get into any of it. What she would rather spend her time on was organizing and designing her home. That and spending her time with Liam. Things that used to matter to her just didn't any longer.

They walked into Sudomo's and were seated out on the patio. Since it was difficult for Morgan to scoot into the booth seat, she sat in a chair beside Kimber while Leanne and Reagan took the seats across from them.

"What's good here?" Morgan asked, looking over the sushi menu. When her three friends remained quiet, she looked up. "What?" she asked when they looked at her funny.

"You've been here like a dozen times," Leanne answered.

"No, I haven't." Morgan glanced around. Nothing looked familiar. She couldn't remember ever being here. The inside seating area was a large room with massive glass garage doors as windows, which were all opened to the street. The patio area had large steel beams overhead with patio lights hanging from them. Long tan booths lined the outside patio walls, with more than a dozen tables and chairs arranged around.

"Yes, you have. We've eaten here with you each time. I think you even brought Liam and Ryder here," Reagan said. "You always get the Sudomo plater."

"I do?" She scanned the menu and found the item and liked that there was a sampling of all of her favorites on it.

"You seriously don't remember being here?" Kimber asked.

"No." She set her menu down as she frowned.

"What other things can't you remember?" Leanne asked, earning chuckles from the rest of them.

"If I knew that," Morgan started with a smile. "I wouldn't be able to tell you."

"I mean, you remember most of the past few years now, unlike when you woke up. Right?" Leanne corrected.

"Yes," Morgan answered. "At least I thought I did." She mentally scanned through her mind. "I guess there's still a few holes."

Her friends schooled her on everything that they could remember happening in the past few years, ranging from social events to celebrity gossip. She remembered most of it, and they filled her in the best they could.

She wasn't all that surprised when they claimed they hung out with her twice a month. Since her accident, and returning home, she'd only seen her friends three times. Even that seemed a little too much for her now.

It wasn't that she didn't like hanging with them, but she felt like she'd changed and they hadn't. It was hard to get excited about the things they did now. She no longer cared who was sleeping with whom, what designer someone wore.

What Morgan was looking forward to probably wouldn't interest them either. Like Liam had mentioned, she wanted a family. She found herself daydreaming about turning the closest guest room into a nursery. She'd even started going through design options and colors.

But the last thing she'd do is tell her friends this. She knew that all of them thought that twenty-six was far too young to ruin your body for a brat.

After they were done eating, her friends continued to gossip, and she zoned out, deep in her own thoughts of starting a family with Liam. She'd lost track of everything and hadn't realized what the flashes were until Leanne gasped and almost dropped her wine glass.

"How dare they come back here," Leanne complained.

Morgan blinked and suddenly realized she was staring down the lenses of more than six cameras. The group of paparazzi stood on the sidewalk just outside the patio, pointing their cameras at her as flashes continued to blind her.

"Come on, let's go." Reagan stood up and helped Morgan stand.

Kimber went to grab Morgan's crutch just as Morgan reached for it. Somehow, Morgan lost her balance. She cried out as she fell face-first onto the floor of the patio as more flashes blinded her.

"We've got you," Leanne said, as she and Reagan each took an arm and helped her stand.

"Here," Kimber said, holding out Morgan's crutches.

"Let's go," Leanne hissed.

Morgan didn't even know if someone had paid their bill. Tears stung her eyes as she hobbled back to Kimber's car. Her knees and hands were scraped up from the fall, and she desperately wanted to go home.

However, Kimber started chatting as if nothing had happened as she drove towards her favorite shops. When she parked on Rodeo Drive, Morgan turned to her friends.

"I think I'm going to get a car and head home," she said, trying not to sound pathetic.

"No," all three of her friends groaned.

"Don't let a few photographers ruin today," Kimber whined.

"I'm not. I'm just tired. You three go on. Have fun." She smiled, holding in her pain and emotions as best she could.

"Are you sure?" Kimber asked, sticking her bottom lip out.

"Yeah, I've already arranged for a ride," she lied as she got out of the car. "It'll be here soon."

"Well, I still need a dress for my event." Kimber sighed as she looked at the other two.

Morgan shifted her bag so that she could hug her friends. "Thanks for today. I needed it," she lied.

After hugging all of her friends, she watched them stroll down the street, arm in arm, and instantly felt relieved.

Pulling out her phone, she tried to log into the Uber app, only to realize that she didn't know her password. After she reset it, it said that her credit card had expired. As she was putting in the new number, trying to balance her phone, her purse, and her credit card all while standing on one leg, a car horn honked at her.

Glancing up, she was slightly relieved to see Grayson pulling up beside Kimber's car.

"Morgan?" Grayson said after he rolled his window down. "Is everything okay?"

"Yes." She smiled.

"You're bleeding." He nodded and she looked down to see that she was indeed dripping blood down her legs from her scraped knees.

"I fell," she admitted as her eyes stung. Suddenly, to her horror, tears started flowing down her cheeks.

She should have called Liam. Why had she bothered with the stupid car app? Maybe because she didn't want to feel like she needed him to rescue her all of the time. Maybe because she didn't want her friends to see him picking her up.

Either way, it was too late now. Grayson was by her side, helping her over to his car.

She was sitting inside the air-conditioned car before she realized it. Then she instantly hated herself for the weakness.

"I'm okay," she said to him when he got in behind the wheel.

"Sure you are," he said with a grin. "Where are you headed?"

"Home," she said, her breath hitching. "I was trying to get a car, but my credit card had expired and... Do you know how hard it is to enter your numbers while standing on a sidewalk on one foot while balancing your phone and a credit card?"

He chuckled. "No, but I saw it firsthand," he said as the

car started moving. "How'd you get down here? Did Liam drop you off?"

"No, I was out with my friends. We went to lunch and then... I fell and they went off shopping," she dropped off, not wanting to rehash the last hour. "Why are you down here?"

He was silent for a moment before answering. "I have a client not far from here." He turned towards her house.

"Oh, right." She relaxed back, holding her phone tightly in her hands. She should call Liam. Tell him what happened. Instead, she allowed the coolness of the car and the humming of the powerful engine to soothe her until her eyelids felt heavy and her head dropped to the side.

Thankfully, she woke moments before Grayson pulled into the long driveway.

"Sorry, I didn't mean to wake you." He smiled over at her.

"I... I'm sorry I fell asleep." She groaned.

"Getting out for the first time after something as traumatic as you've been through can wear you out," he said easily. "You should get some rest. I can come in and look at those cuts?" he offered.

"No, that's okay," she said as he drove up to the house. Liam stood outside the front doors, and the look on his face made her wince. She should have called him or texted him about what had happened. "Thanks," she told Grayson as she gathered her things and tried to quickly get out of his car.

Liam was there, helping her. She felt him tense the moment he noticed the dried blood on her hands and knees.

"What the..." he growled, then he looked up at Grayson, who had gotten out of his car to help.

"I fell during lunch," she said quickly. "Grayson was in

the area and spotted me trying to get a car and offered me a ride home." Her statement basically came out as one long word as she dug her fingernails into Liam's arms to keep him from rushing across the car and killing Grayson. "I'm tired and hurt," she said with a sigh. "And I want to go in and shower."

Liam glanced down at her, then lifted her in his arms in one quick swoop. Without giving Grayson a backwards glance, he carried her inside.

"You should have called me," he growled as he took the stairs two at a time.

"I... was going to, but then I fell asleep in the car on the way back," she admitted.

Liam looked down at her, worry replacing the anger in his eyes.

"I'm sorry," she said as more tears rolled down her cheeks. "I should have called." She laid her head on his shoulder and let the tears flow.

# CHAPTER TWENTY-FOUR

*Every human being is a mixture of light and darkness, trust
and fear, love and hate.*
**Jean Vanier**

There wasn't a lot in life that could instantly stop Liam's anger. Morgan's tears were one of them. He carried her into the bathroom, sat on the bench, and held onto her until her tears dried up.

"Let me look at those cuts," he said softly.

She held out her hand, then tossed her purse down when she realized she was still holding it.

Her palms were scraped up, but nothing too bad. He picked a few pebbles out of her skin without her making a fuss.

Then he set her on the bench and lifted the hem of her skirt to see her knees.

They were bloody and raw. Blood had dripped down her legs to her ankles and had dried.

"What happened?" he asked.

"We went to this place called Sudomo's," she started.

"You took us there once," he said as he went to get the first aid kit. "And?"

"I don't remember." She shook her head. "After we were done eating, there were these photographers. They came out of nowhere and blinded me with their flashes."

His hand tightened on the bottle of antiseptic. "Did they hurt you?"

"No, I was going to get up and reached..." She started and then stopped as she frowned.

"What?" he asked, starting to clean the cuts gently.

Morgan looked up at him. "I was reaching for my crutches, and then Kimber..." She shook her head. "I think she tripped me on purpose."

"What?" he asked, stilling.

She shook her head and then sighed. "I think I'm just tired. I reached for the crutches, and she moved to hand them to me." She closed her eyes and then winced when he removed a pebble from her skin. "I fell right in front of the paparazzi. I'm sure it will be all over the news tonight." She groaned.

"Did you hurt your leg, other than landing on your knees and hands?" he asked as he continued to work to clean her skin.

"No, thankfully. I think the fall in the shower taught me how to fall."

He felt her shiver.

She finished with a weak smile. "Just bruised my skin and my ego."

"And then your friends just left you on the street for anyone to pick up?" he asked, feeling his anger return.

"No, I convinced them I'd already arranged for a car.

They wanted to go shopping. I wanted to come home." She smiled at him, then laid her hand on his cheek. "Besides, I was tired and hurting."

"Why didn't you call me?" he asked, the hurt resurfacing that she hadn't thought to do so when she'd been hurt.

"Pride. I'd mentioned to my friends that I'd called for a car and well... I wanted to be independent." She sighed heavily. "Then I forgot my password for Uber and after I reset it, it said my card had expired. I was hot, tired, hurt, and trying to balance on one leg while I put in my new number."

He stopped working on her knee and took her hand. "That's when you should have called me."

"Yeah, you're right. But then Grayson pulled up and... I lost it." She rolled her eyes. "Trust me, after seeing me cry and then fall asleep in his car, I doubt you have to worry about Grayson having the hots for me any longer," she said with a laugh.

"Morgan." He laid his hands on her legs. "You are stunning even when you're crying or sleeping." When more tears pooled in her eyes, he pulled her close and held onto her. "Come on, I'll finish this up while you lie down." He lifted her in his arms and carried her to the bed, where he gently laid her down.

"I didn't mean to interrupt your work," she said as he finished cleaning her cuts.

"You didn't." He realized that he had yet to tell her about the call he'd received yesterday, or what he and Ryder had found out about Sean. Hell, he hadn't even told her last night that he'd seen Sean.

While he finished cleaning her, he told her everything,

including the call from a woman claiming to be his mother. She seemed excited at first until he mentioned what had happened to Ryder and Sean.

"Do you really think that Sean was behind the call?" she asked as he covered her with a blanket and started running his hands over her arms. He could see that she was tired and almost asleep as he talked.

"I wouldn't put it past him. Remember, in the first year after I sold my company, he sued me, claiming that I knew about the potential deal with IOA before I bought him out." Liam sighed, remembering how he and Ryder had felt betrayed by Sean. It had been like losing a brother. When Ryder had stuck up for Liam, Sean had turned on him as well. "Even after the case was thrown out, he never stopped trying to convince everyone that I'd cheated him somehow."

"I'm sorry Sean put you and Ryder through this." She held in a yawn.

"Even if it had been my real mother, I wouldn't have met with her," he admitted.

"No?" She opened her eyes again. "Why not?"

"Because I don't have time for anyone who doesn't have time for me. She's the one who left me. She's the one who chose her life over mine." His hand stilled on her hip. He had thought a lot about how he would be as a parent. What kind of father he would be. The last thing he'd do was to put his own needs before those of his kids or his wife.

He smiled down at Morgan when he thought about what kind of mother she would be. Unlike her parents, he could tell that Morgan would be a wonderful mother.

Morgan's hand reached over and tightened around his. "Her loss. My gain." Her words slurred slightly.

He smiled. "Get some rest." He leaned down and brushed his lips across hers.

"Liam, I should have called you," she said before falling fast asleep.

He watched her sleep for a few moments before getting up and taking his laptop over to the sitting area to get back to work.

There were a handful of emails that had come in while he'd stepped away. One of them had the subject line "Payback" and was from an unknown email address.

As with anything suspicious, he opened it but didn't open the attachment. There wasn't a message, and after running scans on the file, he knew that it held a virus. It wasn't the first time he'd received such a blatantly obvious attack. It was, however, the first titled "Payback." He moved the email into the trash and went back to work. Less than an hour later, he received three more, all from different emails but all with the same subject line.

He deleted them, but five minutes later his mailbox was full of the same email.

At first, he received a dozen, then fifty. When it hit a hundred, he shut his system down and gave up for the day. First, however, he sent a text message to Rebecca about the emails and asked her to clean them up and block any others that might come in.

Since Morgan was still resting, he climbed in bed next to her and pulled her into his arms. He'd only meant to close down for a while, but when he woke, it was dark.

Then he realized he was alone in the bed. He went to turn on the light, but it didn't go on. Frowning, he figured that it was probably the lightbulb, but then he noticed everything was dark in the house.

The power being out was odd. In the years he'd lived there, not once had they lost power. Reaching around for his cell phone, he realized he must have left it over in the sitting area.

"Morgan?" he called out, trying to make his way over to the coffee table without walking into anything.

When Morgan didn't answer him, he grew worried and called her name several more times. When he reached the table and found his phone, he turned on the flashlight and looked around. The narrow beam of light barely lit up anything but a foot in front of him, somehow making it even harder to see.

When he noticed Morgan's boot sitting by the bed, where he'd removed it after carrying her in from the bathroom, he panicked and started screaming her name as he raced through the house. But each dark room of the massive home was empty. Morgan was gone.

"Liam." Morgan's soft voice shook him from the nightmare. He came awake with a jerk, then his arms tightened around her as he held on to the most important thing in his life.

After the accident, he'd gone through numerous nights fearing that he would lose her. After all, he'd come so close to it.

"Nightmare?" she asked.

"Yeah." He felt his eyes sting. "You were gone."

"I'm right here," she said against his neck.

"Do you know how many times over the past months I feared I'd lose you?" he asked. "Too many to count." He pulled back and looked at her.

It was dark in the room, but not so dark that he couldn't see her smiling at him.

"You won't lose me." She kissed him.

Just then he realized that he could hear the sound of rain outside. A flash of light had Morgan jumping slightly.

"I guess it's storming," she said nervously as she sat up and hugged her knees to her chest.

"You used to like the rain," he said with a frown as he sat up beside her.

"I... did," she agreed. "Now, it's just... I don't know. It makes me feel uneasy."

He thought about it for a moment. "It was raining the night of your accident."

"It was?" She frowned over at him. "I... still can't remember much about it, other than being upset at you as I got in the car."

He put his arm around her and pulled her close. "I'm sorry..."

"No, don't apologize again." She smiled up at him. "Let's go downstairs and get something to eat." She glanced at the clock. "It's past midnight, and we didn't have dinner."

"I can make us some soup and sandwiches?" he offered. She jumped again when lightning flashed.

"Yes, and maybe some of Lynda's tea to calm my nerves." She reached down and strapped on her boot. "The doctor says I can start walking on my leg soon." She continued talking about her last checkup.

He knew she was talking nervously, most likely to take her mind off the storm outside, as they made their way downstairs in the elevator. Both Lynda and Roy had returned to their own homes since they couldn't stay indefinitely. He had persuaded Lynda to be around the house full time on days he went into the office. He didn't want Morgan to be alone in the place while he was gone.

"It's going to be so good to finally use the stairs. I think I'm gaining weight from all this sitting around. Grayson could tell that I hadn't been doing my exercises," she said as they stepped into the kitchen.

Just hearing the man's name made Liam clench his teeth. Despite all the reasons Liam didn't like the man, he knew that Morgan trusted him. He had come to her rescue earlier that day and had brought her home safe. Maybe he should give the guy a break.

Instead of sitting at the bar or the dining table, they took their food into the television room. Liam lit a fire while she flipped through channels, trying to find something to watch. Morgan stopped on a news station after seeing a picture of Theresa on the screen. Turning the volume up, they listened to the latest report on the murders. There wasn't much new information, other than that they appeared to be connected and the police were doing everything they could to find the killer.

The shock came near the end of the story, when it was leaked that Theresa had been two months pregnant.

Morgan hit mute when the station went to commercial.

"I didn't know she was seeing anyone," Liam said.

"Neither did I. I had always assumed..." She shrugged slightly. "That she was a lesbian."

Liam shifted slightly and picked up his sandwich. "You did? Why? Did she hit on you?"

"No, but she was always extremely friendly to me. You know the type, always trying a little too hard," she explained.

"Sure," he nodded, thinking back to a few employees he'd worked with before he'd married Morgan. Hell, even now he avoided a couple of them around the office. Apparently, they didn't care if he was married or not. In his mind, they were just after his wealth and position, which made them ugly no matter how good-looking they were on the outside.

"I wonder if my parents knew that she was pregnant. I mean, they weren't close, but she did come around the house at least twice a week. Three times when I was there after my accident." Morgan took a sip of the cream of potato soup from the mug. "We're supposed to go to this thing this weekend at the country club."

He released a low groan, and Morgan chuckled.

"I feel the same way, but my mother cornered me the other day when she was over here. She was excited that it would be my first real big outing after the accident." Morgan sighed. "Going to an event in this boot"—she motioned to her leg—"is not my idea of fun."

She reached for her sandwich and stilled. He glanced up and saw why. There on the screen was an image of her sitting at the table at Sudomo's next to Kimber.

Morgan yanked the remote up and unmuted the story, which started mid-sentence.

"...been recovering from the car accident caused by the IOA hack known as the dot slash hack. IOA's security systems are run by a company called Electric Security Platform, which is run by Morgan Davenport's husband, Liam Taylor."

Morgan said, "Morgan Taylor," under her breath, and he smiled and took her hand in his.

"Even though her husband was cleared of any wrongdoing, several employees of ESP have been fired from the company. They have not yet been charged with any crimes. This was Morgan's first social outing and apparently she wasn't quite ready for the limelight."

The still images changed to the scene where Morgan was just starting to stand up. Liam watched in horror as she reached for the crutches that Kimber was holding, only to have her friend move them slightly out of reach. In a flash, Morgan fell forward, landing on her hands and knees.

Leanne and Reagan rushed to help Morgan up, while Kimber stood there, holding the crutches as if the scene was very entertaining.

"She did that on purpose," Morgan said, leaning forward. "I thought..." She shook her head. "Why?" Tears started to fill her eyes and, almost immediately, Morgan's phone rang. Morgan looked down at the screen and, seeing Kimber's number, instantly declined the call and tossed her phone down on the sofa.

"Maybe it's not what it appears," he suggested. "Maybe... she was..." He searched his mind for any reason why her friend would have done something like that but came up blank. To him, the move had been very obvious, and he knew that anyone looking at the scene would have thought so too. Yet the reporter continued on with the story as if Morgan had just taken a tumble on her own.

"Maybe she's trying to explain?" He motioned to her phone that continued to ring.

"I just can't..." Morgan shook her head. "Not tonight."

Reaching over, he picked up her phone and answered it.

"Morgan's resting right now," he said without saying hello.

"Liam, I need to talk to her," Kimber said, and he could hear that she was a little breathless. There was loud music in the background, assuring him that she was out some-where and not at home.

"She's resting," he repeated.

"Did she..." Kimber paused. "Please tell her I need to talk to her. It's about... I didn't mean... Just have her call me," she finally said and hung up.

"Well?" Morgan asked when he set her phone down.

"She wants you to call her," he repeated. "She didn't give me any explanation, but she sounded pretty desperate to talk to you."

Morgan sighed and turned the television to a movie channel, and they watched *Alien* while they finished their meal.

Morgan fell asleep a half hour after finishing her meal. He carried her upstairs once the movie was over. Instead of crawling in bed with her, he searched the internet for what people were saying about the incident.

Most agreed that Kimber had purposely caused Morgan to fall. Others claimed that Morgan had caused the incident to gain attention. There was even a meme splitting people into teams, Team Kimber and Team Morgan.

Hopefully, the entire incident would die down soon. He doubted their friendship could withstand much more. In the past year, Morgan had grown farther and farther from her friends. She'd confided in him that they had grown shallow, and she just didn't have that much in common with them any longer.

The truth was that her friends had been like that since the moment he'd met them. Morgan was different. He'd seen it that very first night.

He'd changed himself since he'd met Morgan. She's made him a better man. He didn't know what he would do without her, which is why his nightmares were filled with scenes of losing her.

He'd lost someone he'd thought of as a brother and it had taken him years to get over it. He couldn't imagine losing the only woman he'd ever loved.

The more he thought about it, the more he realized he

would do anything to ensure her protection. Even if it meant cutting one of her best friends out of their lives.

Kimber had crossed a line. One that no friend should ever cross. He knew it was up to Morgan to forgive her for her actions, but that didn't mean he was going to allow Kimber a second chance at hurting his wife.

---

# CHAPTER TWENTY-FIVE

*Peace and negativity cannot coexist, just as light and darkness cannot coexist.*
**S. N. Goenka**

Morgan avoided Kimber's calls the following day. She even avoided Leanne's and Reagan's calls. She had hoped that the story would go away, but apparently now everyone was taking sides and fighting online about who was to blame.

There was a huge group of people who actually blamed her for falling. Like she wanted the attention.

The video of her falling played almost as many times as stories of their wedding had months after they'd been married. She and Liam had been big news. Her face-planting at a restaurant was somehow bigger news. The twist of her closest friend betraying her was probably the biggest draw.

Kimber was all over the stories. Who was she? Who were her family? Where did she come from? Who was she dating? These were just some of the topics discussed.

Most stories dove deep into the Lafyette family. Her great-grandfather had been an oil tycoon, one of the originals in California's boom. Her family history was filled with Hollywood elites, movie stars, and the rich and extremely famous.

Kimber had, in her teens, dallied in acting. She had connections from Leanne's family, who owned several television stations, and Reagan's family, who were almost all A-listers on the big screen and had been chosen for a handful of commercials and shows.

But then reviews of her acting career had started coming in and all of them labeled her a lemon. Quite literally.

"A sour-faced girl who has the brains and acting skills of a lemon." No one would hire her after that.

Morgan had silently agreed with the reviews. Kimber was no actress. Her lines were relayed, not expressed. Her movements were odd at best.

Not that Morgan was a critic herself, but after Reagan had been chosen for a role in a daytime show, the comparison was like night and day. Of course, all the talk had been about how Reagan had inherited the "skill" from Dame Lillianna Hope.

She knew that Kimber hadn't taken the comparisons well. But they did what friends always do—they muddled through it, and Reagan stopped acting. She'd claimed she didn't like the hours or having to deal with moody directors, but ever since then, she'd been posting short little videos on social media, enough to gain her plenty of attention and marketing income.

Every major brand out there sent her free stuff to wear or use. She even gave a lot of the stuff to the rest of them.

Morgan was moping around on the sofa, watching the

news for any signs of herself or Kimber, when the front gate buzzed.

"It's Miss Lafyette, Miss Blyton, and Miss Hope," Lynda said.

Morgan glanced down at the sweat shorts she had thrown on over her swimsuit and groaned.

"Shall I let them through?" Lynda asked.

She thought of turning them away but knew better.

"Yes, tell them I'll be down." She switched off the set and rushed to the elevator for a quick shower and change.

There was no way she was going into this without her war paint on, she thought as she stepped out of the elevator.

Too bad Liam had gone into the office for the day. She could have used his support. They'd talked a lot about what had happened, whether she should forgive Kimber or not. Liam had made it clear to her that it was her decision, but she'd taken his advice.

When Sean had stabbed him in the back, he'd tried to take him back after that first lawsuit. Sean had contacted him and suggested they meet to work things out.

Liam had gone with a broken heart and an open mind. His friend had gone with clear intentions to threaten and strong-arm his way back into the business. He even threatened to claim that he had written the software, not Liam.

Still, as she pulled on a white cotton summer dress, she knew she had to remain true to herself. She was no longer a person to be pushed around. Over the years, she had allowed her friends to pull her in different directions. This was her time to stand strong.

When she stepped out of the elevator, she heard her friends talking quietly in the living room. Lynda had obviously served them drinks. The three of them were sitting around her house as if they were just there for a visit, like normal.

When she stepped inside, their conversation died down. Then Kimber jumped up, rushed over, and wrapped her arms around her.

"I know what it looked like," her friend cried. "I swear that I didn't do it on purpose."

Within the first minute of being in the room, Kimber managed to soak Morgan's shoulder with her tears. Kimber pulled back and then, to Morgan's shock, she said. "You simply have to tell everyone that I didn't mean it."

"Tell everyone?" Morgan shifted away from Kimber and moved to sit down.

"Yes." Kimber wiped the tears from her cheeks. Morgan noticed that her friend's makeup was still perfectly in place. Her friend had thought far enough ahead to put on water-proof mascara. "Do an interview or something..." Kimber sat back down as the tears dried up. "You have to explain that I didn't trip you. That I would never do something like that."

"But you did," Morgan said calmly as she watched Kimber's face very closely.

First shock flashed in her friend's eyes, followed by something close to annoyance. Not once did she see pain or concern there. Morgan was right—her friend was a terrible actress.

"Morgan, I'm sure..." Leanne started, but stopped talking when Reagan took her hand.

"This is between them. All we can do is be supportive of Morgan's decision," Reagan said quietly.

"Thank you," Morgan told the two of them before turning to Kimber. "I don't know what you were thinking, but from what I saw in the video, you had every intention of letting me fall on my face. Maybe you don't understand that there was a real chance of me seriously hurting myself. This boot is not a cast. While it does protect me from some things, a fall could have still seriously damaged my leg. Whatever you had to gain from the show, I hope it was worth the friendship you put second, behind the attention. You have yet to say you are sorry, nor do I think you really are. I'm sorry that our twenty-year friendship has taken this turn. I don't know if I can ever trust you again. I'm not sure I want to, at this point."

Kimber's eyes were completely dry now as she turned to Leanne and Reagan.

"What about you two?" Kimber asked.

"You know our thoughts," Reagan said firmly. "We suggested you apologize and fess up. You chose not to."

"You really wanted her to go on television and explain your actions without apologizing or telling her why you did it?" Leanne asked. When Kimber didn't say anything, Leanne turned to Morgan. "She told me that it was a stunt. That she'd come up with the idea shortly after we'd been seated at Sudomo's. She's the one who called the paparazzi in the first place."

Morgan turned to Kimber, who shrugged. "I thought you would enjoy the attention."

"She told me that you deserved the attention and that this was a good opportunity to show the world how strong you were. I don't know if she knew that you'd fall." Leanne turned to Kimber.

"I never wanted to hurt you," Kimber said. Morgan had a difficult time telling if it was the truth or not.

"We're really sorry," Leanne added with a sniffle. Just looking at Leanne's and Reagan's faces, Morgan could tell that they were concerned.

Kimber, however, was like an ice sculpture. Why had

she never noticed this about her friend before? Had she always been like this?

"I'm expecting my mother for lunch," she said, lying. Her mother was due to stop by, but they hadn't set a time for the visit.

Leanne and Reagan jumped up and rushed over to hug Morgan.

"I'm really sorry," Leanne whispered. "If I'd known..."

"It's okay," Morgan told her. "We'll talk later," she assured her friend.

"Call me later," Reagan added as she hugged her.

When Leanne and Reagan left the room, Kimber stood up.

"So that's it? You're not going to forgive me?"

"You have yet to ask for forgiveness," Morgan pointed out.

"I only did what I did because I thought—"

"You've explained your thoughts," Morgan broke in. "What you haven't done yet is express remorse or concern that I was hurt both physically and emotionally. It was extremely embarrassing to fall like that. I ended up crying in the car on the way home." She hadn't meant to raise her voice.

For the first time since she'd seen her that day, a look of sadness crossed her friend's face.

"Maybe someday, if you ask, I'll forgive you. For now..." Morgan nodded towards the door. "I need some time."

Thankfully, Kimber left without saying anything else.

"Are you alright, Miss?" Lynda asked when she stepped into the room.

"Yes," Morgan answered with a sigh. "I think I'll head up and lie down until my mother gets here."

"Shall I make you some lunch?" Lynda asked.

"No, I'm not hungry." She went upstairs. She didn't care that lying down in the dress would wrinkle it or that she hadn't even removed her boot. Shutting the blinds, she sealed herself in darkness and cried for the loss of a sister.

When she woke, her phone chimed with a message from Lynda that her mother had just pulled through the gate.

She washed her face and refreshed herself, then went downstairs to greet her mother. Her mother took one look at her and frowned.

"You look like you just woke up?" her mother said in a disapproving tone.

"I did," she answered easily. She didn't care what she looked like. It wasn't as if she was going anywhere.

"I was hoping we could head into town for some lunch, but now..." Her mother's eyes ran over her again, then she sighed heavily. "I suppose we'll just have our chat here."

Her mother walked past her and moved into the sitting room. When Lynda appeared, her mother requested some tea and sandwiches. Morgan wanted to explain that Lynda wasn't there to wait on them, but Lynda quickly disappeared, no doubt to get what her mother wanted.

Morgan moved over and sat across from her mother. "What's this all about?" she asked, setting her crutches down. They were getting worn and to ease the discomfort of using them under her arms, she'd taped a hand towel on each of the armpit pieces. She was looking forward to Dr. Ellis telling her she could start putting weight on her leg. He'd mentioned upgrading her to a cane. She was set to go into his office tomorrow so he could do a new X-ray of her leg. She was curious to see a picture of the bones for herself.

"It's about Lynda," her mother said easily.

"Lynda?" Morgan glanced to where Lynda had just disappeared.

"Yes." Her mother shifted and straightened her shirt. "How attached are you to her?"

Morgan didn't know what to say. "Um..."

"As you know, since Ann is gone, your father and I have struggled to find someone to fill her shoes," her mother continued.

"Okay," Morgan said slowly.

"You've been perfectly happy with Lynda, and I wanted to ask you if you'd be willing to let her go."

Morgan couldn't help it, she chuckled.

"What is so funny?" her mother asked.

"Lynda works for Liam, not me. Besides, she's not something that can just be handed off. If she wants to go work for you, that would be up to her. Not me or Liam."

Her mother smiled and nodded. "Very well, I figured I had to ask first."

"Is that it? That's why you came up here?" she asked.

"Yes, well, that and to make sure you and Liam are coming to the event at the country club this weekend," her mother added just as Lynda came in with the tea.

"Yes." Morgan leaned back and waited to say anything more until Lynda was gone. "What sort of event is this again?" she asked. She was sure that her mother had told her before, but with everything happening in the past few days, she'd pushed it to the back of her mind.

"It's a fundraiser." Her mother looked slightly shocked that she couldn't remember the details.

"And it's at the country club?" Morgan asked, already bored with the conversation.

"Yes..." her mother said, a little impatiently. "We are trying to raise money for a children's charity."

"Is Aaron going?" she asked out of the blue. She hadn't seen her brother since he had come over that day after they'd talked to the police.

"Of course," her mother answered. "All hands on deck for this one."

"How is his club doing?" Morgan asked, suddenly concerned.

"Just fine." Her mother waved off her concern. "Now, tell me about what went down between you and Kimber."

For the next hour, she visited with her mother, filling her in on every detail of what had happened to her.

In her memories, she'd never talked to her mother about her and Liam's plans to start a family. Had she and just couldn't remember?

Now, she was nervous just thinking about telling her mother. But she figured that there was no time like the present.

"Mother, Liam and I are trying for children." She practically held her breath.

Her mother didn't look surprised at all.

"You have mentioned it several times now. Is there anything new I should know?"

Morgan was surprised and then shocked when she realized that she couldn't remember if she was late or not. She'd lost track of time since returning home.

"No, at least I don't..." she said, feeling flustered.

Her mother looked interested and leaned forward. "Well, are you late?"

"I..." Morgan pulled up the calendar on her phone and thought back. She relaxed. "No," she said after calculating.

Her mother leaned back. "It will happen when it's time. Until then, don't worry. Children are both a blessing and a curse."

"Oh?" Morgan asked, chuckling.

"Look at the difference in the two of you. You and your brother. You were nothing but a perfect joy to raise," her mother said, shocking her slightly.

"I was?" Morgan asked.

"Yes, you had a few... moments, but for the most part, nothing like your brother. Everything Aaron does is... so exhausting. Just look at his nightclub. If your father hadn't stepped in and paid for the remodel..."

"I thought Aaron used his inheritance?" she asked, trying to think back.

"He lost his inheritance the first year he had control of it," her mother answered.

"What?" Morgan gasped. "All of it?"

"Honey, why on earth do you think he still lives with us?" Her mother shook her head. "Not by our choice, I can assure you."

"So, he's..." She frowned. "But the club is doing well, right?"

Her mother shrugged. "I don't know. I've purposely kept my nose out of it. Your father claims it's doing well, but I'm not even sure he knows. Aaron keeps us in the dark. All we can go off is what the press says about the place. It's packed every night so that has to account for something." Her mother set her teacup down. "I'm surprised he hasn't come to you for cash."

Maybe Aaron had and she just couldn't remember. Maybe he was making enough money to live but wasting it on drugs. Did their parents know that Aaron was using? Did they care? She knew that her father occasionally came home high. Coke, apparently, ran in the family. Maybe that's why Aaron had started using it.

She doubted her mother ever touched anything, being

the health nut she was. But she hadn't condemned her father either. At least not that Morgan ever remembered.

When Liam got home from work later that night, they took a long swim and talked about everything that had happened to her that day. Then he filled her in on the investigation and how, at least for now, it appeared that Dave and the others were being charged. Liam claimed that the process was moving slowly because of the lack of proof. Sure, there was the evidence that the files had been on each of their systems, but the difficult part was coming up with the proof that they were the ones to put them there in the first place.

Then Liam changed gears and told her that he'd bought the building across from Ryder's gym.

"What?" she asked with a chuckle. "What are you going to do with it?"

"Turn it into a halfway home for boys," he explained. "Ryder has this kid, he turned eighteen last week. Marty is a great boxer. Ryder thinks he could go pro, but he has no place to stay now that he's out on his own."

"He was at Wayward?" she asked, remembering seeing the orphanage where Liam and Ryder had grown up.

"Yeah, so I closed on the building today. There was a lot of red tape, which slowed the process down. One of the tenants didn't want to leave and didn't want me renting the place out to a bunch of degenerates. His word, not mine," Liam added with a sigh.

"What did you do?"

"I paid the guy off. Enough money that he could buy a condo along the coast," he added with a smile.

She chuckled and wrapped her arms around his shoulders as they floated. "You're an amazing man."

"Now Marty is living in the guy's apartment. He just

moved in yesterday. He's going to help with the construction too. He's thinking of going to school to become a plumber," Liam added with a big grin.

"I love you," she said, feeling her heart swell with love and happiness. Even if the family and friend portion of her life wasn't going so well, at least this part was perfect.

# CHAPTER TWENTY-SIX

*I think we all have light and dark inside us.*
**Sean Penn**

Liam didn't exactly fit into the country club life. The first time he'd gone to her parents' club, he'd felt so out of sorts, he'd promised himself never to join one himself.

Walking in with Morgan on his arm, however, he felt a lot more at ease. She'd finally been able to ditch the crutches and start putting weight on her leg. She even had a fancy metal cane that she walked with.

Morgan complained that she was faster with the crutches but made a point to tell him how much easier the cane was because now one of her arms was free to hold things like her purse as she walked.

As they made their way to the bar area where her parents said they would meet them, she held onto his arm tightly as she used the cane in her other hand.

"There you two are." Her mother rushed over and hugged and air-kissed Morgan. Then she did the same to him. He knew it was all for show since she never did that when they weren't in the public eye. "You look wonderful," her mother said to Morgan. "You finally dropped those crutches."

Morgan chuckled. "I didn't have them by choice," she said dryly.

Her mother seemed to ignore Morgan's statement. "Come on, the party has already started. You two are late." Her mother waved them towards the bar area where Thomas and Aaron were talking to people and sipping drinks.

"Want something?" he asked Morgan as they approached the bar.

"I won't say no to some champagne."

"Sit." He pulled out a stool for her and then ordered a beer and a champagne for them. He wasn't surprised that neither her father nor brother came over to talk to them in the first half hour they were there.

After that, several of her parents' friends stopped by and chatted with Morgan. Most of them asked her how she was doing or asked when she was going to be hosting events and working with her mother again.

Thankfully, Morgan explained to each of them that her days of event organizing were through. Several of the men tried to chat with him while their wives talked with Morgan.

It wasn't that he couldn't make small talk. He just didn't want to. He didn't have a lot in common with the people here. He hadn't been raised with a silver spoon in his mouth. He didn't attend the country club or even play golf. He didn't know what names to drop or even care who was doing what with whom.

He noticed that Leanne and Reagan had arrived and was happy that they made their way over to Morgan and stuck by her side. He stood next to her, listening to their conversation. He didn't mind, though, since he didn't feel like talking to anyone else that evening.

Finally, Thomas made his way over to him and started talking to him about sports, something he knew they had in common. Probably the only thing.

Aaron stopped by for a moment to complain about having to be there and being missed at the club.

Actually, Kimber was doing everything she could to keep her distance from Morgan and him. He had caught her looking in their direction several times and, whenever she'd spotted him looking her way, she turned her back on him or quickly look away.

"She's being weird," Morgan said to him.

"Yeah," he agreed, knowing that Kimber probably understood that if she came within earshot of him, he wouldn't be able to keep his thoughts to himself. "It's for the best."

Morgan's hand went to his elbow. "We don't have to stay much longer."

"No, it's fine. We can stay as long as you want," he assured her.

"You guys should ditch this party and head to the club with me," Aaron suggested. "You never got to see the club with actual people in it," he said to Morgan.

"That's right." Morgan perked up. "I missed opening night." She turned to him. "Want to go?"

He shrugged. "We're all dressed up. If you're sure…"

She turned to Leanne and Reagan to ask them if they wanted to go too. They both agreed.

"Looks like we're going clubbing," Morgan said cheerfully.

He wanted to remind her that she still hadn't healed all

the way yet but figured that if she felt well enough, it was up to her.

Nightshade was packed when they finally made it through the door. Instantly, Liam had to block several people from knocking Morgan over.

He'd been in plenty of clubs before and, to be honest, there was nothing in particular that made Nightshade stand out other than the fact that it was an old warehouse that someone, most likely Morgan's parents, had paid a whole lot of money to remodel.

The inside was painted black, and long stringy neon lights dangled from the three-story ceiling and changed color with the pulsing music. A massive cluster of lights hung in the middle of the room, like a chandelier of sorts. There were long columns of lights on each of the walls. Even part of the dance floor had flashing lights under it.

They made their way carefully to the bar area, which was completely lit up with a sheer blue glass bar top.

Since there wasn't a stool available for Morgan, Liam asked a couple people to give up their seats. The first two told him to fuck off, and the third one tried to start a fight with him. He was losing what little patience he had when, finally, someone got up and Liam grabbed the seat for Morgan.

Thankfully, Leanne and Reagan arrived shortly after, allowing them to grab even more seats when the men vacated spots for the ladies.

The music was so loud, he couldn't hear the bartender as he ordered them drinks. They were so overpriced that even he balked at the cost.

They must have been standing there for more than fifteen minutes when Aaron finally came by and suggested they head up to the owner's booth, which was a large table upstairs that overlooked the bar and dance floor.

He helped Morgan up the flight of stairs, and she instantly looked more relaxed. Up here, the music wasn't as loud and there weren't people pushing against her.

"Better?" he asked her.

"Yes, much."

They were there less than ten minutes when Kimber found them. She convinced Leanna and Reagan to head back downstairs onto the dance floor with her.

Liam watched for Morgan's reaction when her two friends disappeared.

"What?" Morgan asked him. "I'm not childish enough to think that they're going to choose sides."

He took her hand in his. "But it still stings."

"Yeah," she said with a sigh. "They don't like what Kimber did, they've made that perfectly clear, but..." Morgan shrugged.

"They weren't the ones that were hurt," he finished for her.

"Exactly." She nodded. "So I'm trying to be the better woman."

He wrapped his arm around her. "You are a better person than I am. I wanted to wring Aaron's neck."

When Leanne and Reagan returned, they each had men hanging on them. Reagan spent the rest of the night making out with her guy while Leanne giggled each time the guy that she was with said anything funny.

"I'm going to head to the restroom," Morgan said, standing up. Liam stood up with the intention of making sure she got there okay, but she stopped him by putting a hand on his shoulder. "I can make it."

He frowned up at her.

"I'll go with you," Leanne said, jumping up.

He watched the two of them walk towards the stairs and knew he would worry the entire time she was gone.

"So…" The guy Leanne had been flirting with all night moved closer to him. "Wow, I'm a huge fan of yours."

Liam turned to the man. The guy looked to be barley twenty-one. Honestly, he looked like every other guy in the club—too much hair product and clothes that looked like he hadn't even tried them on but had still spent too much to buy.

"Carl?" he asked, trying to remember the guy's name.

"Cooper," the guy corrected with a smile.

"What exactly have I done for you to be a huge fan?" he asked, glancing towards the stairs again.

"I'm a big nerd. I've been following your career since I was in junior high," Cooper said, causing Liam to wince. He wasn't that much older than the guy. He was only twenty-eight. He quickly did the man and felt his stomach roll when it added up. Shit. He was getting old. Cooper had continued talking about Liam's career and his deal with IOA as if Liam hadn't lived through it himself.

"Thanks," Liam said when Cooper finally had a break in his conversation. "Are you in the industry yourself?"

"No, man, I'm going to college. California Institute of Technology," he added with a grin.

Liam had thought of going back to school at one point after he'd sold out. The year he took off, he even took a few online classes, which he'd found far beneath his abilities.

To him, life was the best school he could attend. Still, he knew that most weren't as lucky as he had been.

"Good, what's your field?" he asked, only half listening to him when he answered.

How long had it been since Morgan and Leanne had

left? A minute? A half hour? He wished he'd looked down at his watch to mark the time when they'd left.

To his surprise, when they returned, her physical therapist was with them and Kimber was hanging on the man's arm. Morgan looked less than pleased, but since she appeared to be physically fine, he was instantly relieved.

"Look who we found," Leanne said, cheerfully.

"Hey." Grayson sat next to Morgan and reached out his hand across Morgan for Liam to shake. Liam didn't want to appear petty, so he shook it.

"Grayton, right?" Liam asked, knowing full well what the man's name was. He even heard Morgan chuckle.

"Grayson," the man corrected.

"Come here often?" Liam asked, shifting Morgan closer to him and wrapping an arm around her shoulder. Morgan settled into his side, and he felt her relax.

"Yeah, at least twice a month. Ya gotta blow off some steam, am I right?" Grayson said.

Liam noticed that Kimber was starting to get agitated that the man she'd been plastered to a moment ago was practically ignoring her now.

"You finally decided to get out," Grayson said to Morgan.

"Yes, we decided it was time." She laid a hand over Liam's chest.

Liam recognized the look of jealousy in the man's eyes instantly and tightened his hold on Morgan.

"I see the doctor finally allowed you to put weight on your leg," Grayson said.

"Yeah, Morgan's almost back to her old self," Kimber said with a tone of sarcasm. "Too bad."

"What does that mean?" Leanne jumped in, staring her friend down.

Kimber shrugged and then laughed. "It's just... Morgan's used to getting attention. When she can't get it because she's a cripple..."

"Leave," Reagan said. "You're drunk, just..." She pointed towards the stairs. "Go home."

Kimber chuckled and then looked shocked when Leanne nodded and added, "Go home, Kimber."

"Come on, Grayson, let's go," Kimber huffed, tugging on Grayson's arm. The man just looked up at Kimber as if he couldn't remember she'd been hanging on his arm moments earlier.

"I'm good here." Grayson turned back to talk to Morgan.

Liam wished the guy would leave but was slightly thankful that even he had snubbed Kimber.

Kimber stomped her foot and then stormed off. The conversation turned to the club and how great everything was going. Then it split off as Leanne continued to flirt with Cooper and Reagan went back to making out with her guy, leaving Morgan and him with Grayson.

The man was trying everything he could to entertain Morgan. Still, he figured it was better than leaving the guy alone with his wife during therapy. This way he could size the man up, figure out just what level of in love with Morgan he was. It was obvious to anyone that the man had the hots for Morgan. The guy was practically drooling.

Almost an hour after Kimber left, Morgan turned to him. "I think it's time we got going," she said softly.

"Sure." He jumped up, then reached down to help her stand, and Grayson did the same thing. Liam hadn't meant to growl, certainly not loud enough that the everyone in the booth would stop and look at him. Grayson dropped his arm from Morgan's and took a step back.

"Sorry, bro," the man said with a shrug. "I guess I'm just used to helping Morgan."

Liam, feeling stupid suddenly, nodded as he took Morgan's arm. "Night," he said to everyone, then walked with Morgan down the stairs.

"What was that?" Morgan asked when they were in the car heading home.

"Self-defense." He chuckled when he realized just how stupid he had been. "Sorry, it was a gut reaction."

Morgan smiled at him. "I thought Grayson was going to pee himself." She chuckled. "Along with the other two guys. Are you sure you're not part werewolf?"

He laughed. "Okay, I might have gone a little overboard."

"Ya think?"

He sobered. "Sorry about Kimber."

Morgan sighed. "She made her choice. I doubt Reagan or Leanne will trust her to not stab them in the backs again."

"Did she hurt you?" he asked, concerned.

"No. After the other day, I've come to terms with the fact that she is who she is. Looking back on the past few years, I realize I should have seen the pattern of her growing farther away. Actually, I'm the one that changed."

"Leanne and Reagan are changing as well," he pointed out.

"Yes." Morgan smiled. "Reagan only picked up one guy tonight, and Leanne didn't even kiss the guy she was with."

"That's because she has the hots for your physical therapist. Like Kimber, but not so... obvious," he pointed out.

"She does?" Morgan asked.

"Yeah, every time the guy she was with made a joke, she would laugh as she looked longingly over at your Grayson."

Morgan was silent for a moment. "That is the first time you've called him by his name."

"It is?" He glanced at her.

"Yes, normally you call him my physical therapist, or the therapist." Morgan smiled. "Maybe all it took was you almost causing the guy to pee himself for you to finally respect him?"

He smiled. "Maybe I should have done it a lot sooner."

Morgan laughed and then sighed as she leaned back. "I'd forgotten how much I hate going out now. I used to love going clubbing."

"I never did like it," he admitted.

"Oh? But that's where we met. At a nightclub," Morgan pointed out.

"Ryder had to drag me there."

"I'm glad he did." She took his hand.

"So am I."

# CHAPTER TWENTY-SEVEN

*However vast the darkness,*
*we must supply our own light.*
**Stanley Kubrick**

Morgan woke shortly after she heard Liam head out for work. He'd kissed her softly before leaving, but she'd been too deep in sleep to wake fully.

Now as she stretched her arms over her head, she smiled up at the ceiling before hugging her arms around herself. Last night was... amazing.

Not the going out part but the after part. Coming home to a man who couldn't wait to pull of the flowing red dress she'd worn out that evening. Even though she had to wear a flat shoe on her good leg, she'd felt sexy for the first time since her accident.

Pulling herself up, she grabbed her phone and realized she'd missed a bunch of messages in the middle of the night.

Worry instantly replaced her euphoria. The first one was a voicemail from Kimber, who was obviously even drunker than when she'd left Nightshade.

"You think you're the shit?" Kimber slurred her words. "You're not. I know things. I could knock your family right off that high horse they sit on. I could destroy you. Just remember that, you fucking bitch."

The next message was pretty much the same, as were the three that followed. She listened to each one as she freshened up in the bathroom. There were also text messages that didn't make any sense.

The last message was from Kimber's phone, but instead of Kimber, a low male voice mumbled something, then the phone went dead.

Even being a total bitch, Kimber had still managed to find a man to be with.

"Good for her," Morgan said as she brushed her hair. She wanted to go for a swim, but she had therapy first thing that morning followed by a session with Marina.

She was looking forward to therapy since she could finally put weight on her leg. She was curious what sorts of things Grayson would have her doing. Maybe she could learn to tackle the stairs instead of using the elevator all the time.

She'd been pretty good at climbing them last night with Liam and Leanne's help. But still, she wanted to be able to climb or descend them by herself.

"Morning," Lynda said cheerfully when she stepped into the kitchen.

"Good morning," Morgan said as she sat down and turned on the television.

"How about I heat you up a breakfast quiche?" Lynda asked.

"That sounds wonderful." She flipped to a news station. The remote fell out of her hands when she saw Kimber's image on the set. The words "Found dead early this morning" flashed at the bottom.

Morgan felt her chest tighten and her vision gray. She heard Lynda scream her name just before she landed on the tile floor with a thud.

When she woke, she was lying in her bed with someone leaning over her.

"Liam?" she said with a groan. "I had such a terrible dream."

"I'm here," the voice said and instantly she knew it wasn't Liam.

Her eyes jerked open and focused on Grayson's face as he leaned over her.

"Oh," she said, quickly sitting up. "Where's Lynda?"

"She's downstairs. I told her I'd carry you up here. Are you okay?" He shifted slightly towards her.

"Yes, I..." She moved to get up, but his hand reached out and touched her lip. She jerked back, only to have his fingers come away with blood on them.

"You cut your lip," he said, showing her.

"Oh." She reached up and wiped the blood away.

"Here," he said, "let me help." He disappeared into the bathroom and came back with a wet washcloth. He wiped her lip with the cold cloth. She held still until he was done cleaning up the blood.

"Thanks," she said, just as Liam rushed in.

"What's happened?" he asked. After seeing Grayson holding a bloody washcloth, he charged at the man.

"I fell," she said, holding up her hands. "He was just cleaning up my lip."

Liam had Grayson by the shirt front.

Then, for the first time since she'd woken from the faint,

the realization of what had happened sank in. "Oh god!" she cried, covering her face with her hands, no longer caring what the two men did. "Kimber's dead," she cried over and over.

She felt Liam's arms wrap around her, and she bawled loudly for the loss of her friend.

"It was on the news," she said into Liam's shirt. "They found her this morning. Why?"

She cried until she couldn't cry any longer. Her eyes stung, her head ached, and she was having a difficult time breathing through her dry sobbing.

"Here," Grayson said. "I carry these for some clients. It's a sleeping pill. It might help."

"No," she said, wiping her eyes and her face with her hands. "I... I need to know what happened." She sat up a little, then winced when her wrist hurt.

"Let me look at it," Grayson suggested. "She might have sprained it when she fell."

Liam scooted side and allowed Grayson to check her wrist. It was tender but didn't feel broken.

"It's okay. I think it's just tender," she said.

"You should put some ice on it, but I think it's okay." Grayson stood up.

"Thanks," she said, then added, "I think I'll skip therapy today."

"Who's Kimber?" Grayson asked as she stood up. "Was that the mean one last night?"

"Yes," Liam answered with a sigh.

"Sorry, were the two of you close?" Grayson asked as Liam helped her stand.

"She was my best friend since second grade," Morgan answered as her eyes watered again. "Oh god." She gasped as Liam wrapped his arms around her.

"I'm so sorry," she heard Grayson say.

"I have to call Leanne and Reagan," she managed to get out.

Just then Lynda came in. "Three detectives are downstairs," she said, then she surprised Morgan by rushing over and hugging her. "You scared me. I'm so sorry about Miss Lafyette."

Morgan hugged the woman for a moment, then composed herself. "Tell the detectives that I'm going to wash my face and then we'll be right down."

"I guess I'll reschedule our session for tomorrow," Grayson said. "See you then."

Morgan nodded. "Thanks."

Lynda motioned for Grayson to head downstairs with her before leaving.

When she stepped into the bathroom, Liam followed her and shut the door behind them, then once more took her in his arms. "I'm so sorry. We will get through this," he promised. "Together."

"Yes." She knew that whatever happened now, she had to be strong. She had to get through this next part. If only to catch whoever had killed her friend.

When they stepped out of the elevator, Detectives Evans, Rhodes, and Carson were all standing around the entryway.

"Mack." Liam moved over and shook his friend's hand.

"Morning, Liam. Wish I was here with better news," Mack said.

"Yeah." Liam motioned to the sitting room. "Let's head in and sit. My wife took a spill this morning upon hearing the news."

"I hope you're okay?" Mack asked.

"She passed out and bounced on the floor," Lynda said, walking in with a tray of tea. "I asked them to sit, they wanted to stand." She set the tray down and then prepared a cup for Morgan. "Drink, it will calm you."

"Is that the cause of the fat lip?" Detective Rhodes asked.

Morgan reached up and touched her lip and winced. "Yes. I suppose I face-planted."

"We won't take up too much of your time. We're only here because of all the calls from Kimber Lafyette's phone to Morgan's last night," Mack said.

Morgan remembered all of the messages and had to bite her lip to stop herself from crying again. "Yes." She pulled out her phone, unlocked it, and set it on the coffee table between them. "I listened to them this morning before I... saw on the news." She closed her eyes as Mack reached over, took her phone, and started playing the messages out loud.

Liam's hand took hers as they listened.

When the last message played, the three of them looked at each other.

"Do you recognize the voice on the last one?" Mack asked.

"No," Morgan answered. "I'd assumed that she'd hooked up with someone last night. Other than Grayson."

"Grayson?" Mack asked.

"My physical therapist. He was just here," she said, motioning to the doorway.

"And Kimber was with him last night?" Detective Carson asked.

"Briefly. But when she asked him to leave with her, he said no."

"He's in the kitchen," Lynda answered. "He wanted to make sure you were okay."

"I'll go talk to him." Detective Carson stood up and left.

"You and Miss Lafyette made a scene last night at your brother's nightclub?" Detective Rhodes asked.

"No, Kimber was…" She cleared her throat when it closed up. "She was drunk, and *she* made a scene. My friends asked her to leave. I don't remember saying a word to her last night."

"You didn't," Liam assured her.

"Your friends, that would be Leanne Blyton and Reagan Hope?" Mack asked, after looking at his notes.

"Yes," Morgan answered.

"And your therapist? He didn't leave with her?" Mack asked.

"No, she left, and he hung around with all of us for about another hour," Liam answered. "He left at the same time we did. He took a cab."

"You never saw Miss Lafyette actually leave the club then?" Mack asked.

Morgan looked at Liam and frowned. "No, I suppose not. She could have remained downstairs."

"Downstairs?" he asked.

"We were upstairs in my brother's private booth the entire time," she answered.

Mack wrote something down.

"My friends, do… do they know?" Morgan asked.

"Yes, we have other detectives questioning them downtown," Mack told them.

"How?" Morgan asked as her stomach rolled. She set the tea down, knowing that if she drank any, she'd probably lose it.

"We're not at liberty to discuss any details at this time," Detective Rhodes said firmly.

Morgan nodded. "Her family?"

"They're downtown at this moment," Mack answered. "We will need a copy of these voice messages."

"I can send them to you." She picked up her phone and sent them to Mack's phone. "Do you think... that was the killer in the last one?" she asked, feeling even more sick to her stomach.

"We'll find out," Mack assured her. "I'm sorry for your loss." He stood up. "If you don't mind, we'll finish questioning your therapist. We may have more questions for you later."

"You know how to get ahold of us," Liam said as the men walked into the kitchen area.

Morgan rested her head on Liam's shoulder. "I feel sick," she said with a groan.

"Want me to take you upstairs?" he asked.

"After they leave." She moaned. "God. Please let this be a dream."

Liam's arms tightened around her shoulders. "I'm so sorry."

Less than fifteen minutes later, the three detectives and Grayson all walked out the front door. Shortly after, Liam lifted Morgan into his arms and carried her back upstairs.

"I'll have Lynda make you some toast," he said, but the thought of eating had her dry heaving. She was about to rush into the bathroom and vomit, but Liam grabbed the trash can and held it out for her. Then he rubbed her back while she emptied whatever contents were in her stomach.

"Oh god. I... can't." She closed her eyes and then lay back.

"Here." Liam handed her a wet washcloth and a glass of water.

"I'm sorry," she said after cleaning herself up.

"Don't be." He brushed her hair aside. "Even though

you two had a falling out, she was your friend. No matter what."

She nodded. "I... I'll take one of those sleeping pills Grayson gave me now," she motioned to the bottle on the nightstand.

Liam handed her one after reading the label. "Get some rest. I'll be right here," he promised her.

Morgan dropped into a dreamless slumber. When she woke, the room was quiet and dark. Still, she could see the sliver of light coming from under the door and knew that it was still daylight out.

The soothing hum of the house sounds calmed her enough that she crawled out of bed and took a long hot shower.

She must have been in there more than fifteen minutes when Liam stepped into the bathroom.

"Are you okay in there?" he called out. Ever since the day when someone had been in the bathroom with her, he had made a point never to walk in without calling out to her. It was just one more thing he did that made her love him even more.

"Yes." She smiled and shut off the water.

He was waiting for her, holding a towel out for her to step into. "Feel a little better?"

"Yes. I'm hungry," she said.

"I've cooked us some lunch."

She stepped into the closet and picked out a pair of yoga pants and a large sweater. She knew that it was probably in the high eighties that day, but for some reason, she was still chilled.

This time when they went downstairs, they were alone.

"I've given Lynda the day off," he told her as she sat on the sofa. "I'll get the food. Drink?" he asked.

"Just tea. Until my stomach settles."

She reached for the remote, unsure if she could handle the news. Then she saw her phone sitting there and realized she'd left it down there after their meeting with the detectives.

She turned on the news channel, but they were playing commercials, she so she browsed through her phone. There were missed calls from her friends as well as text messages that she instantly responded to.

She sent a group message to Leanne and Reagan and told them that she'd taken a sleeping pill and was now up.

Her phone instantly rang.

"We're here, at my place together," Leanne said with a sniffle. "Oh my god. The last thing we said to her was to leave."

"I didn't even say anything to her." Morgan sighed and closed her eyes.

"Did the police question you as well?" Reagan asked.

"Yes, they were here this morning," Morgan answered. "I passed out cold when I saw the news on the television. When I woke up, they were here."

"How are you holding up now?" Leanne asked.

"I'm shaky. You two?" Morgan asked.

"We have each other," Reagan answered. "Did they tell you anything? Where? How? Anything?"

"No, you?" Morgan asked.

"No, but the news is saying she was found in her car. They didn't say it was an accident and by some of the questions they were asking, we think it was murder," Reagan said.

"Yes, I figured as much when they said they'd found her body," Morgan said as Liam set some grilled salmon salad in front of her. The smell of it hit her, and she dropped her phone as she raced to the bathroom and once again threw up.

"Oh god," she cried with her face in the toilet.

Liam was there, rubbing her back. "It's okay, I get that all the time when I cook," he joked.

She chuckled, then threw up again. "It's not that." She mentally told herself not to throw up again. "I..." She stilled. "Oh god." She glanced up at him. "I'm officially late."

"For?" Liam asked with a frown.

"I wasn't when my mother asked, so I didn't think... Then well, I was so upset about Kimber that I'd forgotten." She laid a hand over her flat stomach. "I'm late," she said, and Liam's eyes went wide.

"Are you sure?" he asked.

"I'm sure that I'm late." She nodded. "And I just threw up for the second time today."

"I can run to the store. Get a test?" he asked eagerly.

She smiled. "If you want." She nodded, then gasped. "My phone."

He was smiling as he quickly disappeared into the other room and came back with it as she rinsed out her mouth.

"I'm here," she said to Leanne and Reagan. "Sorry, I've been sick."

Liam mouthed and pointed to the door. "I'll be back."

She nodded and stepped out of the bathroom.

"Are you okay?" Leanne asked.

"Yes, just... upset." She sobered as she stepped out and saw the news talking about Kimber. "It's on the news," she said and hit unmute. She noticed that Liam had cleared away the food for her. Still, she had to swallow a few times and plug her nose to avoid getting sick from the smell as she listened to the report about Kimber.

Several of the photos they showed of her included the

four friends. Others were just of Kimber and Morgan. The reporter talked about their connection and Kimber's connection to each of them.

"Oh god. This is really happening," Leanne said. "Why?"

Morgan hit mute and closed her eyes on a wave of nausea. "I can't..." She sighed. "She left me several voice messages last night," she blurted out.

"She did?" Reagan asked. "What did they say?"

Morgan played them for her friends, then she listened to the ones Kimber had left each of them. Much of the same stuff. She called Leanne a traitor and Reagan a stuck-up, two-timing bitch face.

"She had hit a new low," Reagan said. "I mean, we both knew that she was low, but this low?"

"What do you mean she was low?" Morgan asked.

The line was silent. "We didn't want you to know. You had enough to worry about with the accident and all," Leanne started.

"Kimber was sinking pretty far into drugs," Reagan said.

Morgan thought back to her brother and felt sick to her stomach again.

"Several times when we went out with her, we caught her doing some pretty heavy drugs," Leanne added. "Not that we don't dally in pot, molly, or coke once in a while, but the stuff she was mixing... it just wasn't cool."

Morgan tried to breathe through the sick feeling. "What kinds of drugs? How often?"

"Every time we went out. It's why we stopped going out with her shortly before your accident," Reagan answered.

"She always wanted to go to Nightshade. The drug scene there is unreal. It's the new hot spot for hooking up," Leanne explained.

"It is?" Morgan groaned. Of course it was. Hadn't she warned her brother about that herself?

"Yes, we only go once a month or so ourselves now. Just to score some pot," Leanne added.

"I... need to go," Morgan said, feeling her stomach twist again. She didn't want to be on the phone with her friends while she got sick again.

"Morgan, we're here if you need us," Leanne said.

"Thanks, right back at you. Both of you." She hung up and made it all the way up to her bathroom before dry heaving into the toilet.

# CHAPTER TWENTY-EIGHT

*The darkness declares the glory of light.*
**T. S. Eliot**

It took Liam five minutes less to get to the store and back to the house than it normally did. He had six different types of pregnancy tests in the bag, along with some Saltine crackers and some club soda.

When he walked in, he found Morgan lying on the bathroom floor. From the look of her, she'd obviously gotten sick several more times.

"Babe," he said, rushing over to her. She felt clammy to the touch and moaned when he moved her. "That's it, I'm taking you to the hospital." He hoisted her up in his arms.

"No, I'm fine," she groaned. "I just need to rest."

"No, what you need is a doctor." He continued outside to his car. Morgan pretty much passed out on the car trip down the hill to the hospital.

He called ahead, and thankfully they had a stretcher waiting for her when he pulled up to the ER.

"You can go and park your car in the east lot. Once you

come inside, the desk clerk will show you to where you need to be," the nurse said when he started to get out and follow them inside. Instead, he pulled out his phone, opened the app, and sent his car to the nearest parking spot. "Your car parks itself?" she gasped, but he was too busy holding Morgan's hand as they wheeled her in the doors to answer the woman.

As they moved quickly into a brightly lit room, Morgan's eyes opened. "Liam, I think I need to go to the hospital," she groaned.

"We're already there, babe," he said softly.

"Oh, okay." Her eyes rolled backwards in her head. The nurses started shouting, and he was shoved aside.

"Out." The nurse who had talked to him earlier took his arm and led him outside. "Here, you can wait here." She disappeared back into the room Morgan was in.

He paced for a moment, then pulled out his phone and shot a text message off to her parents. Then he paced some more and sent a text message to Leanne and Reagan. The next message was to Ryder.

"I need you. Morgan's in the hospital." He sent the text and less than a minute later, Ryder replied.

"On my way."

Her friends messaged back as well and said they were on their way. Her parents didn't respond for almost half an hour. By then, he was sitting in the room next to Morgan, who was having her stomach pumped.

The doctor didn't know what kind of substance she had ingested, but whatever it was, it had drained her of all fluids.

The bad news was Morgan was not pregnant. She was, however, poisoned.

The only thing he could think of was the pills Grayson had given them. Sleeping pills. They had seemed to do the trick. Morgan had slept for two hours, undisturbed. She'd seemed fine when she woke, just a little sick.

But he remembered she'd thrown up prior to taking the pills. He didn't think she'd eaten anything that morning, but he sent a text message to Lynda to ask her.

Lynda's reply was almost immediate.

"Nothing. I was heating her a breakfast quiche when she blacked out. I'm on my way down there."

Her parents showed up right after Ryder, Leanne, and Reagan. By then, Morgan was sitting up and joking with him about never letting him cook for her again. He could see the sadness in her eyes upon discovering she wasn't pregnant, but she held back the tears since the small room was now crowded with family and friends.

A few hours later, he carried her back into their bedroom. She'd fallen asleep on the drive home. He picked up the bottle of sleeping pills Grayson had given them and stowed them away in the safe. He was going to give them to Roy to check them out when he saw him next time.

The doctors had claimed that it was a standard food poisoning. The last thing Morgan had eaten was some food at the country club and maybe some chips at the club the night before.

He sat with her until Lynda brought him up a sandwich. He only left her side to use the bathroom or to get a drink from the small fridge in the kitchenette area.

When he returned, Morgan was sitting up, looking down at her phone.

"Hey," he said, setting the club soda down. "How are you feeling?"

"Like I had food poisoning," she joked. Then he saw tears stream down her face. "I had really hoped," she said, and he pulled her into his arms.

"Yeah, me too." He sighed. "Good news is that we get to keep trying," he said, trying to sound hopeful.

Hearing her chuckle, he smiled and pulled back.

"Is that rain?" she asked with a groan.

He hadn't even looked outside since he'd returned home. It had been sprinkling on the way back from the hospital, but now it was thundering and sounding pretty nasty outside again.

"Yes," he answered, and she groaned again.

"How about we stay up here in bed and watch a movie?" he suggested.

"No. I want a shower. Or maybe a bath?" She tilted her head.

"A bath it is."

After filling the tub with water and dropping one of her scented bath bombs in it, he helped her into the bathroom where she stripped and slid into the water. Then he pulled off his own clothes and climbed in behind her. She laughed.

"This thing is too small for the both of us," she said as she moved forward. He was careful to not bump her injured leg.

"Then we'll have to get a bigger one installed." He pulled her back until she rested her back on his chest. "There, this is nice."

His legs were dangling off the edge of the tub. Her right leg was resting on the edge with her left one bent almost to her chest.

"Right," she sighed. "Not exactly the relaxing bath I had in mind," she said with a chuckle.

"I can fix that." He moved his hands slowly over the front of her. When she moaned, he smiled. "Better?"

"Don't stop," she said under her breath. "Don't you dare stop."

"Never," he whispered next to her ear as his fingers dipped into her. She arched and cried out his name, then melted back against him.

"I think that takes the record," he said with a chuckle, "for fastest orgasm."

She sighed. "It was because it was unexpected."

"I'll have to remember that."

"I could..." She started to move, but he stopped her.

"No, today is all about you." He kissed the top of her head.

The following day, he wanted to work from home, but there was an important board meeting that he had to attend mid-morning.

He'd convinced her friends to come over and spend some time with her and knew that Lynda would be there as well.

They were so close to filing actual charges against Dave and the rest of the employees, but he'd almost forgotten all about it with everything else that was going on.

His and Morgan's top concern was Kimber's death.

He had just pulled into the parking lot when Ryder called him. Pulling into his parking spot, he answered the call.

"Hey, what's up?" he asked Ryder.

"Did you hear the news?" Ryder asked.

"About?"

"They've arrested Sean."

Liam jerked. "What? Why?"

"Liam, it was his mother," Ryder said.

"Who was?" Liam asked.

"The other hacked IOA car. The woman that died. It was Sean's mother."

"No, the woman's name was Duffy... something." He tried to remember.

"Karen Duffy. Yes, she'd recently married. Her maiden name was Wilson," Ryder explained.

Liam felt his hands go numb and realized he was gripping the steering wheel too hard and dropped his hands.

"They're sure?" he asked Ryder.

"They've got enough proof that they let the others go. Apparently, Sean had gotten a job at ESP as a part-time IT consultant," Ryder said.

Liam looked around the garage. "Here? He worked here. I... Why did I never see him?"

"He was only there part time. Besides, you've been working from home a lot lately. I bet it wasn't hard to miss him."

"Yeah, I... have to go," Liam said.

"Okay, I just wanted you to know. Talk to you later."

"Thanks," he said and hung up.

If it wasn't for that call, Liam would have walked into the board meeting totally unprepared to see Dave sitting at the head of the table with a huge smirk on his face.

"So, you're back?" he asked Dave.

"Looks like it," he said with a chuckle. "You won't be around much longer to worry about it though."

"Oh?" Liam asked as he sat down.

Dave just shrugged as everyone else filled the room.

"As some of you may have heard, all of the ESP employees accused of the dot slash hack have been cleared of all wrongdoing," Larry said. "Late last night and early this morning we had a surprise visit from the police. There was irrefutable proof that the hack was created and spread throughout this office by Sean Wilson. Liam Taylor's ex business partner."

Several people in the room turned a very accusatory eye to him. He didn't budge or even blink.

"Because of this new evidence," Larry continued, "we have hired back all terminated employees, and both board members who were released have been given back their positions. We hope that we can all put this entire ordeal behind us."

At this point, Dave cleared his throat and stood up. "I call for the dismissal of Liam Taylor."

"On what grounds?" Larry asked.

"Isn't it obvious? He allowed his business partner—"

"Ex," Larry interjected.

Dave nodded with a slight smile. "Into this company. A man he knew and trusted was able to almost take this company down."

"I haven't trusted Sean for years," Liam added. "Nor have I spoken to him. I had no idea he had been hired on as a consultant for the IT department."

"Didn't you? Until we have some proof of this, I suggest Liam be forced to step down," Dave added.

"I second," Dawn called out.

Larry sighed. "There's a motion on the table and it's been seconded."

Liam stood up before the motion could be called for a vote. "Don't bother." He pulled out his resignation. "I had planned on turning this in next week." He tossed it on the table towards Larry. "I'll give this board one warning before I go." He glanced around the table. "If you want this business to stay afloat, you will not allow that man or that woman to become CEO." He pointed to Dave and Dawn.

Without waiting for a reply, he turned and stormed out of the room. He was in his office, collecting his personal things, when security met him there.

"Sorry to do this to you, Mr. Taylor," Roz, one of the long-standing security guards said as he stepped in.

"Yeah, I'm clearing out my things." He tossed the last personal item in a box.

"It's not that. They want you back in the boardroom." Roz motioned.

"What for?" Liam asked.

Roz shrugged. "I just work here," he joked. "Come on."

Liam followed him back down three floors to the conference room. When he stepped in, he noticed that Dave and Dawn were no longer in the room.

Larry stood up and walked over to him.

"The board has decided not to accept your resignation. They've also voted to relieve both Dave and Dawn of their positions."

"I... don't understand," Liam said, looking around.

"Legally, we had to offer them back their positions. But that didn't mean we had to let them keep them." Larry smiled. "In the past month with the pair of them gone, there has been less backstabbing, plotting, and..."

"Fuckery," Regina blurted out, causing several other members of the board to chuckle.

"Right." Larry nodded. "It's been downright wonderful not having them around. Dave's little display earlier gave us the push to vote them out." Larry handed Liam back his resignation. "Later, we'll want to talk about why you had this so readily available to turn in. For now, you are staying."

Liam took a deep breath and then smiled. "Well, shit. I guess I am." Everyone in the room cheered as he sat back down.

"Now, with that business taken care of, how about we discuss what we came here to discuss?" Larry asked.

By the time Liam returned home, the story of Sean

being arrested had blown up all over the news. Cheryl had received more than a hundred calls for Liam to be interviewed, all of which were declined.

The moment he walked in his house, Ryder and Morgan met him at the door.

"I figured you'd need this," Ryder said, handing him a beer.

Liam set his laptop case down and took it, along with the hug from Ryder, then Morgan.

"Come on out back," Morgan suggested. "We're grilling out tonight. Ryder says he's going to put some steaks on."

"Nah, girl. I said Liam would grill some steaks," Ryder joked as he slapped Liam's shoulder.

He knew Morgan and Ryder were trying to cheer him up, and they were doing a wonderful job of it. But in the back of his mind, he kept thinking that he was glad that Sean was only in prison and not being buried, like Kimber would be in two days.

That night, as he and Morgan lay in bed, they talked about the fact that both of them had best friends that had turned on them.

"Never turn on me," she said with a smile, looking down in his eyes.

"Never," he promised, brushing her hair away from her face.

"It's strange, isn't it? When we met, you had suffered the loss of Sean and I had yet to go through something like that with Kimber. Yet here we are." She rested her chin on his chest as she traced a finger over one of his tattoos.

"It does make it hard to trust others," he admitted, causing her to sit up slightly.

"Oh, I still trust Leanne and Reagan. You trust Ryder still, right?"

"With my life." He thought about it. "Along with Mack and Roy."

She smiled and nodded. "I guess there's light and dark in us all." She rested her chin back down and went back to tracing her finger over his chest.

"You have no darkness," he said, brushing his fingers through her hair. "I, on the other hand, have plenty in my past."

"Oh, I have some darkness in me." She laid her head on his chest. "I once stole a lipstick from Macy's."

He faked a gasp and then laughed when she nudged him.

"I kept a secret about my brother from my parents," she said, soberly.

"What secret?" he asked.

"That he and Kimber were sleeping together."

"They were?" Liam sat up. "Seriously?"

"Sure." Morgan sat up a little. "Why?"

Liam thought about it, and tension began to build in his gut. "I think Aaron was sleeping with Theresa too," he said finally. "I've seen them together, flirting and well..." He motioned. "They had to be together."

"What?" Morgan gasped. "No, they weren't."

"Yes." Liam nodded slowly. "It makes sense."

"What are you getting at?" Morgan asked slowly.

"Ann..." he said.

"No. Hell no. Ann was in her late fifties. There is no way my brother and Ann..." Morgan shook her head.

"No, but your dad..." Liam said.

Morgan's face turned sheet white. "Oh my god."

"I'm not saying your father... Or your brother..." Liam started and shook his head. "Hell, at this point, I'm not sure what it is I'm saying."

"I can't process this." Morgan got out of bed and began pacing back and forth, limping slightly on her bad leg. She didn't seem to realize she wasn't using the boot or the cane.

He didn't want to point it out, since she was doing a great job of walking. After all, the doctor had said that she could start putting weight on it as long as she felt comfortable doing so. Then she stopped and gasped. "I told them about Kimber's message."

"And?" he asked slowly.

"And... I don't know." She threw her hands up and went back to pacing. This time when she stopped, she looked down at her leg and smiled.

"Yeah," he said, walking over to her and holding onto her. "You're walking."

She chuckled and hugged him back. "I'm back," she said with a sigh.

"Come on. Let's shut down for the night. Tomorrow morning is Saturday. We'll head over to your parents' place and have a sit-down with them." He pulled her back to the bed. "Have I mentioned how sexy you are when you walk?" He wiggled his eyebrows and she laughed.

# CHAPTER TWENTY-NINE

*I have come to lead you to the other shore; into eternal darkness; into fire and into ice.*
**Dante**

Morgan looked between her parents in disbelief.

"What do you mean you're moving?" she asked in shock.

"Your father has decided that this place is far too big for us. After all, with the success of your brother's club, he'll be moving out soon enough," her mother said dismissively.

"The... success..." Morgan shook her head. "Aaron is broke." She practically screamed it.

Her mother waved her hand. "No, he's not."

"He lost his inheritance then borrowed money to open his club, which is a hot spot for getting illegal drugs. I'm sure it's only a matter of time before the place is shut down and you lose everything." She was practically screaming.

"I'm sure you're exaggerating things," her mother said.

"No, she's not," Liam said firmly. "There were enough drugs being passed around the other night that I'm almost positive that it had something to do with Morgan getting sick."

"What?" Morgan flinched. "You are?" She looked at Liam, who shrugged. "We were careful to watch your drinks, but that doesn't stop someone from slipping it in before it got to you."

She leaned back in the chair and thought about it. She'd had a total of two alcohol drinks and three sodas while she'd been there. She tried to remember if any of them had tasted off but couldn't.

"We've made up our minds," her mother continued. "A nice condo on the beach is just what we need."

Morgan shook her head. She couldn't believe what she was hearing. She'd always thought her parents would die in this house. That one day, she'd inherit it. Then she thought about the logistics and cringed. She didn't want to live here. Hell, she didn't even like the place. Sure, it had been a great home to grow up in, but she really loved Angel Bluff. Loved the home, the scenery, the seclusion of it. Being in the country, yet minutes away from the city.

"Okay," she said, causing her mother's eyebrows to rise.

"Okay?" her mother asked slowly.

"Sure, I mean, it's your home. Do what you want with it." She shrugged.

"We will," her father said, speaking for the first time since they'd arrived for dinner.

"Where's Aaron?" Morgan asked. "We needed to speak with him also."

"He's around here somewhere." Her mother sighed. "Probably still asleep. He came in late. As usual. He usually wakes up about now."

"He does own a nightclub," Liam said.

"What about you two? Why the sudden need to meet

with us?" her mother asked.

"Not until Aaron gets here. I'll go see if he's awake," Morgan said, getting up.

She took the stairs slowly and then knocked on her brother's door. The Go Away sign that he'd made in his teenage years still hung on the door.

"Go away," he called out.

"No, you are needed downstairs."

"Go the fuck away," he yelled.

"Aaron Thomas Davenport. Get your butt out here right now or I'm coming in," Morgan yelled back.

Her brother threw open the door and glared at her. "What?"

She smiled at him. "We want to talk to you and the parent units downstairs."

"About what?" Aaron asked, crossing his arms over his chest. His hair was a mess and there were dark circles under his eyes. He looked sober enough, for now.

"Did you know they're thinking of moving?" She saw the surprise on her brother's face. "See, you really should attend more family meetings." She turned to make her way back downstairs. "Five minutes," she warned over her shoulder. "Or I'm coming back up here and dragging you downstairs."

"You can't even walk without a stupid cane."

"Try me."

When she sat back on the sofa, her mother scowled at her. "Do you kids have to yell? I raised you better than that."

"No, you didn't," Morgan said with a smile. "Otherwise, we wouldn't have just yelled at one another."

Liam chuckled but then covered it up with a cough when her mother's eyes turned towards him.

Five minutes later, Aaron plopped down in a chair.

"What is this all about?" he groaned. "I haven't even had breakfast yet."

Morgan had convinced herself that this was for the best. That confronting her family was going to be good for everyone. Now that she was staring into their familiar faces, she didn't think she could go through with it. She glanced over at Liam and found the strength when he took her hand in his.

Turning to her dad, she asked. "Were you having an affair with Ann?" Her mother gasped, and Aaron burst out laughing. So, Morgan turned to him. "What about you and Theresa and Kimber?"

Her brother's laughter died down.

"Shut the hell up," Aaron barked. He moved to get up.

"Don't," Liam said in a low voice.

"Well?" she asked when no one answered her.

"Your father..." her mother started but stopped when Morgan glared at her.

"I didn't ask you," she said calmly, then she turned to her dad.

Her father swallowed and then nodded. "Ann and I had... an affair. Yes. But your mother knew about it and has long past forgiven me."

"It's the reason I moved in with you a while back," her mother added. "They assured me it was over, and I believed them."

"Why did you allow Ann to continue working here?" Morgan asked.

"What else was I supposed to do? Hire someone else I don't trust? Do you know how long it took me to train Ann to understand our needs around here?" Her mother shook her head. "Really. It's impossible to get good help around here."

"Okay." Morgan shook her head. "So, you claimed it was over. How long ago?" Her father glanced at her mother and winced slightly. "Dad?"

"Two months prior to—"

"What?" her mother gasped. "Two months! Thomas, you promised."

"Yes, but then you started sleeping with... god knows who." Her father sighed. "I felt it was only fair."

Aaron laughed again, gaining Morgan's attention. "And you? What about you and Theresa?"

"So." Aaron shrugged. "I'm not married. It's a free world, and she willingly spread her legs for me."

"Aaron!" their mother yelled. "Do not talk like that about a woman in this house. I raised you better than that."

"No, you didn't," Aaron smirked.

"Were you the father of her baby?" Morgan asked, and her brother's face paled.

"What?" he asked, sitting up. "What baby?"

"She was pregnant when she was killed," Liam answered.

"Hell no. I... didn't know. She never told me." He glanced between Morgan and his mother. "I swear I didn't know."

"Did any of you know she was pregnant?" Morgan asked her parents.

"I hardly knew the girl," her father answered.

Her mother chewed her bottom lip.

"Mother?"

"All right, yes, she told me the week before she disappeared." Her mother sighed and threw up her hands. "I mentioned it to the police. But I had no idea whose baby it was. Besides, I'm sure Aaron wasn't the only man she was sleeping with."

"And yet none of you bothered to show up to either Ann's or Theresa's funerals?" Morgan accused.

"It wouldn't have been proper," her mother said firmly.

"Something tells me that you didn't have to persuade either of them to skip out," Morgan said. "None of you will probably show up for Kimber's services either."

"Of course we will," her mother exclaimed. "It wouldn't be proper of us not to go."

"But Ann and Theresa..." She shook her head. "Oh, I get it. Like Liam said, they were the help. Kimber's family has wealth and connections."

"They are members of the country club," her father said. "Besides, we've known Kimber since she was yea high." Her father held out his hand.

"And Ann was a member of this household for more than twenty years. Not to mention your lover." She glared at her father, who just shrugged.

"What about Kimber?" Morgan asked Aaron, feeling her throat close.

Aaron shrugged. "That was mutual."

"Where you with her the night..." She couldn't say it. She still was in denial that Kimber was gone.

"No." Aaron practically jumped up from the chair. "I was busy."

"With?" Liam asked calmly.

When her brother mumbled, Morgan leaned forward. "What?" she said firmly.

"I hooked up with Reagan, okay?" Her brother rolled his eyes.

"You what?" Morgan stood up. "You... hooked up with..."

"Reagan. It was a one-time thing. She needed a ride

home." He sighed. "And the guy she'd been making out with all night ended up being married."

Morgan held up her finger to stop him as she pulled out her phone. Hitting Reagan's number, she waited a beat until her friend answered.

"Did you hook up with my brother?" she asked when Reagan answered.

Her friend's groan was all the answer she needed before she hung up. "You disgust me."

"Why? Because your friends like to fuck me?" Aaron said, earning him a smack on the back of his head by his mother. "What?" He gawked. "It's not like you're not getting your fix. I'm sure the pool guy and the other guy I've seen hanging around here are just, what? Cleaning the pool and giving you massages?"

Morgan's phone was ringing, but she silenced it and tossed it in her purse. There was no way she could deal with Reagan right now.

"That is enough!" Morgan screamed when her mother, brother, and father all started yelling at one another at the same time. "Let's go," she said to Liam. "I'm so over this mad house."

Liam stood up and followed her out the front door as her family continued to fight.

"That didn't go like I thought it would," she admitted as Liam drove.

"How did you expect it to go?"

She shrugged. "Honestly, I had hoped they would deny it and it would just..." She wiggled her hands. "Go away."

"I'm sorry," he said, taking her hand in his.

"Promise me that you will never cheat on me. If you decide that you're done with me..." She shrugged. "Just break my heart to my face."

"I will never be done with you." He lifted her hand to his lips. "I promise you. What about you? What if you tire of me?"

She smiled. "Tire of the man who made me fall in love with him twice?" She laughed. "What kind of fool do you think I am?"

He laughed. "You make me sound like some kind of Casanova."

She laughed. "You are to me." She sighed. "We didn't eat dinner," she said, feeling her stomach growl. "Mastro's?"

"Sounds like a plan." When the turn came, he got off the highway.

"God, I love this place," she said a half an hour later when a huge plate of pasta had been set in front of her.

"That's enough food for a week," Liam joked.

"Hey, don't knock it. Besides, Raoul loves me." Morgan smiled up at Rose. "Tell him I ate every last bite."

Rose smiled. "It sure is nice to have you back."

"You know," Morgan started as she ate, "if my brother wanted a solid investment, he'd buy out Mastro's and make it a chain restaurant."

"That's not a bad idea," Liam said as he tilted his head slightly.

Morgan waved her fork. "I know Raoul does all he can here, but there's only so much one really amazing chef and owner can do. It's a great location, but the food..." She rolled her eyes. "Most people don't get to experience something like this on the other side of town."

"Okay, then do it," Liam said with a nod.

"What?" she asked, taking a sip of her wine.

"Buy Mastro's and franchise it," Liam said.

Morgan set her fork down and laughed. "Right, like it's that simple."

Liam smiled and then waved Rose over. "Please tell Raoul that Morgan would like to talk to him personally."

Rose smiled. "Right away."

"Raoul is a fool for not making her manager," Morgan added, pointing with her wine glass.

"Tell him so when you talk to him," Liam added.

"I can't just offer to buy him out." Morgan chuckled as she shook her head.

"Why not? It never hurts to ask. Here he comes now." Liam smiled up at the Italian man.

"Raoul." Morgan stood up and hugged the owner and chef.

"It's so good to see you up and about again," Raoul said as he shook Liam's hand. "How is everything?"

"Perfect as usual," Liam answered. "My wife here has a business proposition for you."

"Oh?" Raoul smiled down at her.

Morgan laughed nervously as she sat back down. "My husband is under the assumption that I could simply make you an offer to buy Mastro's and convince you to franchise." She laughed again after she'd said it, but then stopped laughing when Raoul's smile grew.

"For you, mio amore, I would walk to the ends of the earth. You come by when I'm not so busy, and we will sit down to hash out the details," Raoul said.

Morgan almost choked on air. "You're serious?"

Raoul nodded. "I'd be honored. You have saved this establishment once. I am sure that the Mastro name will be in good hands."

"Okay." Morgan took a deep breath.

"I look forward to doing business together," Raoul said with a smile and turned to walk away.

"Oh, and while we're at it, give Rose a management

position," she called out.

Raoul glanced over his shoulder and nodded, then turned to Rose. "That too can be arranged." He winked.

Rose's smile doubled. "Thank you." She poured them each another glass of wine.

"Well, that went better than I expected," she admitted when they were alone.

"You buttered him up before your accident," Liam admitted.

"I did?" Morgan frowned.

Liam chuckled. "Yes. You had met with him once and talked to him shortly after you saved his business the first time."

"Exactly how did I save his business?" she asked.

"Roger is Raoul's son," he said. "Remember? You raised that money for his medical bills. Raoul was about to sell the place to cover the expenses."

She felt stupid, but the moment Liam said it, she remembered every detail. "Right." She nodded. "I guess there are still some holes up here." She tapped the side of her head.

"So, now you have your future all planned out." Liam took a sip of his wine.

"Not all of it. We still need to start working on having children."

By the time they made it home, Morgan was a little more than tipsy. She'd had the first glass of wine to forget her messed up family and the second one in celebration of a possible deal with Raoul.

"Bed?" Liam asked her as he helped her into the house and turned off the alarm that beeped when they'd walked in.

"Bed." She nodded and started removing his shirt as she

kissed him. Liam chuckled as he backstepped inside the house. He was about to shut the door when he pushed her behind his body suddenly, as if to protect her, but the move almost caused her to topple over. She didn't see what caused him to fall after that, but she cried out when she landed on the tile floor with him sprawled on top of her.

"Liam?" she asked, trying to get him to move. His dead weight pinned her to the floor.

"He better not have hurt you," someone growled, causing Morgan to still. Looking around Liam, she saw Grayson standing over them.

"Grayson?" she asked, trying to get herself free from Liam's weight. "What... What happened to Liam?"

"I needed a moment alone with you," Grayson said. He kicked Liam's body off her, then he gripped her arms and easily lifted her to her feet.

"What?" She shook her head and realized that her ears were ringing. She didn't know if it was the alcohol or the fact that she'd hit her head on the floor. Either way, she just couldn't get her brain to work.

Grayson started pulling her towards the door, but she dug her heels in.

"I need to help him," she said, desperately trying to get to Liam.

"He doesn't matter anymore. What matters is the truth is finally out there. We only have a matter of hours before they piece it together," Grayson was saying.

"What? Who?" she asked, not fully understanding.

"The police." Grayson stopped pulling her for a moment and looked at her as if she was slow. Which she was, because up until that moment, she couldn't figure out why he was there. Inside her house. Why Liam was now lying on the ground, unconscious.

Then her heart skipped a beat and in the blink of an eye, she was stone-cold sober.

"You." She felt every fiber of her body tense. All the little hairs everywhere on her body stood on end. "You killed them."

Grayson frowned at her and started tugging on her arm again. "We have to go."

"Where?" she asked, trying to yank her arm free.

"It's all planned," he said with a smile. "You'll see, it's a surprise."

"I'm not going anywhere with you," she said, finally breaking free. Instead of running to her freedom, she rushed back to Liam and started to turn him over.

"We don't have time for him." Grayson yanked her back to her feet. "Now that they know."

"Who?" she asked. "Who knows? What?"

"You had to go and help your family piece it together, didn't you?" he said with a sigh. "I heard you. Heard it all. I had hidden cameras installed all over their place. It was easy. Victoria gave me free rein because I gave her what she needed. I'd planned on only watching out for you, but Victoria had already pieced most of it together before you showed up. She was getting suspicious after Theresa."

Morgan's stomach spun, and she had to swallow bile as she asked. She heard her brother saying something about her mother's lover, one who gave massages. Grayson. Grayson was her mother's lover. Then somehow things fell into place. Like pieces of the puzzle.

No doubt her mother had confided in Grayson about her husband's affair with Ann. He'd found out that Theresa was pregnant with Aaron's baby. How Kimber had hurt Morgan. He could have seen it all on the cameras as well.

There were no secrets in her life, in her family's lives that he didn't already know.

"You killed them all," she said, taking a step back. "Why?"

Grayson was smiling at her and for the first time, she saw the answers in his eyes.

"I did it because I love you." He reached out towards her, but she stepped back again. "I've always loved you. Even when you never noticed me, I was there. I was there, protecting you."

"I... don't understand. Why kill Theresa, Ann, and Kimber?" She cried out her friend's name.

"Theresa was going to blackmail your parents. She would have taken them for everything, leaving you broken. The bitch was all over the cameras blurting about her schemes of how she was going to ruin your entire family and take everything. I couldn't let her do that. By protecting them, I saved you." He smiled. "Ann had to go because it would have destroyed you to have your father's affair exposed. She was at a boiling point. Your father claimed that he was done with your mother. Besides, that woman was always snooping around the house anyway. She knew I was using Victoria to get closer to you. She even found a few of my cameras and then suspected I'd planted them when she caught me watching you when you were asleep. She was going to tell Victoria. Then she found out that I didn't have my PT license yet and threatened to expose me to him." He jerked his gaze to Liam, who was still unconscious on the floor. "I enjoyed getting her out of the way for you. I tried to install cameras here, to watch out for you, but each time I got close to setting them up, he'd be there. I had plans to connect them all in your safe room." He shrugged. "One time you almost caught me sneaking up there."

Morgan processed this information quickly and remembered finding the safe room's door opened several times. It was Grayson sneaking into her room. She shivered at that thought. "Kimber?" she asked quietly.

"That bitch. After what she did to you, she deserved everything she got." Grayson jerked forward and grabbed her arm.

"You're hurting me," she cried out when his fingers dug into her arm.

Suddenly, he dropped his arm. "No, I would never." He looked shocked as he held up his hands. "I'm not the one who hurt you." He glanced at the floor. "He is. Because of him, his friend almost killed you. Because of him, you ended up broken." Grayson glanced back at her. "Because of him. It's all his fault."

"No," Morgan cried. "Liam would never hurt me."

"He has. He left you that night. Abandoned you to drive down the hill all by yourself. It was his old business partner, that he cheated, who hacked your car and forced you off the road. Because of him, you almost died."

"No." Morgan's eyes filled with tears. She realized then that it had been so obvious that the man before her was beyond crazy. From the first moment she'd met him, warning bells had gone off, but she'd been too stupid to pay attention to them. Liam hadn't though. Liam had seen right through the façade.

Grayson's hands wrapped around her arms once again, and he started pulling her out of the house. She no longer had the strength to fight him. As he pulled her outside, she glanced once more at the love of her life and, just like when her car was flying off that cliff, thought about how much she was going to miss him.

# CHAPTER THIRTY

*Deep into that darkness peering, long I stood there,
wondering, fearing, doubting, dreaming dreams no mortal
ever dared to dream before.*
**Edgar Allan Poe**

Liam opened his eyes and then jerked awake suddenly. The memory of seeing the shadow rush toward them forced him into a sheer panic. Morgan!

Her screams still echoed in his ears. Maybe that was just his ears ringing from the blow he'd taken to his head?

Whoever had attacked him had surprised them on purpose.

Plus, like any fool, he'd disabled the alarm. Even now, there would be alarms going off if he hadn't punched in the code and stood in the doorway making out with his wife.

They should have entered their house quickly and locked themselves in, and then enabled the alarms. He knew there was a murderer out there. Knew that someone was after Morgan.

Even though they pretty much got a confession from

Sean about sabotaging the car, there was still the matter of who had killed the three women.

Hearing Morgan cry out his name, he came to his senses and, without thinking, raced out the front door. He saw her being pulled down the driveway by Grayson, and he flew across the pavement.

"Liam!" Morgan cried as he tackled the man to the ground.

"Get to the safe room," he said, pushing her towards the house. "Lock yourself inside."

"No, I'm not leaving you," she said, but Grayson had recovered and was swinging his fists at Liam's head. This time, Liam was ready for the move and easily ducked the blow and jabbed the guy in the gut.

He may have always lost against Ryder, but Liam was a fair enough boxer against anyone else.

"Now," Liam growled. "Morgan, get inside now." He ducked another blow from Grayson. The man was equally matched with Liam's build, but Liam's form was so much more refined.

Still, Liam knew that it wasn't always style that won a fight. Sometimes sheer brute force or willpower won out.

He couldn't spare Morgan a glance but relaxed slightly when he heard her rush back inside. Now, he could focus on the fight and keep the man busy, hopefully long enough for the police to get there. He knew that Morgan was smart enough to call them, or better yet, set off the alarm and possibly scare Grayson away.

The man was a good boxer, but Liam had spent a lifetime boxing and easily ducked or dodged each of the guy's blows. But Liam's head was still spinning from being blindsided, and he doubted he would be able to hold up much longer.

He was already winded, and his vision was going gray around the edges. Thankfully, Grayson appeared slightly winded as well.

"Stop!" he heard Morgan scream behind him. "Grayson, stop," she shouted again when the man threw another blow at Liam's head.

"Morgan, go get help," Liam yelled again. He stilled when he heard a gun click behind him. Grayson must have heard it too because the man instantly stopped moving and held up his hands.

"Morgan, what are you doing?" Grayson turned towards the door. Liam kept his eyes trained on the man instead of turning around to check on his wife.

"The police are on their way, Grayson. It's over," Morgan said with a shaky voice.

"Why?" Grayson asked. "We still have time to escape together. You and me." Grayson held up his hands and took a step towards the door and Morgan.

"Don't," Morgan warned. "Don't come any closer. I'm not going anywhere with you, Grayson. I don't love you. I love Liam and always will."

"But I did this all for you. Everything was for you!" Grayson yelled, waving his hands in the air. "You have to see that. I'll make you understand. I'm the one who nursed you back to health. I'm the one who saved your family and kept them from destroying your life. It was me!" he shouted. "I did it for you. So that you'll love me."

"No," Morgan said, and Liam shifted slightly to see his wife standing in the door holding his gun from the downstairs safe firmly in her hands. How many times had they gone to the shooting range together that first year they'd been dating? How many times had he convinced her that she needed to learn? She'd reluctantly gone with him.

Thankfully. "You're sick," Morgan said, and he saw the gun waver slightly. He wanted to shout a warning to her, but Grayson must have noticed the slight lax in her stance too.

He lunged at that moment and rushed towards Morgan and easily knocked the gun from her hands. It skidded across the tile floor just inside the doorway, far out of reach of either of them.

Liam was two steps away. Two very long steps away. He knew whatever happened now, he wouldn't be able to make it to her in time. There was no way he would be able to protect her from what was coming next.

He was slightly shocked when Morgan balled her left hand into a fist, lowered her arm, and gave the man the most perfect uppercut that he'd ever seen.

The man's chin jerked up so hard that Liam swore he heard it crack. Before Grayson could hit the pavement, Liam was there, standing over him. Liam was so ready and desperately wished that Grayson would get up so that he could finish kicking the shit out of him. Instead, he lay unconscious on the Italian marble tiles of their entryway, bleeding from the lip and nose.

"I..." Morgan said, coming to stand next to Liam. "I just remembered how to box," she said with a slight chuckle.

"My god." Liam laughed and then jerked her into his arms. "My god," he said, holding onto her tightly.

They were both shaking so badly that he didn't know how they remained upright until the police cruiser pulled up into the driveway.

Grayson hadn't moved a muscle the entire time they'd waited. After the third police car arrived, an ambulance pulled in and loaded Grayson on a gurney, still unconscious, and took him away.

When Mack and Roy showed up, they moved inside

and answered their questions. Liam sat by and listened to Morgan explain how Grayson had confessed to all three murders.

Grayson's confession had been caught on their inside security cameras and the new security company had already sent copies over to Roy as evidence.

"Do you think it was Grayson who broke into our bathroom that day?" Morgan asked them.

"If it was, we'll get it out of him when he wakes up," Roy said with a smile. "Did you really clock him?" he asked Morgan.

"Hopefully, that will be on the footage too. If it is, can I get a copy of it?" Liam asked Roy, who chuckled and nodded.

"Will do," Roy said with a smile. "I guess Ryder taught you a thing or two."

"I'm looking forward to starting up my training again," Morgan said with a smile.

"I'm going to make you hit the gun range again," Liam said with a frown. "You should have never let your guard down. It allowed him to knock the gun from your hands."

Morgan frowned. "I still hate guns," she explained to Roy and Mack. "Besides, I took Grayson down without it."

"That you did." Liam smiled.

"We have Sean's confession finally about all of the calls," Mack said suddenly. "All of them over the years. He has confessed to murdering his mother, after finding her. Then he claimed that he thought it was you in the car that night instead of Morgan. When he found out it wasn't you, he hired someone to call you and lure you into a meeting. Hell, he was even going to get rid of Ryder." Mack shook his head. "The bastard is sick."

"Jealousy will do that to the weak-minded," Roy said

with a shake of his head. "Sean was never as strong as you and Ryder were."

"No," Liam agreed with a sigh. "He wasn't."

"What happens now?" Morgan asked Roy and Mack.

"Now, you get some rest while we do our jobs. Grayson will go down for the murders. You can be sure of that," Roy said firmly. "We're searching his place now. There's bound to be some evidence, but if not, his confession is all we need."

Morgan's parents and brother arrived shortly after the police left, sometime after midnight.

They were both surprised to see Aaron there.

"I would have thought you'd be at Nightshade?" Morgan said to him when he walked in after her parents.

"Took the night off," Aaron said, motioning to their parents. "We had some talking to do."

"Was it really Grayson?" her mother asked as they all sat down.

"Yes," Morgan said as he moved into the kitchen to make them all some tea.

"My god, this is all my fault," her mother cried after hearing the story. "Grayson was a friend of the family." She cried on her husband's shoulder. "His mother was my best friend in school."

"And yet you slept with him," Aaron said dryly.

"Shut up. You slept with two of my best friends," Morgan pointed out.

Aaron nodded quickly. "Touché."

"Mom, he was sick. He thought he loved me. He claimed he'd killed them because, in some twisted way, he thought that they would destroy our family and it would in turn destroy me," Morgan said with a sigh. "In a way, he was right. I love you guys." She wrapped her arms around her mother. "Even though you're pretty messed up, you're my family." She motioned for her father to join in the hug. After he did, she nodded to Aaron.

Aaron walked over and wrapped his arms around the three of them.

When they broke apart, Morgan smiled up at her brother.

"You're going to sell your nightclub for a profit and then check into a clinic and get sober. Then you're going to help me franchise Mastro's." She slapped him playfully on the cheek.

"The Italian place?" Aaron asked after a moment.

"Yeah." Morgan smiled.

"I love that place," Aaron said with a nod. "I'm kind of tired of being a vampire anyway. Up all night, sleep all day."

"Parent units." Morgan turned to her parents with a smile. "Sell that massive dinosaur of a home, move into a condo on the beach. Someplace closer to here, because you'll want to be close enough to enjoy all the grandkids you're going to have soon." She walked over and wrapped her arms around Liam. "Very soon," she said as she looked up at him.

Her mother chuckled and then sighed. "I've always liked the beach."

Her father wrapped his arm around Victoria. "Me too. Besides"—her father glanced down at her mom, and she nodded quickly—"after sinking a lot of money into the nightclub, we're..."

"Broke," her mother finished with a sigh. "We couldn't even afford a vacation this year."

"How broke?" Morgan asked.

"Not completely, but enough that the house is a drain.

One we no longer need to worry about," her father explained.

From the moment her parents had met him, they had treated him like some out-of-work nerd orphan. Now, knowing that he was in a much better place financially than they were should have made him gloat. Instead, it made him worry. Somehow, they had gotten under his skin.

He admitted, even if it was just to himself, that he actually liked them. Besides, part of him worried that if they did end up broke, they'd move into his garage. And he wasn't going to go through that again. Last time it had just been Victoria they'd had to deal with. He wasn't sure he could handle all three of them.

"Okay, now that that is settled." Morgan sobered. "We need to all say our goodbyes to Kimber tomorrow. You know where the guest rooms are." She nodded towards the stairs. "I'm tired. My husband and I are heading upstairs."

Morgan laughed as he picked her up and carried her up the stairs.

Holding her in his arms that night, he realized just how lucky he was to have the family he'd always dreamed off. No family was flawless, but he doubted he'd want an ideal one. He wasn't exemplary himself, and he knew that because of it, he fit in perfectly with the Davenports.

While Morgan slept, he grabbed his phone and sent a text to Ryder and quickly explained how he had saved their lives tonight by teaching Morgan an uppercut.

Ryder had instantly texted him back that he would be over first thing in the morning to hear the entire story and to see the video of it firsthand. He had ended the text with a simple, "Love you, brother."

Liam smiled, pulled Morgan into his arms, and fell asleep.

Whatever happened now, Liam knew that they would be able to get through it together.

The following day was hard on all of them. Even though he knew Morgan and her friends had felt betrayed by Kimber, none of them thought for an instant that she'd deserved death.

Even when it was exposed that Kimber herself had been the infamous SM Knight. The author of those terrible articles bashing Morgan and her family. The police had found several unpublished articles labeled SM Knight on Kimber's computer.

Kimber claimed she had been the sixteen-year-old that her father had raped all those years ago. She went into such detail about how she'd been spending the night at the Davenport's house on Morgan's birthday and how her father had attacked her.

Kimber had met with Victoria several times and was trying to blackmail her to keep the story quiet. They met several times in recent months, such as the night that Ann had been murdered.

The police looked into the accusation, however, thanks to proof that her father hadn't even been in the state the night of Morgan's sixteenth birthday, they cleared her father's name quickly enough.

Kimber's parents held one of the most lavish funerals he'd ever witnessed. It almost reminded him of a wedding. After the service, everyone gathered at the country club and, this time, Liam tried very hard to go around the room and talk to people he normally wouldn't have.

He kept telling himself that if the Davenports were that screwed up behind the façade, then more than likely so was everyone else in the room. True enough, there was something about funerals that loosened people's grip on their altered realities. The more Liam talked to someone, the deeper the conversations grew.

In the end, he and Morgan finally felt more welcomed than they had in a long time. The entire day was very somber, and as he held Morgan later that night in bed, she turned to him.

"I'm going to start turning the blue room into a nursery," she said as she rested her chin on his chest.

"Okay." He smiled down at her.

"Not that...well, you know, we're not pregnant yet, but at least we can start preparing."

"I think it's a great idea." He brushed his fingers through her hair.

"What if something happens and we can't have a baby?" she asked, worry causing her nose to wrinkle.

"We'll adopt," he answered smoothly.

Her smile was immediate. "I think that's a wonderful idea. Even if we have our own, I'd like to adopt."

He smiled and leaned down to brush his lips across hers. "It's a good thing I know just the place to go."

## The Pride Series

Finding Pride

Discovering Pride

Returning Pride

Lasting Pride

Serving Pride

Red Hot Christmas

My Sweet Valentine

Return To Me

Rescue Me

A Pride Christmas

## The Secret Series

Secret Seduction

Secret Pleasure

Secret Guardian

Secret Passions

Secret Identity

Secret Sauce

Secret Obsession

Secret Desire

Secret Charm

## The West Series

Loving Lauren

Taming Alex

Holding Haley

Missy's Moment

Breaking Travis

Roping Ryan

Wild Bride

Corey's Catch

Tessa's Turn

Saving Trace

Christmas Holly

## The Grayton Series

Last Resort

Someday Beach

Rip Current

In Too Deep

Swept Away

High Tide

Sunset Dreams

## Lucky Series

Unlucky In Love

Sweet Resolve

Best of Luck

A Little Luck

Christmas Wish

**Silver Cove Series**

Silver Lining

French Kiss

Happy Accident

Hidden Charm

A Silver Cove Christmas

Sweet Surrender

Second Chances

**Entangled Series – Paranormal Romance**

The Awakening

The Beckoning

The Ascension

The Presence

The Calling

The Chosen

**Haven, Montana Series**

Closer to You

Never Let Go

Holding On

Coming Home

The Hard Way

**Pride Oregon Series**

A Dash of Love

My Kind of Love

Season of Love

Tis the Season

Dare to Love

Where I Belong

Because of Love

A Thing Called Love

First Comes Love

Someone to Love

**Wildflowers Series**

Summer Nights

Summer Heat

Summer Secrets

Summer Fling

Summer's End

Summer's Wish

**Distracted Series**

Wake Me

Tame Me

**Stand Alone Books**

Twisted Rock

Hope Harbor

Raven Falls

Angel Bluff

For a complete list of books:

http://JillSanders.com

# ABOUT THE AUTHOR

*Jill Sanders is a New York Times, USA Today, and international bestselling author of Sweet Contemporary Romance, Romantic Suspense, Western Romance, and Paranormal Romance novels. With over 75 books in eleven series, translations into several different languages, and audiobooks there's plenty to choose from. Look for Jill's bestselling stories wherever romance books are sold or visit her at jillsanders.com*

*Jill comes from a large family with six siblings, including an identical twin. She was raised in the Pacific Northwest and later relocated to Colorado for college and a successful IT career before discovering her talent for writing sweet and sexy page-turners. After Colorado, she decided to move south, living in Texas and now making her home along the Emerald Coast of Florida. You will find that the settings of several of her series are inspired by her time spent living in these areas. She has two sons and off-set the testosterone in her house by adopting three furry little ladies that provide her company while she's locked in her writing cave. She enjoys heading to the beach, hiking, swimming, wine-tasting, and pickleball with her husband, and of course writing. If you have read any of her books, you may also notice that there is a love of food, especially sweets! She has been blamed for a few added pounds by her assistant, editor, and fans... donuts or pie anyone?*

facebook.com/JillSandersBooks

twitter.com/JillMSanders

amazon.com/Jill-Sanders/e/B009M2NFD6?tag=jillm-com-20

bookbub.com/authors/jill-sanders

instagram.com/jillsandersauthor